Loyalty'

A novel by

Geoff Kenure

Best Wishes

Geoff

Also by this author

Fiction

Tragic Coincidence. (2020)

Non Fiction

The Heydays of the Independent Probation officer
in England and Wales. (2018)

For

*My special friends, my
grandchildren.*

Zack, Josh, Evin & Maddie

*A good story book can carry you
to different worlds and ways of
thinking, whilst also giving you a
chance to put aside your daily
worries, at least for a while.*

Authors Note

I feel lucky to have grown up when reading and writing were, aside from the spoken word, primary sources of communication and learning about the world. The dog-eared copies of the series of Arthur Ransome children's books are still with me seventy years later. Reading stories on my own transported me to a different world and introduced me to different ideas.

Now in my eighties I wanted to tell some stories for others to, hopefully, enjoy and to both occupy time and be a distraction from the heavy demands of modern life. This book, *Loyalty's Legacy* and its predecessor, my first novel, *Tragic Coincidence,* reflect some of the issues people experience in life, together with what, I suspect, many people hope for, namely a reasonably happy ending.

In *Tragic Coincidence*, the tale covers two years in the life of one man in the 1960s and its enigmatic end is resolved in a Postscript of some forty years later. *Loyalty's Legacy* spans the years 1937 to 2001 and is told through the eyes of seven characters. It has a happy, if enigmatic, ending.

Life is enigmatic; because it cannot just be decided on fact. Mostly in life we make judgements, life is full of them. We use upbringing, education, experience and beliefs. But it is easy to make mistakes, as many of the people with whom I worked discovered, because they were appearing in court.

In writing I drew heavily on the wonderful experience of my working life, first in the merchant navy and later in over thirty years working as a Probation Officer. In this latter vocation I was privileged to hear and, in some cases, be involved in, the life experiences of literally thousands of people who had come before my local courts.

Stories are, perhaps, out of fashion but I wanted to both entertain and reflect life in the periods described. The first book draws on personal experiences in London and northwest Scotland in the 1960s. The second on my understanding of life in World War II, based on childhood memories of the 1950s and the experiences of my parents, who lived through it. Then, as a Probation Officer doing *Guardian ad Litem* work in adoption cases I gained some insight into related issues.

Writing was part of my working life, including preparing many thousands of life histories of offenders for the courts. So, writing has been a lovely hobby in retirement. At my age I did not want to delay by hawking my manuscripts around so decided to self-publish. I did this with my first book, a reflection on my early working life *The Heydays of the Independent Probation officer in England and Wales (2018)*. So I did the same for *Tragic Coincidence* (2020) and now for *Loyalty's Legacy*.

Gratitude goes to my professional artist friend Rick Alred for again providing me with a unique painting to act as a cover. Special and heartfelt thanks to Kathy, my wife of fifty-four years, whose encouragement in all the projects has been constant and is responsible for *Loyalty's Legacy* being published. Finally, I dedicate this book to my four grandchildren, Zack, Josh, Evin and Maddie in the hope that they will find that reading stories can do much to enhance life.

Geoff Kenure 2024

Chapter 1

1997 Gareth - Porthcawl, South Wales

The sprightly, but apparently confused old man, struggling to find his loyalty card and then his wallet for the cash to settle the bill at the supermarket checkout, drawing the 'tut' from an impatient young man in the queue behind, is me.

For most of my working life I have commanded men and regularly made important, sometimes instant, decisions, a few of which potentially involved life and death. Yet now in my eighties my brain seems to have slowed its processing abilities. Oh, as any sailor with a lifetime at sea behind them, I am quite capable. Also, the Good Lord has spared me too much in the way of handicap of health and so I need no carers and happily manage on my own. Washing, ironing, mending were my personal responsibilities even as a young man and I learned them when I first went to sea as a lowly deckhand. These skills, together with cooking, later acquired, now enable me to make all my household chores quite manageable within my weekly routine. And I still drive, though not so far these days and only in the daytime; just little runs you know, out to Aberavon Beach one way or Southerndown Beach in the other.

But loyalty cards and coupons and the hassle of the impatient 'tutter' behind me upset my need to proceed slowly and carefully, just as I would when bringing an ocean-going vessel into a narrow harbour entrance. In those days I was in command. Now organisations such as supermarkets subtly try to command me, to make me fit into their system. I must queue, no problem there as I am a patient man, again born of the patience a professional seaman must sometimes display if he is to ensure the safe passage of his ship. But there, in the supermarket, when the moving counter begins to take the purchases of my predecessor in the queue towards the checkout operator, I am drawn into their system.

I must find the divider which will denote my purchases, a task my predecessor, encumbered with an unhappy two year old child, yelling in a pushchair, has understandably failed to do and the long reach to get it triggers a twinge in my arm muscle. Then I must load my purchases onto the moving counter, it must have a name but I have never asked it, and I must do so sufficiently speedily that I will be ready to move to the business, or bag loading, end once my predecessor has paid. Failure to be ready once my predecessor has done so may result in my purchases being wafted down the stainless-steel slope causing one item to be piled upon another in a disorganised mess. As the harassed mother completes her purchases I ask, and am grudgingly granted, permission to complete my unloading before the cashier commences her personal challenge to ensure that however quick at packing I may be, she will always triumphantly finish long before I complete my task. Already Mr. Tut behind has decided that he has made the wrong choice of queue in getting behind this old guy who is going to take for ever. He should have gone to the ten items or fewer check-out, though to be fair, it is, as usual, unmanned. NO! Strike that. We are in 1997. Unstaffed I should say, lest I am apprehended by the politically correct terminology police.

Now my turn arrives and I am greeted by this particular checkout lady, she of middle years, an apparent sufferer from a metabolic disorder, a casualty of a sedentary occupation or consumer of a vast number of pies; or any combination of any thereof. She is also possibly harbouring a resentment that her Port Talbot steelworker husband is on short time and she is required to prostitute herself by topping up the family income by this mind-blowingly boring work. I move to the position of catcher where she will thrust my purchases at me much faster than I can pack them. She looks at me with her best attempt at a friendly greeting and, quoting verbatim from the company required spiel, she says "And how are we today?" No pause for response. "And do we need any help with our packing?"

My reaction is to thank her and to assert that I will be fine, and I manage to do this without criticising her grammar in that

2

she used the plural 'we' when, self-evidently, I am alone. My preference would not to be alone, but to have the clock turned back, or by other means, have my dear Dyllis restored to me. Ours was a very contented partnership of almost forty five years during almost all of which time I was a professional seaman and she a dedicated nursing sister. Since she was so cruelly taken from me I have relocated from our former large city house to a little bungalow within striking distance of the sea.

As predicted my purchases come at me apace. My 'checkout operative', or so the label situated prominently upon her equally prominent bosom informs me, was apparently Christened 'June' but sadly not apparently accorded with the sunny disposition for which her parents may have hoped. She mindlessly enquires about the weather outside, no doubt ready with a despondent response along the lines of whatever I report about the prevailing conditions she will go on to assert that anything would be better to be out there rather than doing this. To nullify this possible response I remain silent. Many is the crewman who has muttered grumbles about their lot to me in the past and in such situations I used to invite them do as they were told or to sling their hook, they usually did as required, since slinging one's hook in the middle of the Atlantic Ocean is not easy. But in reality I do not engage with her because my goods are coming thick and fast. As a qualified master mariner I have the equivalent of a degree in cargo handling and stowage and the principles of these I use to guide my approach to the loading of my purchases into my bags. Bottles, tins and other heavy items first, followed by more crushable items above. So I am careful. If you only treat yourself to one pack of two cream eclairs per week you do not wish them to be located beneath the 1.5 kilogram bag of red spuds.

Yes, I am slow, but I am the customer and I have a right to pack my stuff as I wish but the Pie Lady has me down as a pain in the proverbial, so does not fill the lengthy silence after she completes scanning the last item whilst I finish packing and before she can rattle off the amount demanded in payment. I search for my coupon; after all I only come here to ensure getting a regular small rebate in coupon form. Then I search my wallet for sufficient notes and count them out to cover the amount, adding, as an afterthought, a small coin to avoid my having a vast

3

amount of change. Too late; she has entered the total of the notes and not noticed the coin and I am presented with a veritable bucket load of 'shrapnel' together with a long curl of till receipt. I struggle to fit the newly acquired metalwork into my purse, and before I can start to push my trolley away Mr. Tut is already at my side itching to complete the purchase of his lunch.

The thought "Won't be so bloody keen to get into my grave with me," occurs to me but unfortunately, although I thought it was a thought, I must have muttered it out loud, and Mr. Tut retorts, quite belligerently.

"What did you say?"

"I said 'I think I have failed to get some gravy.'" I reply. I have not yet lost my ability to react to comments, as one learns to do as part of survival amongst a group of seamen thrown randomly together on a ship for a short period until they are relieved and go on leave or join another ship.

He self-evidently does not believe me but it's hard for him to take it further and so I move off with a small grin leaving Mr. Tut and Mrs. Pie to mutually complain that silly old buggers who are losing the plot ought not to be let out on their own.

It is unfortunate that today, of all days, when I normally do my weekly shop that I felt a little under the weather when I got up as usual at just after six in the morning. Normally on a Saturday I get to the supermarket for bang on seven when they open but I just did not feel like it today and so it's close to midday when I get back to my car. I make a mental resolve to never, ever, to come in the middle of the day again. If I am not up to it then I must defer my trip and go early doors another day, never go with the crowd. Apart from the till incident, my normally swift progress with my written list, meticulously set out in the order in which the store is laid out, was impeded by couples and families wandering aimlessly picking up and studying items, some even discussing the merits of a purchase or otherwise.

It is, therefore, with some relief that I make it back to my little hatchback car and stow my bags in such a way that they will not shift as I round the corners on my way home. I return my trolley and with relief enter the security of my car and can again regain some more control of my life. The trip home is all of six minutes and I turn into my road looking forward to preparing myself a

4

sandwich for a late lunch and the thought that, given that the day is so nice, I might, after my post lunch-nap, go for a little jaunt to Rest Bay and walk by the sea.

"Who is parked outside my house?" I definitely say that out loud in the car and this time it does not cause me any trouble. Outside my garden wall a large vehicle in the form of what, I believe they call a people carrier, is parked. A stupid name really since I am not aware of other motor cars called pig carriers or sheep carriers or even idiot carriers. Though in my experience people carriers are more popular with the latter category, those who cannot really cope with the width of their vehicle, but that is another story. I swing into the driveway of my semi-detached two bedroomed bungalow which has its front door to the side, accessed via the driveway. Standing beside the door is a tall woman in late middle age who has obviously been ringing my doorbell and awaiting a reply that could not come, since I live alone and I was out.

She waits patiently whilst I exit the car, brownie points for that lady for not immediately engaging me. I wonder whom she might represent, since, as I do not know her, she must be engaged in business of some sort. Not a member of the Church of the Latter Day Saints because they are usually male, be-suited and work in pairs. Not a Witness of Jehovah because they always arrive in packs in our road. Possibly, I wondered, Christian Aid or other charitable donation seeker.

"I wonder if you can help me," she starts, "I am looking for a Mr O'Shaughnessy, in fact one who may once have been Lieutenant 'Taff' O'Shaughnessy."

Now that is undoubtedly me. But I am wary.

"And who is it that is looking for him?" I ask as neutrally as possible, not wishing to have another Mr Tut incident on my hands.

"Oh. I am sorry it is a long story but my name is Rose Crowther and I am trying to trace my origins. You see, I was adopted as a baby during the war and it is just possible, although a long shot, that this Lieutenant "Taff" O'Shaughnessy might be able to add to what little I have been able to find out so far about my birth mother."

5

I looked at her; she was a well presented, quite matter of fact woman and her story was quite reasonable and despite a slight unease I could see no point in not responding so I said.

"Well, since you are apparently not selling something, attempting to proselytize me, or trying to collect on my very many debts, I can say that once upon a time many, many moons ago I might well have been addressed as Lieutenant "Taff" O'Shaughnessy RNVR." She laughed and I continued. "Perhaps you would like to come in and have a seat."

"Well thanks. But you see I have the family here, well my son-in-law and two grandchildren." She pointed at the vehicle and the driver's door was opened and a young man in early middle age got out and came towards us and Rose turned to him.

"Michael. Success! This gentleman is the one I was seeking," then, turning to me, "this is my son-in-law Dr Michael Trotter."

I shook the proffered hand.

"Well, come in." I said, moving to open the door with my key. But Michael indicated the children in the car and so I invited them in as well.

I explained that I had been to the shop and there were some frozen things that needed to go into the fridge, especially as the car was now parked in the sunshine, and so after I was introduced to Ewan, eight and Maggie, four, they all turned to and helped in getting my stuff from the car and helping me to unpack.

"Sorry to have turned up without warning," said Michael, "but Mum (nice, I thought, that he referred in this way to his mother-in-law) has only come down for the weekend and my wife Sally and I arranged our weekends off to coincide, but unfortunately there was a big pile up on the M4 on Friday night and we had an emergency call in to the hospital in Bristol, where we both work. Fortunately for us Mum was able to look after the kids. But Sally is needed today as she works in orthopaedics whereas, once the emergency was over, I was released at about midnight and am not required today."

"Added to which, I am only able to be here for the weekend myself," put in Rose, "and, whilst I come down as often as I can, this trip was only about following the lead to try and trace you, so Michael agreed to bring me down instead of Sally, as I have to go home tomorrow to be in work on Monday."

Shopping unpacked and stowage having been completed it was obvious that the children were getting a bit restless and Michael looked at Rose but turned to me.

"We bought some sandwiches in the town and I think the kids have been in the car for long enough and as the sun is shining do you think I could take them to the beach?"

"Well." I said. "You are welcome to have them here."

"The main purpose of today," said Michael, "was to help Mum see if we could find you and, to be honest, I was very doubtful that she would manage to do that and I was primed by Sally to look after her if our mission failed and she was disappointed, as I think you may be her last lead. But now that she has found you it might be better for her to be able to talk to you without two travel-weary, and slightly over warm, children fratching and we have promised them time on the beach. After all it is the most beautiful late September, Indian Summer's day."

Turning to Rose, he enquired if that would suit her, and she nodded vigorously.

"You are not leaving this nice lady all alone with this unknown old man are you?" I asked.

Rose replied, "I think that Michael has judged that I will be safe enough and I agree."

"Do not always judge a book by its cover; why I almost created a fight in the supermarket this very morning, so I could be the South Wales version of Jack the Ripper!"

Rose laughed and said, "I will take a risk on the basis that I can tell your speed of running is probably not what it used to be and what is it Confucius said? 'Man with trousers down does not run as fast as woman with skirt up.' Added to that, and like my daughter, I am a nurse who has worked many a shift in Accident and Emergency in the past and have experience of dealing with roaring drunks and other awkward customers. Anyway, I have my mobile phone and can dial 999. Or if you behave properly, I can use it to locate Michael and the children when we finish."

"Fine." I said, "As long as you are alright with that then, may I suggest we make a little sandwich for our lunch as my tummy thinks my throat may have gone off duty."

Having given Michael directions to the Rest Bay car park from my bungalow in Sandpiper Road, and explaining that it was

7

only a few minutes away, Rose went out to wave Michael and the children off and to rescue her own sandwich whilst I busied myself making my lunch and brewing some tea. On return she helped set the table in my kitchen diner and we chatted about the children and the journey down.

Over our meal she told me a bit about herself and her mission.

She was brought up on a smallholding on the edge of Otley Chevin in Yorkshire. She explained that the word 'chevin' describes a large steep hillside and the origin of the name may come from the Welsh word 'cefn' which she told me she had looked up and apparently it means a ridge of high ground. The town of Otley, she told me, lies beneath such a steep hill. Her parents Bill and Alice Longstaff ran a small farm, not much more than a smallholding really. In later years her father also had a regular term-time job driving school busses for a local coach company which meant split shifts but enabled him to do things on the farm as well. She said that she had a really happy childhood as an only child surrounded by, and caring for, animals and chickens. Possibly in caring for poorly animals she became interested in caring generally and it was no surprise to her parents that she went into nursing pretty much straight from school. Much of her working life was spent in the hospitals of two adjacent cities; the Infirmaries, first Bradford Royal and then after her maternity break, Leeds General. Currently she worked as a senior carer, with a commercial company, providing support to the elderly and disabled in their own homes and it was to this work she needed to return on the following day.

She married Harry Crowther, a joiner, in 1963. A happy marriage producing one child, a girl Sally now aged 34. Sally had followed her mother into nursing and was now a Ward Sister and was married to Michael, the doctor, whom I had met. They were both working in Bristol, but the plan was to return to Yorkshire when the right job for Michael came up.

A lovely family story of achievement and general happiness but, of course, life is never without its trials and tribulations, and for Rose they related to her roots.

And here, just to clarify, we are not talking hair dye.

Chapter 2

1943 Alice - Otley, Yorkshire

The last vestiges of daylight were still in the western sky, yet it was well past ten on that clear summer evening as I settled the baby to, what I hoped, would be the feed to last her until morning. I had grabbed a couple of hours sleep before the cries from the cot in the next room had awoken me and quite happily I had risen, lifted the squirming noisy baby and taken her downstairs to see to her needs. The initial decibel levels of cries were partially subdued as, whilst the bottle of formula milk warmed, I changed the soiled nappy and dropped it in the stone sink for later attention. I had then successfully negotiated what was, for me, the worst part of the nappy change, namely the insertion of the nappy pin through the terry material of the nappy, whilst contending with a wriggling child. Since that very first nappy change, nearly three months ago now, I had been terrified of accidentally stabbing the infant.

After testing the temperature of the milk I took baby to the rocking chair to sit and enjoy that peaceful moment of silence and contentment as feeding progressed. Sitting there and looking out at the sky, through the kitchen window, I reflected on my journey to this point in my life. How fate had indeed brought me to this location and the status of motherhood, in a most unexpected manner. Here I was in the middle of a war, husband absent in the army, sitting peacefully in a rural setting, looking out of a farmhouse window at a very settled evening sky and nursing a child of my own. A child I had, in recent years, got used to thinking I may never have, yet here she was, sucking contentedly on her bottle. Not that life had been bad, indeed I had always thought of myself as very lucky compared to many of the girls with whom I had worked at the mill in Lockwood.

First the luck that had me born as the youngest of a family of five living on a small farm on the edge of Clayton West, a small village loosely at the centre of the triangle made by the towns of Huddersfield, Wakefield and Barnsley. Although there were links with both the latter places and they were marginally nearer, the bus and train services were both better to Huddersfield than to the other two towns and so it was the most used big centre by most of the villagers. From the age of five I had attended the Council School, known as Kayes County School, in the village leaving at fourteen to work in the local Beanland's Mill. That work was enjoyable enough, especially with the camaraderie of the other mill girls, but I was always glad to get home to the family farm, where I could help out with my older sisters and brother. Being the youngest of the five I saw my elder sisters get married and of course the farm, which could only really support one family, would eventually go to my brother.

Then I recollected those days when I was aged about eighteen and Bill Longstaff, who was a couple of years older than me, came to the mill to work as a trainee engineer. I smiled as I remembered the shy exchange of glances at work through which we had shown our potential attraction to one another. But little had progressed until we both found ourselves coming face to face at Skelmanthorpe fair, which was known locally as the 'feast'. In the small local villages roundabout Clayton West there were not many meeting places aside from churches and chapels and the events which they organised. So like many others of my age I looked forward to the annual visit of the feast, and at eighteen I had made my usual trip to the Clayton West feast and had a great time. When it's week in Clayton West was over it moved on to Skelmanthorpe, the next and bigger village, on the way to Huddersfield. In this slightly bigger location it joined with another small feast to make one of twice the size. It also ran for two weeks rather than one so, I had taken my trip to that bigger event on the middle Saturday of the following week.

I could still recall, with pleasure, that first accidental meeting where I had almost literally bumped into Bill and after that we had spent quite some time together walking round and talking. Through our conversations we found ourselves to be in fairly similar circumstances. Like me, Bill was a farmer's son and, also

10

like me, his elder brother would inherit the farm, so he had started mill work straight from school and after other experiences he then got his trainee engineer's post at Beanland's. Our blossoming romance went on to lead to visits to one another's family farm houses and, after a year's courting and a second year's engagement, our wedding had taken place in 1929. It had been possible because, by this time, Bill had obtained full time engineer's job at a mill in Lockwood near the centre of 'town', as Huddersfield was locally known. As a result he had been able to rent a back terrace house nearby and, when I joined him as his wife; it was not long before he was able to get me a job at the mill where he worked too.

Our life as a young married couple had gradually developed there; making local friends and joining a local chapel and various clubs and we were a happy pair satisfied by each other's company. Our sex life had been, and still was, a very enjoyable part of the relationship but, despite all attempts, pregnancy never occurred. For a few years the subject was never discussed but then, after we had been married for about five years, a chance, and somewhat stinging comment from a drunken acquaintance in the local club, made us sit down and discuss the issue. We reached the conclusion that we were happy together and if it was God's will that we were not to be blessed with children then we would accept that fact, and just enjoy life together.

In breaks at the mill there was always chatter and gossip which occasionally included stories of women, often very young lasses, who got pregnant and how their various situations were dealt with. From this we learned that there were ways of arranging for coping with the arrival of unplanned children. Grandparents sometimes cared for the baby of a very young mother as their own or, in other cases, help in finding a home for a baby that a mother could not keep may be given by a local doctor and these seemed two of the most common choices. Bill and I had discussed whether or not to make it known to the local doctor that we might have an be interest in offering our services in terms of adoptive parents, but the conclusion was that we were fatalists and should do nothing. After all there were also a few stories about families who apparently could not have a child, who took on the care of somebody else's, only to find that a child of their own was soon on the way after all and perhaps our incomes did not allow us to support two children if I could not work full time.

We had always been careful with money and as a pipe dream we had agreed to save towards a better and more semi-rural home, with enough room for a small garden. Then there came Mr. Hitler and his megalomania, leading to war; and to start with Bill had not been called up because of his work as an engineer in the mill. But in late 1941 he had decided to join up and with his engineering background he initially went into the Royal Engineers and later, when they were established in late 1942, he moved to the Royal Electrical and Mechanical Engineers or R.E.M.E as it was called. I remembered those first months of missing Bill immensely, but I had received a lot of support from good friends and neighbours and my work mates, many of whom were in the same boat with their husbands being away. I felt I had managed well enough and Bill was good at writing to me, and I to him, being, as he was, stationed in the south of England so we could keep up a regular correspondence.

Then in late April 1942 there arrived that unexpected letter from my mother's brother Ernest Brayshaw who had written to say that now, into his seventies, he was struggling to manage his small farm on the edge of Otley Chevin. His farmhand had been conscripted and he had been unable to get a Land Girl to help him and he wondered if, having been brought up on a farm, I might be able to do so. The offer was that I went to the farm to live in a small two bedroomed cottage attached to the main building, and formerly let to the farmhand. Ernest could only afford to pay me a nominal wage but there would be no rent to pay and all meals would be found and any reasonable requests for clothing and any other essentials would be met. From deep in my memory I had vaguely remembered Ernest from a family gathering when I was in my teens and I had also recalled that Ernest, and his wife Agnes, had suffered bereavement when their only child had died of some childhood ailment like measles, at about the age of six.

Life was good in Lockwood, but I remembered thinking that whilst I was happy with my present life the war was dragging on, even after the entry of the Americans the previous year, and it

12

was lonely without Bill whom I knew would not be home till the war was over. So, I had sent a holding letter in reply to Ernest to say that I was interested in coming to help him but needed to get Bill's thoughts before taking it further.

As Bill was stationed in England his reply was prompt and he said that he knew how much I missed the open air of the farming life of my childhood and as for us being together he was happy to be with me anywhere. He said that the decision was mine and practicalities were a secondary consideration. Our present home was rented, and it sounded as though our possessions could go to Otley and my lack of income was not an issue because I would be living rent free and given board. Furthermore, and in any case, all of Bill's pay was going into the bank. But despite all of that he had said that I should make no decision before spending a little time with the Brayshaw's, checking to see if I could get on with them and clarifying the arrangements.

So, I had correspondence with Ernest over a couple of exchanges of letters and eventually I had arranged to take a week off work on the pretext that I was going to help a poorly relative. I travelled to Otley and, with my small bag of clothes; I followed Ernest's directions of not going down into the town from the station, but instead walking round and up the edge of the Chevin until I came to what was then Ernest's small farm.

From the start I had found Ernest and Agnes to be a lovely old couple, he an active seventy two year old and she a couple of years younger, but not as sprightly as a result of the restrictions placed on her mobility due to mildly arthritic knees. Having arrived in the early afternoon the first thing I had been shown was the cottage which had immediately endeared itself to me. Attached to the main house, but with its own doors to the front and back, the inside was clean and bright and despite it not being any bigger than our mill cottage it was much more airy and with a wonderful outlook from the front window. The farm buildings in the yard were old but well maintained and a tour of the farm itself showed me that it had milking cows and a couple of pigsties and some arable areas for potatoes and other vegetables. The main income was from the milking cows, then pigs reared for slaughter together with the sale of seasonal vegetables and of course a large penned area for chickens, leading to the sale of eggs and some of the birds themselves for meat.

As I had walked part of the farm land on that very first time a couple of low flying planes could be seen off to the right and Ernest told me that they were toing and froing from Yeadon Aerodrome, which was not far away, in fact just over the hill. As well as a small airfield it apparently also housed a large 'hush hush' Avro engine factory, concealed under a huge area of camouflage netting. This aside, the farm was a wonderfully peaceful location and, whilst by no means a large holding, it could easily be seen to represent something far too big for a single ageing man to operate to anything like its maximum potential. It also took me back in my thoughts to my own happy childhood, on my Mum and Dad's farm. For the rest of the week, armed with borrowed overalls and boots I remembered getting up at five in the morning to milk the cows and then after breakfast to let out and feed the chickens and pigs. Ernest harnessed the farm horse to a small cart and took the milk churns to a wooden stand, at the farm gate, where they would later be collected and sent to Otley station for onward transport to Leeds by train. A small amount of the day's milk was left in the dairy to be sold to, and collected by, neighbours without cows. I helped with hoeing the vegetables and various other tasks and it was such a wonderful week, working hard all day and sitting down to lovely meals with my uncle and aunt each evening.

The week had sped by and over the evening meal, on my last planned night there, Ernest had told me, sitting at the farmhouse table, that he could see that I had not lost the farming skills that I had learned in childhood on my parent's farm when growing up. Because of that he thought that he felt sure I would make a tremendous contribution to the efficiency of the farm which, incidentally, the Government was keen to see happen in order to help feed the nation. For my part, I was excited to get back on to the land and fresh air and away from the enclosed space of the mill. Of course, I knew that I would miss my friends in the mill and amongst the neighbours in those cheek-by-jowl little mill cottages, but the fresh air and quiet would more than make up for that. So, they being pleased with me and I with them, and with the already granted permission from Bill, a move to the farm was agreed as soon as it could all be arranged.

Having returned to Lockwood and written out my notice I handed it in to my overlooker on my first day back, telling him that I was leaving to undertake other war work on a farm and my notice was accepted. Only one weeks' notice was required, but I had agreed to two weeks when they requested extra time to try to train another worker to fill my place. Life then got very busy making arrangements for removing. Every evening had been spent sorting and packing all the smaller items of our clothing and possessions. Fortunately, there was not much in the way of furniture to move from the tiny two bedroomed back terrace house, with its one room downstairs into which the front door opened and there was access to a cellar head kitchen. My brother, now fully in charge of our family farm, knew a fellow farmer with a horsebox and he felt that the bed, table, wardrobes, kitchen and easy chairs, together with our other curtains, rugs and possessions, would easily fit into it. On the appointed day my brother and his friend had come with the horsebox, specially swept out for the occasion, and loaded everything apart from my suitcase, which only held my overnight clothes and toiletries. They then went back to Clayton West and would travel directly to Otley the following day, whilst I had awaited a visit from the landlord, who came to inspect the state of the house and collect the keys. He came at about five in the evening and I then went to Susan my friend next door, as arranged, to sleep on her couch until six the next morning when, having dressed and said cheerio to Susan, I had set off to catch the bus to town.

Even now I could remember in detail that amazing moving day, when I alighted from the bus near the George Hotel in town and had walked towards the neo-classical portico of the Huddersfield train station, its aesthetic beauty considerably diminished by the wartime sandbag protections between the pillars. This time I had purchased only a single ticket to Otley and carried my suitcase down through the underpass to await the arrival of the train from Manchester, which would carry me first to Leeds. It had soon appeared out of the tunnel to my right, as I faced back across the line to the booking office, and it came, clanking and belching steam and smoke, past me. The size and the weight of the mighty beast had made the platform shake. Being early on a Saturday morning it was not too busy and I found a corner window seat in a second class carriage. There were a couple of soldiers who looked tired and worn and were obviously using this trip as a way to catch up on some sleep, an elderly couple happy in their own company and two younger girls happy to chat together on their way to work in Leeds. Settling myself to the treat of another journey by train, I remembered reflecting on this potentially life changing opportunity that lay before me.

At the start of that journey, in June 1942, I remembered thinking that I was on my way to a very different life to the one I had been living for the last dozen or so years. As the train had left its call at Dewsbury station and chugged slowly across the viaduct, it enabled me to look down on the town which was probably the centre of the 'heavy woollen' area of the West Riding, I did wonder whether this return to farming was really for the best. After all, I had enjoyed my life in Lockwood and the wonderful community spirit with hard working colleagues, many of whom had family duties as well as having to work. But in many cases help was provided by extended family members or neighbours and community loyalty was extended to most. Those too foolish to understand the unwritten rules and who 'offended' against the normal range of accepted behaviour were ostracised. It was fear of that ostracism which kept most folk in line, so the police were rarely needed. For all that relative happiness of the past twelve years, however, I did harbour the hope that a return to farming roots might move me on from just treading water, to a point where life became a little more dynamic.

After changing trains in Leeds I travelled to Otley station where Ernest was waiting for me and he had given me a smiling welcome and taken my case and loaded it into the pony trap. On the slow climb up the hill he told me that my brother and his friend had arrived just before he had left to collect me and that, when last seen, they were prioritising getting the bed upstairs and reconstructed. And I remembered with great clarity that arrival day at the farm.

Ernest had reminded me of that of which I was already well aware, namely, that early summer on a farm is a very busy time and of course even a small dairy herd needs attention twice a day. Nevertheless, he suggested that he did not want me to start work until I had my new home set up as I wanted it. He said he really meant that because, as he put it, 'once you do start there is never any stopping with this sort of farming life'. But I was of the view that there would not be a lot for me to do and I was expecting to be ready to start work from Monday morning milking onwards.

When I arrived at the farm my brother John and his friend, who turned out to go by the name of Ronald, were sitting on a bench outside the farmhouse munching on sandwiches and with big mugs of tea in their hands chatting to Agnes. Both men looked warm and tired and I noticed for the first time that my brother, now into his late forties, was looking so much older and more worn. I could remember clearly my arrival and his greeting.

"Nah then our Alice. Me an' Ronald 'ere 'ave got yer bed all fixed up and yer clothes cupboard and drawers upstairs. An' dahnnstairs we've put t' dresser, table and chairs in as well. When we've supped us tea and snap, what our Agnes 'as done for us we'll come wi' ye and if tha wants owt shiftin' we can do it afore we go. Cos all 'ats left in 'orse box is drapes, beddin', suitcases and bits and bobs in boxes, like. And we'd like ter get on't road as soon as."

I can hear him now and I remembered smiling at my brother's broad accent which, whilst very local to Clayton West in its own way, was now much more tinged with the broad Barnsley accent of his wife Doreen, who had been one of the Beanland's mill girls before she married John. The men were as good as their word and had everything placed as I requested before I had waved them off. Agnes and I were joined by Ernest for a quick cup of tea and a bite before Agnes asked if she could help in any way and then she and I had spent a happy couple of hours chatting whilst making up the bed and hanging curtains before Agnes went to start the evening meal. Left alone I felt that I would be able to get along with Agnes very well, as the older woman had helped with the fairly impersonal things that were to be done but she had not interfered by involving herself in unpacking the personal things like clothing, nor had she interfered in the kitchen, so that I was free to put things where I wanted them to go.

By the time I went for my evening meal on the Sunday, I had everything just as I wanted it and so at five on Monday morning I was, as promised, in the milking parlour and beginning my informal 'land girl' work; milking twice a day, haymaking, feeding chickens and pigs, keeping an eye on the vegetables and later on ploughing. Ernest and I divided the labour on the basis of what I was best able to do. So, maintenance of walls and fences were his task. He also insisted that he did both sets of milking one day of the week to give me a rest day, and I reciprocated. Otherwise we both did morning milking (except for respective days off) and then we would alternate doing the afternoons unless there was a pressing job he was finishing, when I would do a number of afternoons on the trot.

On several occasions I had been offered the opportunity to take eggs to market, or go on errands, or for shopping into Otley, but I rarely did for two reasons; first contentment with my own company and the farming life, and second I could also see that these trips to Otley were Ernest and Agnes' only opportunity to meet their friends and socialise. And so they would often go off together, with our produce in the little farm trap, leaving me feeling sorry for the little horse, it would be alright going down there but the long steep pull up the hill, on the return journey, was quite taxing for the poor little thing.

Agnes was a good cook and I soon became great friends with her as every meal was taken with them in the farmhouse. Bill's long hoped for leave did not materialise and so over the summer and autumn the three of us had become a very happy unit, almost like parents and daughter. I was not unfit as a woman mill worker, but I still found myself becoming fitter and healthier than I had been for years. Working hard from dawn till dusk, much of it in the open air, I did indeed ensure that the farm's productivity increased. In many ways the farming life made up for not having Bill around and I was content with farm work and with the company of Ernest and Agnes and we clearly held one another other in mutual respect living, as we did, as a close knit family sharing work and meals.

The older couple had tried to persuade me to take some time off from the farm, but I had little interest in doing so. To keep them quiet on that subject I made one trip to Leeds on the train,

18

but having walked round for an hour or two in the centre, I was more than happy to catch the return train to Otley. One autumn day I did go into Otley with them, on market day, and left them to their trading and talking to their friends whilst I went to explore the little back streets and ginnels of the town. Then I walked down to the river Wharfe and over the bridge and along to the adjacent weir. It was nice and of interest but it was nowhere near enough to draw me away from what I was beginning to see as my second childhood days of farm work, no matter how hard it was.

True, I recalled, how it became harder in the winter; there was less to do apart from the milking and of course the need to feed the animals and the cattle that had to be brought into the barn by early November. So, I did a little decoration in the cottage and made the place more homely. Just as well, because in early December Bill got five days leave and travelled up overnight from his unit, in the overcrowded trains of those wartime days, arriving in Leeds in the early hours and catching the first train of the day to Otley. On the very day he arrived, just after lunch, and unbeknown to us, Ernest had been up mending a small hole in the barn roof when he slipped and fell. We heard a clatter and some yelling and the three of us had run out to find him laid on the ground by the barn. The left side of his face and arm had borne the brunt of the fall and as well as some lacerations on his face, which looked the worst to start with, but turned out to be the least of his worries, he was clutching his arm. It was obvious that there was a lot of blood in his upper arm where some metal protrusion, on the route of his slithering or subsequent fall, had caused a nasty gash and his sleeve was covered in blood.

We had got him back to the farmhouse with great difficulty, indeed without Bill's presence it would have been a real struggle. Ernest was shocked and bruised and we wondered if he had bumped his head in the fall, though he said not. Agnes got hot water going and Bill, who had been given first aid training in the army, had a look at the wound, but there was no doubt that he would need the doctor. Taking Agnes' old cycle, Bill rode downhill to one of the Otley doctors' houses, in just a few minutes. Less than twenty minutes after the accident the doctor arrived in his car – in fact it took Bill a further half an hour to get

19

the bike back up the hill, sometimes riding and more often pushing. By the time of his return Doctor Lynch, who was even then in his seventies, had finished cleaning, stitching and dressing the wound and was pronouncing Ernest to be a very lucky man not to have sustained worse injuries. He forbade manual work for a fortnight on the basis that a man in his mid-seventies like Ernest, healed slowly and he had applied over twenty seven stitches in the long cut and told him that any manual work was likely to open the wound. It was arranged for Ernest to see him in ten days when a decision would be made about removing the stitches and only then was there a possibility of a return to work. At that time also there would also be opportunity for the settlement of the medical bill.

Doctor Lynch, it had turned out, was clearly in no hurry and happily accepted Agnes' suggestion of a cuppa and some recently made cheese scones. And this decision was to turn out to be a life changing one for Bill and me, although we did not realise it at the time.

The doctor asked how Ernest would manage the farm for the two weeks he should refrain from work. Ernest explained that I was a relative, brought up on a farm now run by my elder brother, and explained that I had been working in a mill in Huddersfield, but had agreed to come and help Ernest when his farmhand had been conscripted. Ernest was very complimentary about my abilities and his complete confidence that I could manage all the manual work required on the farm in this season of the year. The doctor went on to ask me about how I was finding this life and after I told him how much I was enjoying it he asked Bill about his army life. He was obviously in no rush and somehow, as the conversation went on; during that the length of time we had been married came up and that was how our childlessness came to be discussed.

At this point the sensitive Agnes had suggested that she take Ernest up for a rest on the bed and to find different clothes to the blood soaked garments he was wearing. After they had left the doctor just asked if we had considered adoption and we explained that we had discussed it some time ago and had not been motivated to pursue the idea. But Doctor Lynch continued the informal discussion about a subject which we confessed we had never really explored and neither had we really reached a conclusion, beyond just saying 'we await fate'. This, he pointed out, was not actually a decision one way or another. Whatever, we found ourselves saying that in due course we may be interested and the good doctor said he would bear us in mind if an appropriate case ever came to his attention.

It was a lovely few days with Bill at home and even better because we could work together on the farm, and he was so happy doing so that he was reluctant to return to his unit and he said so on his last evening of leave. Agnes had done a special meal of roast chicken, baked potatoes, carrots and sprouts and Ernest had obtained some cider and so it was a very happy evening. Towards the end Bill said that though, just then, in late 1942, things were in somewhat of a stalemate in the war with all the fighting in North Africa and in Russia around Leningrad it was going to take a long time for the war to end. Ernest said that he looked forward to the day that Bill could return and then he and Agnes could retire to the cottage and we could have the farmhouse and run the farm because, in the absence of children of their own, they had decided that upon the death of the second of them that the farm would be ours. Whilst we were delighted we were both stunned by this announcement, and completely lost for words.

Bill returned to the army and the three of us remaining had a quiet Christmas in 1942. Ernest was out of action effectively until the end of the following January and I managed everything singlehandedly and enjoyed it greatly. Gradually Ernest got fully back to work by Easter which fell in early April just before the cattle were ready to go out to grass again. Not long after Easter I remembered that I had been working in the barn when a car came into the farmyard. As there were never many callers I had gone out to see who it was and found Doctor Lynch in conversation with Agnes. Seeing me he hurried over and said he would like to have a word in private, so we went into the farmhouse kitchen and Agnes kept out of the way.

He told me that he had attended a birth in the Otley County Hospital and the mother had subsequently abandoned the baby and, after police enquiries, she could not be found and the child was therefore, what he referred to as, effectively a foundling. Doctor Lynch remembered the discussion he had with us and so

21

he had come to ask if we could help. Apparently there was a shortage of potential fosterers and adopters at that time as a result of the strain on families due to the war. Many women were working to help the war effort and without husbands around they could not afford to give up to their job to take care of a child. Given that we had agreed in principle to consider adoption, and he was also aware that there was wider family support to help me he had come to ask whether we would now actually be prepared to help. My understanding was that Bill and I had agreed in principle to caring for a child and so I thought it was my right to make, what was the fairly instant, decision needed. So, I agreed and experienced an immediate excitement, but then there were all the practical issues that would need to be faced. The farm needed attention to the point of working full time on a year round dawn till dusk basis and spring was a hectic period. How would caring for a tiny baby fit into that? So there was discussion first with Ernest and Agnes to get their views and advice.

No doubt the older couple were influenced by the fact that their only child had died and no doubt too their grief over that persisted and, more altruistically perhaps, they felt that they did not wish us to be childless like them. Then, there was the fact that the farm would have a family member to carry it forward and that too would have been a nice thought for them. There was absolutely no doubt that they were very much in favour. When the issue of the practicalities was raised they saw these as mundane issues being subservient to the main issue of a family future. In short order they dealt with the practicalities. Agnes was still fit enough to care for the child during the day, and in fact she said that it would be something that she could do to be useful as she was limited in her ability to do farm work and had few other things to occupy her except for cooking our meals. Ernest was now basically recovered and had resumed the sharing of farm duties as before.

So, it was agreed that I would take the child and the Doctor went off to make the arrangements and thought that the child, a little girl, would arrive within the week. I rushed down to the post office in Otley to telegraph Bill of my decision and by the following morning I had his one word reply, no doubt limited by the fact that telegrams were charged by the word, 'Wonderful' it simply said. I wrote immediately to Bill that evening in somewhat of a daze to tell him how happy I was that he had agreed to be an instant 'father' to a child which had, so far as we were concerned, an apparent gestation period of less than nine days never mind nine months. I also explained the arrangements with Agnes to help with child care. Agnes got Ernest to go into the loft and resurrect a Moses basket, a cot and tin baby bath stored since the loss of their own child and then the following day, whilst I was finishing the milking, they went off in the trap to Otley to buy some terry nappies and returned with them and some good quality second hand baby clothes which they had sourced in the market. Later I learned that they had told friends that their niece who had come to stay with them to help on the farm was due to have a baby. Of course, since I had rarely been in town nobody would have known if I was pregnant or not.

And so it was unintentionally established locally, that Ernest and Agnes' young niece who had come to help on the farm, whilst her husband was off in the Army, was having a baby. Just one day later on Thursday 9th April Doctor Lynch came early in the morning to say that he had arranged that the baby girl would be brought to the farm later that afternoon. There was then a frantic rush to get everything reorganised. For my part I moved into the spare room in the farmhouse so that when I was about my work Agnes could easily get to keep an eye on, and see to, the child. That shifting of furniture and clothes, together with other jobs, made the morning fly by and about two o'clock, long before we were ready, a car drove into the farmyard. Its driver turned out to be some member of the hospital management committee, a well-dressed lady with a plummy voice to boot, who was clearly doing this job as a duty, being one of the few with a vehicle.

A nurse was in the back of the car and it turned out that she had been holding on to a sort of travel cot to prevent it from moving around on the back seat. After a brief greeting the 'her ladyship' woman established that I was indeed Mrs. Longstaff and was expecting to care for the child as arranged by Doctor Lynch. That done she summoned the nurse and the baby was brought into the farmhouse in the travel cot. The journey had obviously been to baby's liking as we learnt that she had quickly fallen asleep, but now the motion of the car had stopped the child became restless and soon realised that she was uncomfortably damp and probably hungry as well. So, her entry into the farmhouse was a noisy demanding one.

'Her Ladyship' was keen to be shot of this task and ignoring the child's demands she wanted to see what arrangements had been made and Ernest took her off to inspect the room we had been preparing. The nurse, or midwife as it turned out, was much more friendly and practical and asked if I was used to children and, when I explained the situation soon had me practicing the arts of holding and changing the baby. She told me how to prepare the bottle and suddenly I had realised that this was an item we had not thought to purchase. The midwife said that she would leave the bottle they had brought but that I was not to mention this to the management committee lady who would no doubt seek to charge for it.

As the milk was warming I had my first lesson in nappy changing and that was when I first experienced the terror of inserting the nappy pin, for fear of stabbing the wriggling infant. Fortunately, Agnes had come to my aid and the nurse had nodded and told me that I would soon get the hang of it and no doubt grandma would help. This clearly cheered Agnes and it was she who gave the baby her first bottle, as by this time Ernest had returned from leading the tour of inspection.

"Is there anything I should know about the little girl's background?" I asked and 'her ladyship' thought for a moment.

"A young woman in the late stages of pregnancy turned up on the doorstep of the hospital." She replied. "She was quite uncommunicative and possibly mentally slow or ill, and stayed long enough to be delivered of this child, but not long afterwards she disappeared. Enquiries by the Police have not resulted in identifying the woman. There is nothing more that can be said and if you have further questions please address them to Doctor Lynch. And now I must return this nurse to her duties."

With that she made for the door followed by Ernest and the nurse said to her departing back. "I will just be a moment and gather up our things so I will see you at the car, Lady Smeeton."

Turning to us, after her companion had left, the nurse said.

"Has anybody told you that staff at the hospital gave her the name of Primrose because they were in flower in the Hospital grounds? Also, in cases like these nothing much is ever revealed but me and some of the other staff believe that it might just be possible that in years to come she might need to know more about her start in life. Of course, the decision is yours as to knowing anything about the mother and really there was not much known more than you have been told already. But if ever it comes to pass that you or Primrose need any more details about the first few days of her life then I have made some notes from the official medical and nursing notes. Please do not say anything or I will be in trouble. Essentially what you have just been told is quite correct but in case it was ever of any interest or help I will leave you this."

She reached under the blanket that formed the base of the carry cot and withdrew a sealed brown manila envelope and handed it over, picked up the carry cot and left.

And sitting there on that July evening, nursing the now sleeping baby who had become my 'Rose' I gave half a thought to that unopened manila envelope which I had squirreled away to a secret hiding place.

But, there and then, I decided that it was unlikely for it ever to need to be opened.

Chapter 3

1997 Rose – Porthcawl

Gareth, the old gentleman, I say old, for he was probably in his eighties I would guess, if he had been in active service in the Second World War, had been welcoming, hospitable, attentive and was clearly 'all there'. Having dealt with, or nursed, many older people in my long career, I had come across a variety of octogenarians who were failing; some physically, others mentally and not a few in both aspects. Of course, in nursing you can get a skewed impression of the elderly population, because you only see those classed as the elderly who need care or treatment and so, by definition, have physical or mental health issues. You can easily forget that many of those you do not see are relatively heathy and mentally alert and functioning much as they had all their adult lives, save perhaps for episodic issues, minor ailments and relatively insignificant physical limitations. Gareth appeared to be one of this latter group of people.

So, I judged that I should treat him with due regard to his being a man in full command of his faculties and therefore I could safely address my issues head on. And given, that earlier in our discussions, he had invited me to use his forename I looked him in the eye and asked directly.

"Gareth, tell me, what do you know about 'foundlings' and 'adoption'?"

If shocked by my directness he did not let it show, and after only a moment's hesitation for thought he replied, hesitantly and carefully.

"Well adoption is a legal thing where a child who has lost their parents, or been taken away from them by the authorities, is given to new parents to bring them up and the courts are involved at the end of the process and, if they approve, sanction it with an official order, I believe. As to foundlings well, I am not sure, that feels to me like a Dickensian term applying to lost children."

"Very good." I said. "Well, you did a lot better than I would have done before the day my mother effectively told me I was an adopted foundling. But since then I have learned an awful lot more about those two topics in general, but, nowhere near enough in particular to find out how I personally fit into them. Perhaps, if I give you an idea of what I have learned overall, you may better see why I am turning to you to see whether you can add another piece to my very incomplete jigsaw puzzle.

But before I tell you about my personal story, can I first tell you what I have discovered about the general history of adoption in this country, that is if I have correctly understood what I have learned. It will allow you, as it did me, to better understand the climate in which my parents were operating and making decisions at the time I entered this world. Armed with this information you may see why, when I tell you my personal story, my adoptive parents ended up having to wrestle with such a serious dilemma. Furthermore, to have some sympathy with my poor mother, when she engaged me in that fateful conversation on, what was effectively, her death bed.

From time immemorial the coming together of any fertile man and woman can potentially create a child. In the beginning maybe humans behaved in the way animals, like cattle and sheep do today, living in loose extended family groups where surviving young were kept safe and reared within the group. At some point the idea of family grew up where a man and woman – or women – living together might stay with one another in order to bring up their children in a potentially, though not always an actually, supportive group. But of course, human nature and differential sexual drives and opportunities meant that liaisons outside the family, sect, tribe, etc., had the potential to produce a child whose presence was not acceptable, for whatever reason. These children might then be abandoned to their fate, and most might die, or they could potentially be found and cared for by some person or group who, for whatever reason, was able and motivated to help.

As society developed and social rules and mores were created by custom, religion or government, so the pressure to discard children who were the generally unexpected or an unwanted product of a liaison, grew. A general instinct, particularly but not exclusively of women, to feel sorry for an unwanted child, did mean that sometimes others would step in to bring the child up. Mothers of very young girls who were raped or, to use the old-fashioned term, ill-used, would sometimes bring up their grandchild as their own, and indeed that was quite common, it is still not at all unheard of even in this day and age. Nevertheless, there were children who were just abandoned by a woman who could see no way of surviving if she were to keep this child. In the growing urban society of the 1700s, in England, there were increasing numbers of such children who were abandoned, either as tiny babies or even after the mother had supported them through infancy but could no longer go on doing so. Such an abandoned child who was found by some person or authority became known as a foundling.

Only a couple of hundred years before my birth, in 1741 Thomas Coram founded the first Foundlings Hospital and, as I have read, over the years his initial work developed and gradually he was joined by many other organisations concerned in the welfare of children, which really developed in the age of British philanthropy between the 1850s and the First World War. These organisations included the work of the Catholic and other churches as well as other charities like Dr Barnardo's for example. Many of these secured placements for the unwanted child or baby in the homes of those willing to take them and whose personal philosophy accorded with the vision of the placing agency; so, for example, the Catholic Church favoured Catholic people to care for the child, irrespective of the possible background of that child. But it was all done on an ad hoc basis of personal assessment by a particular group or set of individuals. Such unregulated arrangements even extended to the local doctor organising for the unwanted child of some upper or middle class person to be spirited away to the care of a farm labourer's wife some distance away in another doctor friend's area. Sometimes money changed hands and not all of that may have gone with the child. The main focus was the protection of the mother's good name; the care of the child was not a particular matter of interest and it was assumed that the people accepting the child would act in good faith.

In this climate the rights of an abandoning mother over the rights of a child were very much a basis of the first Adoption Act in England and Wales just over seventy years ago in 1926, and indeed there is a register of all legal adoptions since 1927. However, the Act was more about ensuring that those who went through the formal process, and by no means all did, resulted in the natural mother being written out of the child's life and, furthermore, the adoptive parents were protected from her interference.

After that there were some changes which affected the climate of opinion which concerned the care of children and marginally impacted on adoption practices. A lot of the Poor Law responsibilities for welfare of people and children were passed to local authorities including city and county councils. Public Assistance related to finance was managed through Means Testing and applications were scrutinised by the, often hated, local 'Means Test Man'. But, at the same time, improvements were being made to the provision of social care and many local areas set up 'Councils of Social Service' who would get involved in social welfare issues including childcare matters.

By 1939, and the outbreak of war, local authorities had for a while been linking with local voluntary hospitals and any foundlings, in the old sense, were now, in the absence of other agencies or remedies, sometimes dealt with by hospital almoners liaising with the local authority welfare departments to arrange fostering and then subsequently an adoption agency may be asked to become involved. However, there was still a large market in informal fostering and adoption often facilitated by caring and altruistic professionals, including doctors, who very much practiced independently. That, as I understand it, was the background of attitudes to adoption as we entered the war. And of course, the very fact that we were at war relegated the niceties and even the legalities of many things to a very low level on the list of survival.

Gareth, I am giving you this background because it became fundamental for me to understand sufficiently the thinking that might have laid behind the mind-set of a childless couple in 1943 in so far that they may have understood the 'rules of adoption'. An adoption formally would, in their then understanding, as far as I can establish it, have meant that by adopting this abandoned child, they, as adopters, would henceforth be in sole charge of the child and the natural mother, even if she miraculously re-appeared, would have absolutely no rights to contact or see the child. An understanding, incidentally, that would most certainly have been confirmed by the Courts of the day.

Furthermore, in the paternalistic world of that era they would probably have been encouraged to think along the lines that as the natural mother cannot now interfere in any way, that they may as well just consider the child to be their own. To any question which they may have raised, such as 'should we tell the child', the authorities of whatever ilk would more than likely have told them quite clearly that it was simply a matter for them to use their judgement about. But equally there might have been a rider along the lines of 'well after all she was only a few days old when she came to you, so to all intents and purposes she is yours'.

Some six years elapsed after I was born before the next Adoption Act, in 1949, and if my parents had considered its provisions, they would still have found that it, in effect, reiterated that the purpose of adoption was to sever the child from its natural mother and endow the adopters with full parental rights. It maintained the principle that the natural mother had no rights to pursue the child and similarly the child had no right to find and contact a natural parent. It was not for another twenty-seven years that the rights of the child finally became more central in law.

As I understand it the main effect of the new law of 1976 was to completely move the goalposts in respect of the former rights of the adoptive parents to prevent the natural mother having any contact with her natural child, albeit that rules about how this could be arranged were made. And, at the same time, it opened the door for the adoptive child to have the opportunity, again with certain safeguards, to get to understand what had happened to bring them into this new family and even, potentially, to seek to establish contact with their birth mother.

All very laudable, unless you happened to be one of the parties to that earlier adoption 'contract' of many years previous; one which had provided for rights of anonymity from the birth mother. In that former adoption climate people made decisions on what to tell a child based on the then placement of the legal adoption goalposts. So, with particular regard to the issue of what they chose to tell the child about their adoptive status they could have decided to be quite open or to say nothing to the child about their adoption. Either would have been perfectly legally proper and within the spirit of the then law.

The change in legal goalposts caused by this new Act was based on the greater understanding of the issues, especially the rights and interests of the child, and they were well signalled and debated and passed with good intent. However, the arrangements were not confined to adoptions subsequent to the passing of the Act, they were to apply retrospectively as well. Therefore, some people who had acted under the principles of the old legislation now found their earlier decisions in conflict with, or challenged by, the new rules.

As far as I can see it my adoptive parents were amongst those caught up in the effective shifting of the principles of adoption. And there were some consequences for them, as I guess for many others too.

Chapter 4

1980 Alice – Otley

The staff at St Jimmy's in Leeds, in the oncology department, had all been absolutely wonderful ever since I had started going there for treatment, the better part of two years ago now. Even more so in the last couple of months whilst I had been an inpatient and they had been giving me, as it turned out to be, their last shot at enabling me to beat this horrible cancer which has been afflicting me. But now I was delighted to be on my way out; out of the hospital and in due course, as I was now well aware, it would also be out of this world. Just last week they had told me that there was nothing more they could do and it was just a matter of time, a short time, before I would meet my maker.

When my cancer was first diagnosed, I was up for the fight. And I have fought a very good fight and put up stoically with all the demands the treatments have made of me, with a firm goal of wanting to see my fifteen year old granddaughter have her eighteenth birthday before I leave her. But there comes a time in any fight, long after the point where you begin to feel the balance shift against you, when ultimately you have to come to terms with the fact that the chances of winning that particular round are disappearing and inevitably all chances of victory disappear completely. I had recognised this, long before the day last week when my lovely consultant faced me with the truth that this was coming and mentally I had already begun to make plans.

I told him that I thought this was likely to be the news that he brought me and if that was to be the case then I wanted to ask if I could go home, and he readily agreed but said it would take a little while to make arrangements for me to receive the pain relief that I would require at home. I pointed out that my daughter, Rose, was a state registered nurse and maybe that would make the arrangements easier. He responded that, unfortunately, professional procedures required that pain relief, in the circumstances in which I found myself, should only be offered by independent professionals. I could understand that but was nevertheless disappointed that it would take a couple more days than otherwise to make the necessary arrangements. But now the day was here, and so was Bill, and I was enjoying the journey in the car out through Headingley towards the farm that had been my home for thirty-eight years.

Of course I was not returning to a working farm anymore. Rose had been set on becoming a nurse and as Bill got older and farm work became heavier, even though we had long since cut back on the milking herd. Accordingly, we had decided to sell some of the farming land and just retain the farmhouse and a couple of acres. The sale of the land allowed us enough money to modernise the old farmhouse and incorporate the adjoining cottage into it and also to demolish most of the farm buildings and replace them with a house for Rose, who by this time was married to Walter. There was also enough money to build a bungalow where the old brick-built pigsty's had been, set a little distance from our two houses and which we used as a holiday let, to provide us with another income. Rose and Walter paid all the utility bills for both our properties as we had gifted them the house itself.

I was very much looking forward to getting back to my own home again where, in addition to two nursing visits a day, I would also have support from Bill, Rose, Walter and Sally my lovely granddaughter. I was well aware that my time with them would not be lengthy, but I was so looking forward to treasuring every single minute that I had with each of them. But there was one thing that I did not look forward to and it was something so important that it needed doing urgently and I had resolved to get it out of the way as quickly as possible. In fact, I had decided to lay the groundwork for that particular ordeal on the journey home from the hospital.

"Bill." I said quite casually. "I want to thank you for looking after me all these years and especially these last two, which cannot have been easy for you. You know how much I love you, but you also know that there is one thing where we have differed in our views. It has not been a big problem I suppose until now, because we have avoided it as a topic. But I must tell you that I cannot in all honestly leave our family without telling Rose the truth."

"Oh! Please let's not go over this again," he responded, crossly, "I don't think that having kept a secret for nearly 40 years now that it is going to benefit anybody, least of all Rose, by raking the past up at this particular juncture. You know that I told you about a conversation I had with that solicitor bloke in the pub about the criminal law and the way that sometimes it's only the sentences that were available for the crime on the day that you did it, that apply. If they change the law to make a punishment more severe for some offence, then they sometimes set a date and only if you commit your crime after that date can you be liable to the heavier sentence.

So those politicians that changed the adoption law in 1976 got it all wrong. Okay, society might have grown up and it might have been felt better for there to be greater rights for adoptive children, but that should only have applied to adoptions after the time they changed the law. You know full well we were told, at the time we took Rose on, that the natural mother could never ever be involved in her life from that time forward. You know also that we understood there was no duty for us to tell Rose anything about her birth and its circumstances. What is more you know that you have been her mother from the age of about one week. There are many mothers who, through the difficulties of birth, or being ill at the time of the birth, have been unable to care for their child for a week or two, or even longer, until they were well enough. That could have been you, incapable of caring for her for a few days. So, I wish you would just leave things as they are."

"I had half expected this to still be your view and so I can say that there are just two things that trump that view as far as I am concerned. To the best of my knowledge, I have never, ever, not told Rose the truth. Because of that I cannot face leaving this life whilst there remains a chance, however minuscule, that something will occur that reveals Rose's origins to her and for her then to realise that her mother had allowed this lie to continue."

34

"Whatever's going to happen that could possibly reveal that if we don't say anything?"

"Well, we have seen how medical science has developed, look how they've kept me alive so long. And what would happen if Rose, or even Sally, develop an illness, something that is deemed to be an hereditary illness, but which is nothing to do with either of our families. Equally you could become ill and lose your reason with something like, say Alzheimer's, and completely unintentionally something could be said which again revealed the truth. But then, and I hope you might accept this is the best argument, it is Rose's life and she has the right to know about her background. She is a wonderful young woman and mature enough to handle what I have to tell her. She's got the support of you, Water and Sally but I am quite confident she will not need that."

There was a silence which must have lasted for about a mile or more.

"When we were younger," said Bill, "and got to the point after five or more years of marriage without children coming along, we decided to leave things to fate. I wish you would again leave things to fate and not be starting off a hare running that may lead to all sorts of unforeseen consequences."

"Yes, we did say we would leave things to fate, but fate intervened in the form of Ernest falling off a roof and Doctor Lynch coming to see him and having time to spend talking to us over a cup of tea. Then us sort of making another of our well-known non-decisions by going along with the idea that maybe, possibly, perhaps, we might, one day, adopt. Fate brought Doctor Lynch back to see us and that then let Rose into our lives, and we did make a decision at the end of the day and that decision was to care for this wonderful girl of ours. And whilst I realise that for one of the few times in our lives we are at odds with one another, I have made my decision. I'm going to tell Rose because it is her right to know and not our right to withhold that knowledge from her."

"So, you are going to fire your Parthian Shot," said Bill angrily, "and gallop off so that you do not have to deal with the consequences?"

"Oh! I see. It's about you feeling you have to deal with the consequences. To me that just seems like another way of putting the adoptive parents' rights and feelings above that of the adopted child, just as all the adoption law before 1976 did."

I could see Bill was really angry.

"Don't you think I have enough on my plate without having to deal with an issue that does not have to even be an issue?"

"Yes. You have the issue of me to deal with and I recognise that will be very hard. But we have colluded together to avoid the issue of Rose over the years and it has always been you that has taken the 'let sleeping dogs lie' approach and like with the big issues in our lives we have failed to make a decision."

"Don't you see?" He said banging the steering wheel with one hand. "That it is a non-issue anyway because she is not adopted."

Now it was my turn for a short silence

"What do you mean?"

"Well, you are so bloody full on about truthfulness and taking responsibility so ask yourself what did you do about sorting out the legalities and the paperwork? Who do you think got sent to get the Birth Certificate at the end of the war, when one was needed for us to needed to enrol Rose at school?" He paused. "Me! Did you ever study it? No!" He shouted. Then more calmly.

"Did you think an adopted child's birth certificate would name the adoptive parents as mother and father without any reference to them having adopted? I know I did. And I carefully studied the certificate I brought home. Did you?"

"You told me that it was all in order and that there was no mention of adoption because that was the way the system was in those days so that the birth mother could not follow up on things."

"Yes, but did you ever bother to look at it closely?"

I said nothing just looked at this man I thought I knew so well and who had never, to my knowledge, ever lied or cheated on me in all our years together.

"Yes, I told you that all was in order and in one sense it was, but did you look closely at the full certificate, the person named as the informant, and who signed the register? Doctor Lynch did, reporting as one who was present at the birth. He puts down 'Name of Father' me, and occupation 'L/Corporal Royal

36

Electrical and Mechanical Engineers' and the mother is you Alice Longstaff (nee Trantor). Place of birth and dates all correct and signed by some 'Asst. Registrar'. The registration date was about the end of April. But the thing is that we, that is you and me, are named as father and mother."

"You said there never was an adoption hearing or whatever because of the war."

"Yes, I said that because for anybody to find out that there was not would have got folk into trouble. Doctor Lynch for one and you and me for not saying when we noticed that it was wrong, even though, by then, the worthy Doctor was dead himself."

"Why didn't' you say something?"

"I suppose I just thought that it would open a can of worms and because I thought it would cause upset for you and Rose. And let me say, that this was still at the time when your precious 'rights of the adoptive child' were on nobody's lips. The doctor thought he was doing everyone a favour. Bloody Hitler may have been running the country within a few months. Who knows who would care in wartime? What I do know is that in the eyes of the Law, our Rose was registered as being born naturally to you and there is a full birth certificate to prove it. How that was done I have no idea, from some limited enquiries I know that a person present at the birth, and the good doctor was, can in some circumstances register a birth. Maybe he said that I was serving in the army and you were too poorly to register in the required period; I do not know. But the deed was done and if we say anything to Rose about her beginnings all of this may come back to haunt us."

I was silent again for a while, then.

"So, over all these years you have never really taken the trouble to spell that out to me?"

"Agreed that's true; but on the few occasions when Rose has needed her birth certificate you have never expressed a concern that she may detect something was amiss."

"But you have never spelt out the flaws in the process you had found."

"No and now I have; what does that mean to you?"

"It means you have bee……….."

"Lying?"

"……… no not that. But not completely open and truthful either and I find that disappointing."

"Well, that is both interesting and hypocritical because that seems to me to be a mirror image of the way Rose is going to feel when we reveal that we have not been 'open and truthful' about her own beginnings. And," he said triumphantly, "it nicely makes my case for us saying nothing to her. The time for those explanations is long gone, SO LEAVE THINGS BE."

Although we were approaching Bramhope and only a couple of miles from home at that point, we completed the journey in silence. I felt all my plans and good intentions of sorting the issue out before I left Rose were thrown into turmoil.

Sally and Rose came rushing out to greet us when we pulled into the courtyard between our two houses: formerly the farmyard. Welcomes and smiles abounded and I got caught up in their enthusiasm and of course I was excited to be home too. Sally disappeared and collected a wheelchair and I was ushered inside. The old front parlour which had been our lounge was now transformed with a big 'hospital' bed installed where I could easily look our past Rose's new home, which was almost at right angles to ours and I could see our remaining field and our former fields beyond, still farmed by our neighbour. When the adaptations were made to the house a toilet and washbasin had been fitted downstairs and I could use that. The only shower was upstairs and I guessed I would not be climbing those.

Bill busied himself unloading the car and the girls were all ready with tea and home-made fruit scones and I was fussed over far too much for my independent-minded liking. But I recognised the emotional stress for them as well as me. They were welcoming a mum and a grandma home for the last time. Oh! They would not have so described it, but subconsciously it was there. They were making life as perfect for me as possible today, because in just a few weeks they would never be able to do anything for me ever again.

Bill remained scarce and after a while Sally, who had sought and been given permission for a day off school, went off to complete the assignment she had agreed to finish, as part of the time off arrangement. Rose saw that I was tiring and got me into bed.

"Are you OK Mum? You did not look too happy when you arrived today, and dad has gone off somewhere. Have you two fallen out?"

"Not really. It's a difficult adjustment for us all. Not just the practical changes you have made, and, by the way, thanks for organising all this." I said waving my hand around the room. "This is lovely and I know I will be happy being here with you all and having this lovely view. It's going to be an emotional time for us all, and of course you know that better than anyone here from your own nursing experience. Your dad is going to have a hard time coming to terms with it all and he and I love each other a great deal yet there are things that we, even after all our wonderful years together, have to come to terms with."

"Like what?"

"Oh no, darling; not today. Maybe another day; let me now just rest a while in the unbelievable delight of being home and of having my two precious girls to look after me."

In that way I sidestepped the issue and bought myself a little thinking time.

But ten wonderful days on from coming home I feel as though things are beginning to take a turn for the worse. I feel weaker by the day and much more reliant on the pain relief. And, as I anticipated, going up to the shower has not been an option and reluctantly I have agreed to let Rose bed bath me today. I cannot really be bothered but I recognise the need. So, prevarication time is now more than past and decision time is here. I have heard Rose telling Bill that he should make himself scarce whilst she attends to my needs, so we will have uninterrupted time together, as Sally is off at school and Walter at work. I had intended to do the deed whilst Rose was bathing me but in the end I have waited until she has finished and we are sitting together holding hands.

"Rose, you know I love you and have always loved you from the moment you came into my life and I will love you for ever. And you also know that I have always insisted on telling the truth and I have never knowing lied to you. But there are two sets of lies in my book those of commission and those of omission. I have never told you a lie of commission, that is to say told you

39

something that I knew to be untrue or dishonest or whatever. But maybe I have been guilty of a lie of omission, which is to say that I knew something affecting you, which I could, and arguably should, have told you, and I failed to do.

When your father and I took a decision that the thing we knew about you was something that might be unsettling for you and perhaps was better left unsaid, it was a decision based on what was the accepted wisdom of the day. In recent years that wisdom has been replaced with a new set of values and ideas, which, if they had been around when we made our original decision would no doubt have changed the way we approached things. I cannot leave you, as it looks like I soon may, without telling the truth on our misguided lie of omission."

"Is this the thing that has seems to have got between you and dad?" She asked; and I nodded.

"Nothing can ever really come between that lovely man and me, but he will be mad at me talking to you about this, yet I know that if I do not say anything then he will not broach the subject and my decision is based on every single person's right to expect to be told the truth by the people they trust most. I should have told you this many years ago but the Law in 1943 gave me a clear steer that encouraged me to say nothing. Then for the last few years there has been a big debate about the morality and rights of individuals in your situation, a debate which I have followed closely and with whose conclusions I agree, even though it puts me in this dilemma.

There is no easy way to say this other than to say that until you became an adult I never hardly let you out of my sight. You were, and are, so precious that I did not want to miss another day with you because there were a few missing days from your birth until you came into my care."

"Are you saying I was adopted?"

"In essence, yes. Dad and I had been married for over a decade and it was clear we would not have children naturally so yes, we took on another person's unwanted child and we wanted that child and we have loved her, you, with all our hearts and all our beings."

"But mum, I have seen my birth certificate and it names you as mother and dad as father."

"Yes, it does, and here I must say I have been remiss because I never bothered to study it and it was only when dad was bringing me home from hospital that he pointed out that it is apparently a 'real' birth certificate, but it is not correct in many ways. Your date and place of birth is correct. But you were never an issue from my body, as I have never borne a child, yet it says I was the mother. I always assumed that was what an adoption related birth certificate looked like so as to keep the natural mother out of it, as was the way in those days. But dad pointed out that you were registered by the doctor who was present at the birth, three weeks after you were born and two weeks after you came to me.

And I remember that doctor, Doctor Lynch, coming to see me on my own a couple of weeks after you arrived and saying something like 'now, are you going to keep this little girl or not as I need to sort out the paperwork'. Of course, by this time you were mine and I could never have let you go. I know he talked to Uncle Ernest and Aunt Agnes and I thought little about it. But when I started talking about telling you around the time of the Adoption Act debate in 1975, Dad had studied the birth certificate, and although he never told me about its apparent discrepancy, he made it clear that he was dead against telling you and in my weakness, he managed to stop me. But when I raised it on the way home from the hospital the other day, he told me what he had later discovered something about the Birth Certificate which I had not known about."

Rose's face looked to have gone pale and her shock was evident but we were still holding hands so I hurried on.

"When you were first nursing and you were doing assignments, I recall you doing something on psychology and I remember it relating to child development and the issue of what, if I remember correctly, were the theories of nature and nurture as elements in childhood development. How much was innate in the child, reflex responses or coming from its genetics and how much was in the nurture, or the training, love and help given by the parent figure. But whilst that matter which you were researching and writing your essay about gave pause me for thought at that time, we were still years in advance of the debate

41

about the rights of the adopted child and the change in the law, just four years ago.

As I recall it you seemed, in your assignment, to conclude that the way the child was treated by the parent was the most important factor in a healthy development and that encouraged me to think that, having done our best for you, Dad and I would have overcome any deficiencies which your natural mother may, or may not, have passed on to you."

"This has been a huge issue for you personally, hasn't it?" Rose said and I nodded. "Well. I will not say I am not completely taken aback, and I am sure that there will need to be some time for me to think it all through, but here is my first reaction. You and Dad have 'nurtured' me so incredibly well and I am happy and secure with a good marriage of my own and a lovely daughter and I cannot see at this stage that this information is going to knock me off my life course. It will certainly not stop me loving you and Dad for all the love you have given to me. I guess that if you had told me at Sally's age, fifteen, with exams and hormones and peers ready to pounce on anything out of the ordinary, it could have led to problems.

Right now, I want to give you back the love you gave me as a child and to keep you with us as long as possible and in doing so make things as good for you as they can be. And I think that maybe we should just keep this between us as it may not be so easy for Dad to deal with me knowing what you have just told me, given what you say about how he sees things."

"Oh! Rose. Thank you so much for hearing this from me, it is such a relief for me to at last tell you and to not find that you are really mad at me. I think you may be right about Dad needing to let sleeping dogs lie, but there is something important related to all this that you must know. Neither Dad nor I were ever told anything about your beginnings. We did not really ask that much and to be honest I do not think there is much to know. You were delivered to us by a very kindly 'do gooder' lady and a nurse. The lady was led on an inspection tour of the house whilst I was shown how to care for this beautiful little baby girl. When leaving, the nurse, well I guess midwife really, said that she thought that there may be a time in the future when we, or you, might want to know a little bit more about the circumstances of

42

your birth and she had thoughtfully, and I suspect against regulations, written some things down, culled from the medical and nursing notes of the hospital. She had put them into a sealed brown manila envelope which she passed to me. That envelope is as sealed today as it was when it was handed to me, and I have no interest in its contents. It is in my underwear drawer in the bedroom dressing table, underneath the lining paper. So, it's up to you now to decide what to do about that."

Chapter 5

1997 Rose – Porthcawl

"I am sorry." I said to Gareth. "I think that I can see from your face that you are wondering what all this is about."

"There, dear lady, you are completely wrong. These last few years my life has been quite regulated and, in many ways, I rather like routine. But even so sometimes it is nice to have an unexpected change. And to have a very attractive young woman call to your door and start telling you a lovely, long and interesting story is absolutely delightful and will be a source of memories for me, for a long time to come."

"It's nice of you to say so, and the flattery is rather nice, but a little over the top for a grandmother like me. But thank you anyway"

"So, you opened the envelope?" Said Gareth.

"Well no. Not then nor indeed for another fifteen years. There was too much emotion around already, because mum died within about five weeks and dad was distraught and became a bit lost and needed my support. I talked about the revelation with Walter, my husband, of course and he encouraged me to leave the issue, whilst I was grieving and also supporting dad. Dad never really got over losing mum and within about three years he went too. Mum was correct in that he never broached the subject of my origins or ever asked me if Mum had ever said anything to me. I guess he may have thought if I never raised it then probably he had convinced her to keep her own counsel. Even then I might have begun to think about it but hard on the heels of Dad's demise my husband Walter, an apparently healthy individual, had a heart attack at work and I never had chance to even say goodbye to him in the way I had with Mum.

Throughout all of this Sally was growing and working hard at her own nursing career and then she met Michael, they married

44

and had the kids and my life was constantly filled with family issues of one sort or another. I gave up full time nursing and got a job as a carer with a local private homecare company. My background and experience in nursing made me the most qualified person on their books and I sought, and got, a good deal from them. I said I was willing to work hard and give them something special, in terms of the qualifications and experience to deal with those care cases that required a really high degree of expertise. In return I specified the working times I could offer which I tailored around supporting the children, so that Sally was able to return to work.

My life was so hectic, and all thoughts of my origins were firmly relegated to a future, 'to think about' list. And so it remained until Michael got his first step on the promotion ladder with his move to Bristol couple of years ago. Then my frenetic lifestyle was suddenly changed. No more childcare for me was the biggest miss in my life, and although I increased my work commitments to fill some of the time I was still left with lots of unfilled, not at work, time. There is only so much decoration and sorting of stuff you can do and then you are reduced to the telly, books and quiet meals on your own. So then in 1995 I finally decided to open the envelope and that then led to giving me a lot of work over the last two years, which eventually has led me to your door.

Inside the envelope were two sheets of lined paper which looked as though they could have been torn from an exercise book or the like. Neither had any identification marks or headings and was, apparently, written in the same neat hand.

The first sheet gave simple facts apparently copied from hospital notes and here it is." I said, handing Gareth two pages of typewritten copies which I had transcribed from the handwritten originals which had been within the brown envelope. I then read to him from my copy.

"*Friday 2 April 1943. 8-13 pm. Woman arrives at hospital. Presents as unkempt and in apparently confused mental state, but she is self-evidently in labour. Admitted and attended by nursing staff. Delivered of healthy girl weighing 7lbs 3ozs at 6-44 am Saturday 3 April 1943. On call GP, Dr C Lynch, present at the birth.*

Apart from feeding baby, mother rests till Saturday lunchtime at which point duty sister seeks to get some history from mother. Name Sheila Johnson, date of birth 7 June 1920. No identification or ration cards. No previous children. No given address. States she has been living variously with friends. Has no settled accommodation. Informed by Sister Jones that her case will be referred to the hospital voluntary almoner and it was hoped that she would be seen on Monday next. Apart from feeding the child she spends little other time with the baby and appears uncommunicative with staff, sleeps a lot and eats all meals provided.

Sunday 4 April. Asks if she can have a 'breather' outside is allowed to get dressed and spends half an hour walking in the grounds observed by a nurse.

Monday 5 April. Feeds baby at approx. 6 am. At 8 am she requests another 'breather' and is allowed to go unaccompanied, as staff members are very busy. At 9-30am the almoner arrives and mother cannot be found. After a search of the grounds proves unsuccessful the police are notified and attend at 10-15 to make enquiries.

Wednesday 7 April. Police inform hospital that they are unable to find any trace of a woman of the description they were given.

Thursday 8 April. Meeting. Ward Sister, Almoner, Chair of Governors and Dr. Lynch. Where it is resolved that Dr Lynch will make initial arrangements for the care of the baby.

Friday 9 April. Baby, earlier named Primrose by staff as mother had not named the child, is, later in the afternoon, discharged to foster parents as arranged by Doctor Lynch.'

"The actual place," I told Gareth, "is not mentioned but it was Otley County Infirmary, and I discovered that it was originally an infirmary under the Poor Law, as I understand it, then it became Otley County Hospital in 1948 after the National Health Service was created. Now it comes under the Leeds Hospitals and needs upgrading and in fact there are discussions about redeveloping it all.

However, interesting though that page was in terms of the actual records and a clear chronology it tells us almost nothing about the mother.

46

My mother!

But the second sheet is less formal and is clearly just someone trying to capture something of this woman who arrives, gives birth and disappears leaving the child abandoned.

'*Sheila had limited her contact with nursing staff but after she disappeared, I was talking about her to the mother in the next bed who had been delivered the same day as Sheila. It seems that this other mother tried to be friendly and at first, just like with nursing staff, Sheila was reluctant to engage. But whilst the staff members were very busy and worked shifts, that other mother was beside Sheila day and night for two days. After a while Sheila did begin to engage with this other mother at least to the extent of being civil. Then, on the Sunday, the day before she disappeared, there was a slightly more personal exchange, from which other mother learned that Sheila had obviously lived abroad for part of her life and she had said that she had been a fool and made lots of mistakes. But last year she was affected by an incident where the brave crew of a naval ship called the* Loyalty *saved another ship called the* Atlantic *something or other and that incident, she said, had brought her to her senses. As a result, she had managed to change her life but unfortunately she realised that the clock could not be turned back and therefore she would just have to learn how to carry on paying for her mistakes. It was such an unusually personal conversation that the other mother wrote it in her diary later the following day when Sheila was found to have disappeared. Looking through Sheila's bedside drawer the police found a note addressed to the other mother which wished her every happiness and that she would often think of her and both their children as they grew up.*'

"So!" Said Gareth. "Now I immediately see where you think I might be able to assist you with your story, because you have somehow discovered that I was on the *Loyalty* at the time of the incident that was mentioned."

"You were? How wonderful." I said. "I had discovered that you were on that ship during the time it was requisitioned by the Navy, but I had not gleaned that you were also involved in that particular incident. You see I began my search by contacting the local British Legion and they referred me to the Soldiers, Sailors and Air Force charity and they gave me suggestions as to where

47

to start my search. The National Archives, Royal Navy Archives, Forces War records all had letters and, or, visits from me. Some had a lot of contact and I travelled to London quite a few times following leads. I can tell you that it has been hard work. I tried first to see if the 'incident' of the two ships mentioned was listed somewhere and there I drew a blank, in fact it was almost as if it had never happened. Then trying to trace information about the *Loyalty* itself was hard because she was never fully integrated into the Navy even though she was requisitioned for war work. The company that owned her effectively leased her to the Navy. Eventually though a trip to the company offices in Liverpool led to the information the *Loyalty* was only in the employ of the Navy for about four years and during that time there were four commanders I eventually discovered.

These were Baker, Hopkins, Morrison and O'Shaughnessy. I tried starting in alphabetical order, but I was soon struggling to locate these people and I enlisted the help of a local genealogist, without his input I would not be here today. Baker was hard, but after about six months we were convinced that he had died in the sixties. Hopkins seems to have drowned when the ship, on which he was gunnery officer, was torpedoed escorting an Atlantic convoy."

"Ah. That I did not know." Said Gareth. "He was a lovely young man and my second in command indeed he actually succeeded me as Acting Commander when I left the *Loyalty*. I did not know of his fate, and I am saddened to hear that he did not even make it through the war. Sorry, I interrupted you, do go on."

"Well, Morrison took less time and he had survived until 1988 when he died of a heart attack. So, we turned to the last on my alphabetical list; that is you. Fairly quickly we were able to trace you to an address in Penarth."

"My parents' home, that would probably be." Said Gareth and I nodded.

"Then to an address in Lisvane, Cardiff where the trail went cold because you had apparently sold the house to a couple who only lived there for a few months before the husband was unexpectedly offered a good job in London and they sold the house to the present people. They gave me the address of the

48

owners who had bought it from you and I wrote to them, and in due course I had a short telephone call to the effect that you had not left a forwarding address, and they couldn't help me and goodbye. As one final effort a couple of months ago I came down to Sally and Michael's in Bristol and Sally brought me to Cardiff. Together we tried all the doors of the neighbours, and I got lucky with an elderly lady across the road."

"Barbara Jenkins." Said Gareth, and I nodded. "Yes, Barbara always kept up with gossip, she was a friend of my late wife, though I never really took to her, and I told her when I was leaving that I was going to temporary accommodation but looking to settle either back in Penarth or maybe in Porthcawl. I had no interest in getting Christmas cards from her, so I never let her know my address."

"Exactly." I said. "I was given Penarth or Porthcawl as possible places and I returned to Otley and with my genealogist friend started searches of voting registrations and a few weeks ago your address came up, and........ . Well, here I am."

"Well! Congratulations on all your detective work........."

My mobile phone rang and it was Michael to say that the kids were having a whale of a time but that he wanted to beat the teatime motorway traffic round Cardiff and Newport so he would come for me in about half an hour if I was still OK. I told him that was fine. Gareth had gone off to the kitchen whilst I was on the phone, and I could hear the kettle boiling and went to join him.

"Thought another cuppa would be in order." He said.

"Lovely." I replied and looking at him I could see that he was pensive.

"In reality," he said, "the only link, tenuous at best, to discovering something of the woman who apparently and possibly bore you into this world is the hearsay evidence of a colleague mother, if I can put it that way, who shared a room over a weekend whilst both she and her contact in the next bed were exhausted from childbirth and also meeting the demands of their respective new born children. Sorry, I worked for three years after my retirement as a court usher and got into the legalistic way of things as they were presented in trials."

49

"Yes, you could put it like that I suppose." I said. "But hearsay or not it's all I have at present to link me to her."

"Yes, and despite its hearsay element, there is the fact that the reporting mother wrote down what the other mother, possibly your mother, told her pretty much straight away, again in the legal sense fairly contemporaneous notes. Good evidence. Although, as against that we do not have the notes, we only have the hearsay evidence of the nurse who says she had seen the original notes related to her by the woman who wrote them. Another problem would be if the other mother got her facts right about the ships involved in this incident in the first place.

Well, I will stop being silly and my attempts to be quasi legalistic and I will tell you straight away that there was indeed such an incident. To use the favourite line of South Wales's most famous singer and songwriter of recent years, Max Boyce, 'I know cos I was there'. So yes, I was there and in command of the *Loyalty* on that fateful day. However, when I start to think about it, there was also, quite coincidentally, a young woman who would have much more reason to remember all that transpired in that particular rescue than any other woman.

That, in itself, begs the question of why your mother, if indeed that was her, saw such significance in that incident to the extent that she might have referred to it in in the circumstances you describe. On that particular point I have not got a clue. But let's take this tea through to a comfy seat and let me review that incident in my mind and see where it takes us."

Chapter 6

1942 Gareth - Loch Ewe, Northwest Scotland

For a seaman the weather defines his moment. He must deal with every twist and turn of its vagaries. My predecessor generation of seamen, those whose ships were propelled by wind power, were, to a much greater extent, hampered in having to deal with those vagaries of weather. However, they were probably more in tune with those elements than us modern sailors whose ships are driven by engines and, in many cases, we have the bonus of a covered wheelhouse in which to shelter from the worst of those elements. But we still, albeit to a somewhat lesser extent, face the weather and its many moods, sometimes benign, sometimes malevolent, and today had been one of the latter weather experiences. And also today, Wednesday 1st July 1942, I had managed to face the violence of the weather whilst providing assistance to other seafarers in distress and, by the Grace of God, I am still here to tell the tale.

Just.

Coming down to earth after the day's experiences I was sitting in the wheelhouse as we lay at anchor. Looking forward, the tide was on the ebb and so we were bows in towards the landward end of the loch, I sat idly watching as the watery evening sun, which was setting astern of me, lit the hillsides at the head of the loch. It was turning into a peaceful evening after the ravages of the short-lived storm which had spent its force here and was moving on to the east to give some other poor seamen bother in the Moray Firth or North Sea. In that peace, that had only recently descended, I reflected on the life experiences which had brought me here and, arguably, had saved the lives of myself and others today, whilst at the same time doing my country a service.

My father had been a dock pilot in Penarth, South Wales, and I was one of my parent's five children to achieve adulthood;

unlike three more of my siblings who sadly did not make it that far. A pretty heavy contra score for my parents but, by the standards of child mortality of their day, three deaths in childhood in one family was no worse than many other families and certainly not extreme. My Irish grandfather had divided his time working as an inshore fisherman and tending his meagre crops on the small parcel of land next to the one roomed thatched cottage in which his family lived. But he and his family became part of the Irish diaspora spread by the onset of the potato famine of the previous century. Many of that generation went to America and other overseas places and some others made the short crossing to Fishguard and many of those walked penniless in search of work. Some only went as far as that industrial area of South Wales which might provide employment in shipping, manufacturing and mining. In some ways they reversed the old myth of the exodus of the Saxons who could swim; whom, albeit doubtful legend says, were driven west by the Romans or Danes and those that could swim went to Ireland so to become the Irish race. Nice story, but apocryphal of course.

My father and grandfather had links to the sea but I was fortunate in that one of father's friends, John Francis (I never knew his family name), was a Bristol Channel Pilot. In those days these pilots were self-employed and they would sail their small pilot cutters down the Bristol Channel and offer their services to inbound ships. In the pilot cutter there was just John Francis and his assistant whose job it was to bring the cutter back single handed, when he got a ship to pilot. As a boy I had been out with him a few times and through that I learned a bit about boat handling as I got to help sail the cutter home with his assistant. John Francis took me under his wing and it was he that got me my first berth on a Reardon Smith's ship, a Cardiff based shipping company, not long after I left school in 1927. Like many small companies of the day it was what was known as a tramping company, meaning that it went with a locally loaded cargo to a distant port and there, through local agents secured another cargo. If you had gone abroad you may be lucky to get a return cargo to the United Kingdom, where shipping laws of the day allowed you to leave the ship, or 'pay off' as it was known, but just as likely you might be off to a completely different part of the world. My first ship kept me crisscrossing the world and away from home for fourteen months before I could 'pay off' and during that time I graduated quickly from Ordinary to Able Seaman with the added bonus of a Steering Certificate.

John Francis had told me that to get ahead I needed to study. He warned me that at sea there were men of many kinds, from the ordinary honest lad making a living to the idiot who was avoiding jail or even those who ought to be in an asylum. I found his words to be true, though in the main most were in the first category he described. He exhorted me to not spend my seagoing life in the fo'c'sle, in other words not just to stay as an ordinary sailor but aim to become a merchant navy officer. To that end he gave me a much battered copy of 'Nicholl's Seamanship and Nautical Knowledge' which, the inside of the cover advised, would be of 'great assistance in helping the reader to pass the 'Second Mates', Mates', and Masters' Examinations'. I think this book had first been published in 1905 and my edition was updated in about 1920. Possession of such a book often led to a lot of ribbing by fellow mariners whose main focus in life was to earn money and then spend as much as they could in the bars and brothels of the ports visited.

After about three years I had the good fortune to serve on a ship called the 'Norwich City' and the master was a former HMS Conway Merchant Navy Training Ship cadet and he took an interest in my intentions to try to qualify as a deck officer. It was he who helped me with the celestial navigation issues which were not easy to learn, just from books. We traded for about ten months in the Pacific and during that time he taught me and his company sponsored Deck Apprentice to take sun sights every day; much to the anger of the Bo'sun who had to let me off duties to do this. In order to gain the Board of Trade maritime qualifications you had to pass examinations, including an oral examination, but before that you had to have achieved the required amount of four years 'sea time' in other words you had gained some experience. Anyway, alongside all my sea time experience, my book learning and the time I paid to attend a crash course before my exams, I got my Second Mates 'ticket', or to give it the proper name, 'Certificate of Competency, Second Mate (Foreign Going)'. That was in 1933 and by gaining the necessary sea time in between each of my next two tickets I qualified as Mate in 1935 and then went on to get my Masters in 1938.

However, even though I was qualified as a Master and therefore legally able to have a ship of my own, there had been hard times in the post-depression years and in fact there were men with master's tickets even sailing as able seamen, just to get a job. I had been lucky that this period was ending and, as the country moved towards war, work became more plentiful and, just before the war began, I manged to get a Mates job. Whilst awaiting a ship I had applied to join the Royal Naval Volunteer Reserve (RNVR) and had been accepted but before I could go for training I got a ship and deferred my training until my return home. When the war in Europe broke out, I was on the other side of the world and it took me until the middle of 1941 before I could get back home and fulfil obligation to serve my country in uniform.

After a few days at home with my parents in Penarth I went off to the King Alfred's Training 'ship', which was actually a shore establishment on the south coast, in Hove, next door to Brighton. It was not far off Christmas 1941 before I was approaching the end of my training at King Alfred's when the Commanding Officer sent for me and told me I was being posted to command an inshore vessel and I was to travel to Liverpool and report for final instructions. I recalled the winter's day of my arrival at Liverpool Lime Street and walking the short distance to Derby House, the Headquarters of the naval director of the then Western Approaches Command. I was sent to see an aged Lieutenant Commander who was in charge of inshore vessels. He was a real throwback to the days of Admiral Jellicoe and the First World War, which after all had ended less than twenty-five years before. I could almost still hear his plummy voice saying.

"Ah, O'Shaughnessy. My dear boy. Sealed Orders are here for you in this envelope. You are off north sailing on tomorrow's morning tide. Off you go. You have the *Loyalty*, join her in the Overcoat Yard."

Of course, he knew that I would reply where is that? And when I did, he triumphantly explained.

"In Cammell Laird's shipyard of course, don't'cha see……….. Cammell Laird. Get it ….camel haired so camel haired …….overcoat! Ha. Ha. Ha"

Of course, he was referring to the famous Birkenhead shipyard of Cammell Laird and Company, on the other side of the river Mersey, and this most awful play on words was his little joke. It obviously made an old man happy, so I left him to it.

Off I went across town to the river and down to the Liverpool Pier Head and, after a twenty-minute wait, took the next ferry to Birkenhead. As we crossed the river, I noticed that the training ship HMS Conway was not at her moorings off Rock Ferry, where I had seen her on previous visits to the Mersey. My former captain, the one who had helped me with my celestial navigation, had spent two years training on her and referred to the old black and white painted, wooden walled relic of the time of the Napoleonic wars, as his 'old wooden mother', which, he explained, was part of the ship's song. In answer to my enquiry a ferry deckhand told me she had been moved in May to moorings off Bangor, in the Menai Straits, because of all the air raids on Liverpool. From the ferry I made my way to the dockyard and after showing my pass I was directed to a large basin adjacent to the lock gates. By the time I arrived it the light was fading and in that darkening December afternoon I was looking for my first command. First, I passed one of Alfred Holts ships that had been in for repair and the next was a small corvette, so I straightened my back in anticipation of arrival at 'my ship' only to find that the gangway notice did not provide me with the ship's name I was after. On I went, acknowledging the salute of the corvette's gangway guard and just beyond was the rounded stern of a tug with the name *Loyalty* emblazoned on it.

Somewhat disappointingly my first command was to be a tug, 145 feet long, 31 feet beam and drawing 12 feet with a tonnage of 740, whereas my first ship on going to sea in 1927 had a tonnage of over ten times that.

Still, it was to be my ship. And a modern vessel of its type, I noticed. High bluff bows with the inevitable myriad of tyre fenders, a short foredeck just to give access to a small windlass to operate the anchor and a working area for docking. Then the forepart of the accommodation housing had five round port holes across the forward-facing part, none of which would have a view forward of the vessel because of the high bow. Above the one level of the main deck, in effect in the upper of the two storeys of housing, was a raised walkway to enable the master to move out of either side of the wheelhouse and walk a few paces towards the stern, to better view what was happening whilst towing. Abaft the accommodation was a much smaller funnel than I was used to, and this was because this tug was so relatively modern that it ran on fuel oil, rather than being powered by coal and steam. Then, further aft still, comprising well over a third of the length of the vessel was the towing deck fitted with two towing arches to prevent towlines from snagging. I realised that she had modern lines and, of her type, she was a smart little vessel.

Looking back those seven months, to when I first took command, I remembered how happy I was that this little ship was mine. That the oddballs whom I had discovered made up the crew, had turned from such an eclectic bunch of individuals, many of whom thought serving on this 'tub' as opposed to tug, was beneath them, had become such an interdependent unit that had enabled us, working together, to be able to achieve what we had today. And I smiled as I remembered throwing my kit bag on board and climbing, unchallenged and unwelcomed, over the gunwale to be greeted by a man in his sixties covered in grease and oil who said, "Come to join the fun." In the inevitable Glaswegian accent that was ubiquitous in the engine rooms of that era, or so it seemed to me.

"Yes. Jock." I replied. "And you must be the Chief Engineer?" I immediately returned.

"Welcome to the madhouse then, Taffy. And thank God for a real merchant navy man."

"How do you know that?" I asked.

"Well, your tone showed some respect to a person who might be a Chief Engineer, as opposed to being written off as some 'greaser' of an Engine Room Artificer, that dreadful Navy term. Anyway, you have wavy navy rings on your arm, so it was a good guess. Chief Engineer Gordon McKay, and I'll not shake your hand for obvious reasons." He said wiping his oily palms vigorously on some cotton waste.

That set us off on a happy footing and he said that he was just going for his tea and maybe I would like to meet the rest of the idiots chosen to crew this commandeered tug. We went into the accommodation via its entrance in the after end of the housing. This was a large tug by design; perfectly capable of seagoing and in commercial service, it would probably have had a crew of five or six, now, to suit its requisitioned needs changes had been made to accommodate a much larger permanent crew. As I moved forward the first door on the port (left) side were the heads or toilets, next came a galley and then stretching to well over half of the forward end of the housing was a mess room with table. Then most of the other starboard side had been made into two four berth sleeping quarters with bunk beds and finally, beside the entrance to the accommodation, was a large shower room, also equipped with a big dhobi sink in which to do your clothes washing.

Generous helpings of 'lobscouse', the sailors name for what was originally a Norwegian sailor's stew recipe, was being served in the mess room. Very apt I thought, as a scouse or scouser was the sailors name for a Liverpudlian and we were just across the river from that great port. The youthful cook, looking at my Lieutenant's stripes asked if I would like some and I was delighted to accept. None of the others, as one might have expected with the arrival of an officer, acknowledged me they just continued their chatter whilst they ate. Now, there is discipline and discipline, and that which existed in the mercantile marine, where I had all my experience, rested more on co-operation and the mutual acceptance of power, but did not require its demonstration on a daily basis. It is unlike the military version of discipline which is much more overt and requires salutes and formal demonstration of position, normally the junior acknowledging the superior. As a Mate on a merchant ship, I gave orders in a reasonable expectation that they would be carried out and any deliberate failure to comply would first be dealt with informally by the bo'sun or myself 'having a word' but repeated, or very serious misdemeanours would allow me to have the offender 'logged'. If an offender was logged by the Master then in effect he was charged and convicted of an offence, and this would normally mean that they would lose pay.

Merchant seamen hated this loss of pay above all, so most would avoid taking things to that level and would do as instructed.

Therefore, I made no fuss about being ignored, as a Royal Navy officer might have done, and I just took off my jacket and ate my meal and joined in the conversation. During this I discovered a little about my shipmates. The Chief Engineer I had already met. Despite the boyish looks the cook had actually served as second cook and baker on a merchant ship, there were two Royal Navy radio operators, as it later transpired that was how we were to receive our orders, via radio telegraphy, and the only other full time navy man was there to handle our very limited light armament of Bren and hand guns, which were for use in boarding any vessel that needed to be examined. There were two civilian able seamen, employed for undertaking helmsman duties and a very spotty and youthful Sub Lieutenant Hopkins RN on his first seagoing appointment since training, and my second in command. At the end of the meal I told them that we would be sailing sometime before high tide which was at ten past ten the following the morning and said I would see them all for breakfast at six thirty. After breakfast and before sailing I would meet them all and inspect the vessel.

I learned then that the crew quarters only held eight bunks in two cabins of four and there were nine of us. But I was told that at the rear of the wheelhouse was a bunk, around which heavy blackout drapes had been fitted and that was my space, all ten feet by five feet of it. I unpacked my kit into lockers beneath the bunk and spent some time looking through the ship's papers under the light at the chart table, situated behind the wheelhouse, before turning in early ready for an exciting day to come.

The following day I completed my threatened inspection of the vessel and found my crew to be polite to, but wary of, me, as one might expect. Hopkins had been advised in advance of my arrival that the tug was to sail imminently and so was able to report that our provisions and bunkers were complete and that we were ready to sail. So it was, on a grey morning that I went to the bridge and prepared to take my first ever command out of the locks from the shipyard basin and into the river Mersey.

There was a little bit of pressure as I had not had chance to handle the vessel before this undocking and we were right at the forward end of the basin beside the lock gates, moored starboard side on to the quayside. It was an awkward position. It would have been possible to warp the tug, in other words used ropes, to get her round the knuckle and into the entrance to the lock. But any seaman worth his salt would not do that if his engines were working. I knew the crew would see this as a test of my ability to manoeuvre the tug astern in the crowded basin, so that I could line up to sail into the lock. Also, it was clear that all the other vessels in that confined space would be watching how I did, especially the Royal Navy corvette astern who would doubt the abilities of a wavy navy commander. In the event I was confident in my small boat handling skills and felt they were quite transferrable to this situation. I ordered all my shorelines to be cast off except the spring leading astern from the bow. I rang for slow ahead and immediately slow astern. The initial short burst pushed the tug against the spring, causing the bow nip gently in towards the dockside whilst the stern came out. Casting off the spring we went astern between the moored vessels and I brought the head round pointing into the lock and ringing slow ahead neatly ensuring a deft move into the lock itself without bumping anything. Just the looks and nods from the crew members showed me that they could see that on the evidence of that first exercise I was no dummy when it came to seamanship and undoubtedly gave me some important kudos in their eyes.

Once clear of the river estuary we turned north and I felt able to open my orders. The elderly Lieutenant Commander had told me that they were to remain sealed until I was in the Irish Sea heading north. As far as I was aware this 'sealed orders' approach was dispensed with not long after Admiral Lord Nelson's time and may just have been another of the elderly man's little jokes. Anyway, I had obeyed my instructions. The orders were to the effect that I was to head for Greenock, in the Clyde, there to collect a lighter full of munitions for transfer to Loch Ewe, just below Ullapool, high up on the northwest coast of Scotland. We accomplished our mission and a week later, after delays due to weather, I reported as required to the Officer commanding HMS Helicon in Aultbea, Loch Ewe, which was known in those days as Port A. There I learned that we were to be part of a 'gofer' gang of working boats servicing the many naval and merchant ships which used the loch as a safe haven and for the assembly of convoys. We were tasked to assist vessels berthing for bunkers and supplies, which was sort of proper tug duties, but then we were to check on incoming vessels entering Loch Ewe through the anti-submarine nets, take supplies to anchored ships, transfer crew who needed medical or other attention, in short everything and anything.

No two days were the same, that is no two days and nights were the same, for we were often busy for many hours at a stretch. I tended to take the night watches because young Hopkins was not, to start with, very experienced and able at manoeuvring the vessel; but he learned. And we all learned. Our work was varied and included transferring, by rope strops, 45-gallon oil drums from our towing deck to another ship's deck 20 feet or more above our own, taking sailors with broken bones and split heads to the jetty for sick bay transfer, even taking sailors ashore to visit the NAAFI or the Aultbea hotel. Together with an armed trawler, we took responsibility in boarding, checking and marshalling merchant ships arriving to assemble for convoys and meeting their requirements for stores as well. It was a busy life. But the business and its variety soon enabled our small crew to gel as a team, and it felt that we became a happy ship.

The port commander was a forward-thinking man with excellent management skills and not long after we had arrived, about Easter 1942 he called me to his office and explained that he wanted to give some of his shore-based staff an opportunity to spend some time afloat. He particularly had in mind the members of his staff who were in the Women's Royal Naval Service (WRNS), or Wrens as they were known, who never got the chance to go to sea. He proposed that he would allocate by rota several of these young women, to spend a day seeing what we did and asked if I would be alright with that, which I was. I mentioned it to the crew one day, when we were at anchor and eating together and, after the usual ribald comments, there were no complaints. I said that there would need to be a programme which, I suggested, would involve the Wren spending time with each member of the crew, who could explain their particular role on the tug. I proposed a start with an engine room tour with the Chief. Then they would move on to the signallers, the gunner, the cook and, finally then to the bridge with the helmsmen, the Sub-Lieutenant and me. This to be spread out over the day only interrupted by whatever tasks the vessel and we were required to perform on the day. This programme meant that everyone had a chance to be involved.

The first woman allocated to the scheme was a Petty Officer Wren and she was a lovely lass, she not only filled her uniform, but she also clearly overflowed in it. Chubby and happy might well describe her and she really enjoyed her day with us, and we all enjoyed the laugh we had with her. It was a standard day for us involving tug work and 'gofer' duties, as we had come to know them, all of which she really enjoyed. There was then a succession of others, on the basis of about one a week; and the latest had arrived at 0600 this morning, in the form of an Ordinary Wren. From the start she was a much more formal, almost buttoned up, young woman whose interaction with us all was very limited. Nevertheless, she was interested in all the Chief had to say about the engine room. But then we got a call to attend a cargo ship to remove a suspected appendicitis case to one of the cross-channel ferries, the *St. David*, which had recently arrived, having been requisitioned as a hospital ship. Apparently our regular 'floating ambulance', the drifter *Craig Alvah*, was having engine trouble and was not available. We had just delivered the sick man and had manoeuvred off when the duty signaller came to say that we were to proceed with all speed to take in tow a disabled American oil tanker, the *Atlantic Catalyst*, whose steering gear had failed about five miles off the mouth of Loch Ewe. She was apparently drifting towards the rocky headland at Greenstone Point.

It was by now about ten thirty hours on an increasingly darkening summer's day, with the wind which had been rising since the early morning creating quite a little chop on the waters of the Loch. A westerly gale was gaining strength. Clearly time was of the essence. Loch Ewe was protected from submarines by three anti-submarine nets across the mouth of the loch with a 'gate' operated by two trawlers. One opened the inner or third net and the other opened the outer two, they were advised in advance of our mission and as we steamed at full speed towards them and the open sea, they opened the route for us to pass through. Even after nearly six months on station we had only been out to sea a few times since our arrival.

On our way to the 'gate' to pass through the nets and before I would need to take the conn I gave orders to ensure that all watertight doors were closed, deadlights fixed especially to forward facing portholes as we had very little freeboard and in the seas we were likely to experience I did not want to end up swamped, through water getting into the accommodation or engine room. Then I left young Hopkins in charge and consulted the tide times and looked up information on the current direction and rate of flow for the state of the tide. It was flowing northwards and so it would be taking the stricken vessel, which turned out to have steerage problems and its rudder was jammed to starboard, towards headland of which Greenstone Point was the extremity. On a calm day there was even a chance the set of that powerful Minch tide might even have let her drift round the point and into Loch Broom. But not so on a day like today; with this westerly gale intent in driving her ashore. Then I called the chief engineer and the non-duty helmsman to the bridge where, with the Wren present, as it seemed the safest place for her, I explained that we would need to try to get a line aboard the tanker, which was not going to be easy given that the sea was going to be lively. I instructed the second helmsman to inform all the crew and then to ready a towing hawser. Then I told Hopkins to find the breeches buoy equipment in case we needed to use a rocket from that to effect the transfer of a line.

We went through the gate and within minutes the sea became very rough and confused. I estimated we were about three miles from the casualty, but with the wind whipping spray from the crests of waves we did not see her for fully five minutes, until we were abeam of Slaggan Bay. Ten minutes later we were closing the tanker, one of the new T2 types that the Americans were mass producing for the war, and I got the signaller to contact her, reminding him to send his words very slowly, as these were merchant officers who would not be able to read the Morse Code from the flashes of his Aldis signal lamp if he went too quickly, as the vastly more well practiced Royal Navy signallers were prone to do. I said send, 'WILL SEND HEAVING LINE BY ROCKET'

The Aldis lamp clattered and after a while a reply blinked back.

'NO ROCKET. OIL LEAK'

I said to the signaller, "Send 'ROCKET WILL PASS OVER. NO DANGER. JUST GRAB LINE'."

After a while came the reply. 'NO. REPEAT. NO ROCKET. COME CLOSER'

"There is no helping some folk." I muttered.

"Shall I send that?" Asked the signaller, and I shook my head.

By this time I had reduced speed to get as near as I dared. I noted that we were about two miles off the land and the chart had indicated deep water till quite close inshore. On the other hand the tide was setting at three knots and the wind was towards the shore so time was of the essence.

I manoeuvred *Loyalty* as close as I dared in the heavy seas and carefully watched the motion of the tanker, which was of course broadside to the seas and rolling fearfully with each wave. If I got too close and was in a wave trough following the wave that lifted her, she would then slide down into the trough and endanger us. I needed to manoeuvre so that I was near the bow of the tanker and as a wave came power forward to rise up the crest and pass in front of her at the crest of the wave and hopefully a heaving line could be put aboard her. I waited my chance and rang 'full ahead' at the point I judged to be right and we surged forward and passed close by the tanker, at the crest of the wave and the able seaman on the towing deck threw a heaving line but it fell well short. And I realised that there was only one shot more that we had and after that the tanker would be on the rocks.

I shouted to the able seaman on the towing deck who was retrieving his heaving line.

"Get a cork life ring. Fix your longest heaving line securely to it leaving two fathoms free at the end. Get another long heaving line and coil the first four fathoms and hang onto it."

"Mr Hopkins!"

"Yes Sir."

"I am going to manoeuvre directly to windward of the tanker, with our head into the sea then I need you to veer down towards her, but never at any time must you endanger this vessel. I am

63

going to take a heaving line to them. When I signal to stop the engines you will do so for just long enough for me to clear the propeller and do the same for the return. Oh, and by the way if this attempt to get a line aboard her fails, then she will be done for and your responsibility will be to ensure the safety of this vessel and its remaining crew and you will abort this rescue and return to base." You there," I said looking at those on the bridge, the helmsman and the Wren (whose presence I had completely overlooked), "you heard me issue those orders?" And they nodded. "You will stand witness for Mr Hopkins that if he follows those orders so that he cannot be reprimanded for abandoning the tanker to her fate."

I stripped off my uniform and other clothes except underwear and socks and ran down onto the towing deck where I explained to the able seaman, the cook and one of the signallers whom he had recruited to help him, what was to be done. I was going to tie the spare two fathoms from the life ring around my middle with a running bowline knot, so that I was secured to the ring which was itself linked to the tug by the remainder of the heaving line. Then I would take the second heaving line myself and jump overboard with it and they would pay out the heaving line attached to the ring and also the one I was holding. Being to windward of the casualty I would swim and drift down towards her with the tide helping too. When I got to the tanker, I would attempt to pass the heaving line I was holding onto the tanker's deck. Because she was loaded she had freeboard of only about ten feet, and I would hold a couple of fathoms of heaving line ready to throw up to them on their deck. Then our crew could haul me back by pulling on the heaving line fixed to the life ring. Meanwhile the tanker crew could attach the other heaving line to their steam winch and haul our towing hawser aboard.

They looked at me as though I was mad, but I gave them no chance to say anything before I started by attaching the heaving line to the life ring with enough to spare to knot around my middle to ensure that, if I lost grip on the ring, I would be able to regain it as it could not float far from me. Then I took the second line and coiled a few fathoms. Then I looked up at the bridge and signalled to Hopkins to begin the process of veering down to the stricken vessel. He did well and the gap reduced until I judged we were as close as we dare get when I signalled him to stop. I waited till I heard the engine room telegraph ring, counted to ten to hope that by then the propeller would have stopped turning and stepped off the unprotected stern end of the towing deck, with the ring and the second heaving line in my hand and began to swim to the tanker allowing the wind and seas to take me down wind towards her.

The seas of the Minch do get up to about fifteen degrees centigrade in the summer, but it was still a long way off summer and it felt cold. Fortunately, as a lad I had been swimming in all weathers off the beach at Penarth and so the exercise was not completely outside my experience. Still, looking back I was far more than lucky. It took just a few minutes with the pushing of the waves and the tide and the letting out of the line for me to come close to the tanker. I became this terrified small bobbing head by this floating cork ring and I was towered over by this enormous steel side of this huge tanker. I realised that my idea had been quite wrong and that I had not anticipated that this leviathan would simply reach the top of a wave and then come down onto me and crush me. I was about to die right now and there was nothing I could do to avert it.

People who win medals for bravery, in the heat of battle, often have an individual plan or rush of blood to the head and they take an action, as I did, on the impulse of a good idea in general terms, but perhaps not entirely fully considered. Many suffer the ultimate fate and if rewarded for their act it is posthumously done. Just a few find the Fates take a hand and with extreme good fortune the ridiculous 'good plan' actually comes off. So, incredibly, it was with me that day.

Sure enough the tanker reached the crest of the wave, her vast sides and underbelly towering above me as she rolled to port lifted by the huge wave. Then as the wave moved on she began her roll to starboard towards me. Down into the wave trough and the huge metal crusher that she was came slowly but inexorably towards me, and by rights would have done for me. But my distance from her was just perfect to allow her metal railings, on the cargo deck, to pass just a foot from my head and as she buried her side into the oncoming next wave so I slid onto her deck. As the sea began to drain, when the tanker started its next rise, two crew men raced to me and I was able to pass them the heaving line attached to the tug's hawser and they rushed forward with it. I followed them and a couple of rolls later I waved to the tug and signalled like a participant in a game of tug-of-war that I wanted them to heave me back. By this time I had worked myself forward on the tanker, to near the bow and as she buried her side into the next wave and the cargo deck again was covered in water, I jumped into the sea from about six feet and immediately felt the life ring pull as I was being hauled back towards the tug.

The whole episode probably lasted about ten minutes, but it seemed a lifetime until I was back alongside the tug and, catching a line from the towing deck, I was hauled aboard. Somewhere along the way I had lost my underpants and one of my socks, but I still rushed up to the bridge to oversee the connection of the hawser and to begin the towing process. Soon I felt a towel being wrapped over my shoulders and as I stood shivering somebody was using another towel to dry my legs and I glanced down to see the Wren vigorously towelling my legs before standing up to start drying my hair. It must have presented a very comic spectacle as I dashed, mainly unclothed, from one side of the wheelhouse to the other supervising the commencement of the tow attended by a Wren trying to rub me dry. After things had begun to settle she disappeared and then soon returned with a shirt and pants, as somebody must have indicated the location of my clothes drawers, and I got the shirt and a jumper on and then she offered me the towel and said.

"Perhaps there are some places you may wish to dry personally." And she grinned at me.

We had a difficult return journey, albeit only about six miles but we successfully towed the '*Atlantic Catalyst*' through the anti-submarine net gate and took her to safe anchorage in Loch Ewe. Her Captain invited me aboard and he and his officers were fulsome in their thanks and commented on my bravery and said that they would make a report to the Officer Commanding. They sent two cases of bottled beer and five packs of two hundred cigarettes for my crew. I returned to the tug with the accepted gifts a hero, not for my activities in the sea, but for procuring such a bounty from the 'Yanks'. Then, at about nineteen hundred hours, we took the Wren to the jetty I escorted her ashore and turned to offer my hand, which she shook, and said.

"I cannot tell you what a wonderful experience I have had today, and I thank you and your men. You have helped me to come to some decisions about the meaning of life, that is to say the meaning of my life, and you can never know how important today has been for me."

Retracting her hand she turned to go and, on an amazing and completely out of my character impulse, I replied.

"I don't suppose you would like a drink sometime at the Aultbea hotel?"

"No. I would rather not."

"That's fine."

"But I am free to go for a walk on Saturday afternoon which, according to your Chief Engineer is when you ship is next scheduled for a few hours off. Meet me outside the Wrenery accommodation at thirteen hundred hours?"

"Err. Yes." I managed and with that she saluted me and turned to walk off up the pier.

Cook had postponed our meal, but the men were all tucking in as I entered the mess room and there were some comments about 'showing your tackle to get a date with a Wren', followed by 'not having much to show after a long immersion in such cold water'. I smiled and pulled a face and things fell good humouredly quiet until the Chief rose, lifted his bottle of beer and said.

"Stand up you miserable bastards and drink the health of a very brave man under whom we are proud to serve."

This resulted in all of the assembled crew standing and drinking my good health.

Much later in the peace of the wheelhouse, with the tug lying peacefully at anchor, I thought how all the years of seamanship training and experience at sea had been crucial in my being able to do what was needed today. It had cemented an already good relationship with my men, and I even had a date with a quite attractive young woman to look forward to on Saturday.

I turned into my bunk a happy man.

Sadly, a prematurely happy man.

Chapter 7

1997 Rose -Porthcawl

"So, just to be clear that I understand you, this Wren woman was actually aboard the tug *Loyalty* at the time of the incident and that could be a reason as to why she may have seen this as a special incident?"

"Well, of course other women in the Wrens on that base at that time would have known about the event, but, yes, she was the only female present on either of the vessels involved, and so she would have had more reason than any to remember it." Said Gareth.

There was a momentary silence which was broken by the sound outside of the slamming of vehicle doors and moments later by the 'ping pong' of the doorbell.

"That sounds like your chauffeur and his very excited assistants." Gareth said, as he went to the door.

The children were in high spirits, talking over one another as they told me, in a rush, all about a lovely beach, sandcastles, wet feet and ice cream. When the first burst of energy drained Michael stepped in.

"You can see that some folk have had a lovely time, and were hard to prise away, but as I said on the phone I would like to get home to prepare some tea for Mummy as she has had a pig of a couple of days. But I must ask Mum – sorry – Gran, if that is OK and if you have had enough time to get your information."

"Yes, we have done very well and indeed just as you arrived we have just discovered that there was one woman in particular who would have had reason to recall the incident that, you will remember, was the one my natural mother mentioned to that other mother in the next bed not long after giving birth to me. Whilst there were probably several women who might have reason to know about of the incident, Gareth has told me that this woman would most certainly have had a more significant reason than most to have it imprinted on her mind."

Whilst I was making these comments to Michael, Gareth himself was looking very serious and thoughtful and as I finished my comment to Michael and I turned to him, he hesitated before saying.

"Well, I have been thinking that somewhere in my attic I have boxes of notes and mementos from all my many years at sea and they will include, somewhere near the bottom of the pile in one box, some notes on my time on the *Loyalty*, my very first command. Over the years I have kept notes on the people I have sailed with and the *Loyalty* would be no exception, Now I have not had time to tell Rose this yet, and it is something we cannot do today, but I am more than happy to spend some time looking through and seeing what more I can find out about the time of the incident and that Wren girl in particular. What I suggest is that I do some looking and then write to you with any information I unearth."

Really? You may have more details then?" I asked and he nodded. "Oh. That would be wonderful."

We spent some time making notes of our respective contact details, postal addresses and landline phone numbers, since he was not into electronic communications of any other sort. Then as we made to leave, Gareth remarked.

"It has been such a lovely afternoon, Rose. Thank you for coming I have been fascinated by your story and I will do what I can to help you in any way in your quest. Do bear with me as there are many boxes to go through and I fear it will not be a speedy process."

"If it would help I could arrange to come and assist." I offered.

"My dear, for starters it will give me great pleasure to have a reason to look back over the 'treasures' of my seagoing past and I have ordered things to my own satisfaction so I would much prefer to do it myself, but I assure you that I will find the relevant papers and I will be in touch with you as soon as I can."

We all moved to the door and out into the balmy, sunny, but autumnal afternoon air and went through the process of goodbyes. The kids first, then as Michael went to shepherd them into their seats and fix the seat belts Gareth turned to me and put out his hand and said.

"Thank you for a lovely, unexpected afternoon and I am sure that I can help you a little bit more, once I have found the papers which I am sure that I still have. But I do not want to raise your hopes too high because, as I am sure you are only too well aware, we are looking for things half a century or so old."

"Yes, I know." I said grasping his firm handshake. "But I was at a dead end until today and you have opened what I expect, one way or another, may be a final door in my quest, just a fraction, but it means that there is still one avenue of enquiry left to me, so that is more hope than I had begun to believe was ever possible, when we set out this morning."

On impulse I leant forward and briefly kissed his weather-beaten face.

Michael came to see me into the car and also shook hands with Gareth before returning to the driving seat and encouraging the children to wave as we set off. The children continued their excited stories of the seaside afternoon until we got onto the M4 Motorway when, after a while a post excitement silence kicked in, and they both fell asleep.

"He seemed a nice man?" Michael opined; and I nodded.

"Very nice indeed. He has been a seaman all his working life ending up as a ship's captain in the merchant navy. And he was the officer in command of the *Loyalty* when she was involved in the episode with the other ship, which is referred to in the papers the nurse or midwife gave to my mum. What is more he told me that there was a young Wren who was, just by chance, on the ship, actually it turns out to be a tug, on that very day of the incident. So, whilst other Wren personnel on the base, and maybe even other local women in the area, or even I guess wives or sweethearts of crews of the ships involved who may have heard about what may have been a dramatic rescue, there was one particular woman who was most likely to have the incident indelibly imprinted upon her."

"So do you think she could be your mother?" Asked Michael.

"Well, of course it is possible, but at this stage it is far too big a leap to make and, as you heard, Gareth says he has papers from his seagoing life and he is going to go through them, to see if he can find some more information from his time on that ship. And I am not sure, and he did not say anything, but I think he knew something more and he wanted to look things up before he committed himself."

"Why do you think that?"

"Oh! It's silly, I just have this feeling that when I showed him the letter, he went thoughtful, you know the way you do when you have an idea that you know something but you need to check your facts before you actually commit yourself.

Just a hunch,

Nothing more."

Chapter 8

1937 Stella - Essen, Germany

Returning to our family home in Essen in time to for Hanukkah in the late November of 1937, I was not immediately struck by the changes. My bus from Essen station to our home, in the district of Horst, held chattering local folk who apparently paid no attention to the smart young woman with the suitcase. If any had felt that I looked a little overdressed for the bus and wondered why I was not in a family car then nobody said anything. Had I been asked I would cheerfully have explained that I had, from a young age, learned to be independent because my lovely parents were heads in the cloud's dreamers, totally immersed in their respective works. Daddy, for I used that English nomenclature since I was born and raised in England, was a brilliant electrical design engineer yet socially he was the epitome of the 'absent minded professor'. Whilst Mummy was a classical musician for whom life was completely filled with study, practice and performance. I sometimes wondered how they had ever come to beget a child since they operated on seemingly different planes.

They had met in London just before the First War when both were studying, and being German nationals they should have been interned, at the very least Daddy should have been. But already he had established himself as brilliant designer of electronic components for naval vessels and with typical British pragmatism he had escaped internment on some pretext of his being crucial to the National Interest. Their marriage was happy as a sort of mutual friendship and a social partnership and, I assume, some sexual satisfaction. It is hard to think of your parents copulating, but by definition they must have done, since otherwise I for one would not be here. I can imagine that their absorption with their respective work may have restricted their engagement in sex, although they might have been like rabbits for all I know, but whatever the reason it was not until 1919, when Mummy was in her late 30s, that she became pregnant, and I was born the following year. By this time we were very settled in a house in Surrey with an older housekeeper, Mrs Beatrice McMillan, whom I called Auntie Bea.

I loved my Mummy, and I was desperate for her to be more engaged with me, but her music was all consuming to her and if not practicing or teaching then often she would be out, performing, and so Auntie Bea became a surrogate mother, and I loved her too. I was devastated when, at the end of 1927, at just seven years old, after two and a half happy years in the local village school we left England, and I lost Auntie Bea for ever. It so happened that my father accepted a very well-paid job in Germany, for which he had been recruited to work in their growing electronics industry. Both he and my mother were from well to do upper middle class Jewish German families, although they were only nominally Jewish, and by no means strict or devout. As it happened both their sets of parents were deceased. Mother was pleased with the move as she was somewhat well known for her study and performance of Beethoven sonatas, and she expected to be in demand for recital performances in Germany. Father's job was in the industrial region of the Ruhr and so Essen was selected for our home base.

After the shock of the upheaval and losing of Auntie Bea I adjusted fairly quickly to my new lifestyle, and a new, less significant, carer entered my life and although the new housekeeper was friendly enough, I had not the same ties to her as to my English 'auntie'. But as a child you deal with what is put before you and of course, although my first language was English, I was bilingual and soon nearly fitted into my local school. I say nearly because I was always just that bit different from the other girls because, whereas my English was completely unaccented, my German was not and neither, in those impressionable days, was it colloquial. In those early days I was not really affected by the growing influence of Hitler and his anti-Semitic agenda. Neither did my parents appear to take much notice and this was probably because of their respective dedication to work, and I suspect that they both saw themselves

73

as Germans and not Jews. We did not attend Synagogue and were entirely secular so they might have argued that they were not really being Jewish either.

Towards the end of 1935, when I was fifteen, we began to hear of 'incidents' involving the attacking of Jews and indeed there was a rather annoying member of my school class who picked on another Jewish girl, and I reported this incident at home. Whether that was a factor I do not know but my father took the course of sending me to a finishing school in Geneva for what was planned for three years. This involved a train journey of about five hundred miles and so it was arranged that I stay in Geneva during the holidays, even for the Christmas break. In the first summer break Mummy and Daddy took an apartment in Avenue de Corzent in Thonon-les-Bains, an easy boat ride from the centre of Geneva, but they said that they had not been able to do so this last year because of work commitments and I had spent a lovely summer in Italy with a friend from school. My finishing school was not just concerned with teaching the social graces and developing secretarial skills. Already proficient in English and German I now developed my Italian, especially after my Italian summer holiday, and French. I was taught practical things like cooking and needlework, in fact I found I had a particular ability in the latter, and I even learned the fundamentals of dress design. The time passed enjoyably and quickly but during this autumn term of 1937, I began to hear disturbing reports about what was happening in Germany with regards to the overt views about Jewish people. Consequently, I had begun to research a little about Judaism to see what was, so apparently and allegedly, bad about my race and religion. It was the unsettling news from home which made me decide to take an early Christmas break and the festival of Hanukkah seemed like a good, if nominal, excuse to make the journey to my parents' house.

Despite the fact that I had written to say that I would be arriving I knew that my parents would be too busy to meet me so the need to take the bus was expected. What was not expected was the fact that when I rang the bell at my parent's front door there was no answer from the housekeeper, as I would normally have expected. Off I went round the back only to find that all there was locked too and of course I had no key to either door. I

74

went to the next house to see our neighbour Mrs. Epstein, who had always been friendly towards me as a child, and I waited a long time after knocking and then I saw a saw a curtain twitch and then I heard several bolts being drawn and finally the door was opened.

"Stella? Stella, is it really you? How you have grown into a beautiful girl." Said Mrs. Epstein.

"I am locked out." I said and she nodded.

"The doors must be kept locked and only opened to those you trust."

"But where is Clara the maid?" I asked.

"Come, come and sit and let me tell you." She said and took me through into her very untidy front room, carefully bolting the front door behind us.

"Your mother's Clara and my Hannah are long gone, Hannah did not want to leave me, but she was told that if she continued to work for a Jew then she would be in trouble. Best part of six months we have had no help in the house your mother and me. Anyway, I am too old to continue like this, so my boy Paul he comes for me in two weeks. I tell everyone he takes me to his home in Amsterdam for just Christmas. He comes by train and takes me home with him; it's only a little over 200 kilometres, I think. For weeks now I go regularly to the bank and draw money in small sums, and we will take that with us, when he comes, also my jewellery but then just clothes for a holiday trip, no more otherwise I may be questioned he says."

"Are Mum and Dad planning to leave too?" I asked.

"Many times I say to your mother she must go but you know her 'I am important teacher and performer of German music', as if that helps her to hold back this groundswell of anti-Jewish hysteria that the madman Hitler has whipped up. Your Dad I think may be beginning to realise that things are not as they should be, but also, he must be a brilliant man in his field but not perhaps so brilliant in life skills. Does he stop, like all hunted wild animals should do, to frequently sniff the air for danger? No. If he did then surely he must see that we Jews are becoming hunted, and he needs to start to react to the smell in the air and realise that it is a smell of danger.

But you will be tired from your journey and will need to go into your home, although, a bit like mine, it may not be as tidy as you would expect"

She passed me a key which she retrieved from a drawer and I went to our house and, after collecting my suitcase from where I had left it at the back door, I went inside. There too I was met by a stark warning of the changes that were happening to my parents' life and which Mrs. Epstein had warned me about. Mummy had never been either a housewife or a cook and the whole house was in a complete mess. The place was dusty, the wooden floors upswept, the kitchen was full of dirty pots and dishes and upstairs their room sported an unmade bed and a variety of clothing draped here and there. My room was dusty but otherwise in order. My schooling had taught me linguistics – I spoke four languages – secretarial and bookkeeping skills and also social skills including cooking and entertaining. Accordingly, I set to work and soon got cleanliness and order into the kitchen and dining room and I was just part way through an overhaul of the lounge when my father arrived home. I threw my arms around his neck and hugged him.

"Daddy, are you alright? What's been going on? Mrs Epstein says things are getting bad for Jewish people. She thinks you should sense the building danger and leave"

"Stella; not to worry," he said, "I have a very important job, and they tell me I must not be concerned, they say they know I never go to the Synagogue and that I live for my work and your mother is still an important teacher of music and gives recitals, so we will be OK."

We sat and talked until it was time to get a meal, which I volunteered to do, but there was not much by way of foodstuffs, so I volunteered to go to the shops in the centre of our village, just a few minutes' walk away. I knew the grocer there stayed open late, but on the way there I was passing Ulrich's the travel agents and he seemed to be getting ready to shut up shop for the day and on impulse I went in to see him. In the past I had found him pleasant enough, obsequious even, until he secured a sale and then he became a little more terse. He glanced up as I entered, and I thought perhaps his eyes narrowed.

"Hello Mr Ulrich. I was thinking of taking my mother and father to visit our old home in England for a week or two in the spring, would you be able to make the arrangements for us if I give you some dates. I am approaching you because you were so helpful in arranging for them to stay near me the summer before last when I was in Geneva."

"Why do you ask Fräulein Goldman? Surely it should be your father who comes to me and also with dates and the precise location of your destination. There may also be a requirement for your parents to have a travel visa and he would need to approach his employers about that."

"But it's just a holiday to see our old home in Surrey where I was born and where I lived for over the first seven years of my life." He shrugged.

"Nevertheless, your father will need to come and see me with the information which I outlined. And now if you will excuse me, I must shut my shop."

I thought to make a sarcastic comment about his attitude, but in the event, I restrained myself and went to the grocers to buy food for our evening meal.

Little did I realise that a spur of the moment general enquiry, trying to see if I could get my parents away from the awful climate of hate that had developed, would probably amount to the signing of the death warrants for both of them.

There is the old adage which says that schooldays are the happiest days of your life, and I was about to find out how true that was, but before that realisation became clear to me there was one final week of my family life to be treasured. During that next week I had a wonderful time with my parents, of course they had to work in the day but each evening and the one wonderful weekend we had together, they enjoyed my presence because it had been so long since we had spent time in one another's company. I played at housekeeper and prepared the evening meals and at the weekend, a dry cold weekend, we went for a walk by the river on the Saturday and to eat out on the Sunday.

Monday passed normally and my parents were home for a six o'clock meal which we all enjoyed, and we went to bed about ten o'clock. At five the following morning there was a loud banging on the front door with shouts of 'Police, open the door.' Daddy went down and as soon as he opened the door several policemen and two men in suits pushed their way into the house, as I came downstairs in my dressing gown.

"Stella Goldman?" They asked, looking directly at me; and I nodded.

"There have been reports of enquiries about this family planning an unauthorised journey abroad whilst Mr. Goldman here is employed as a top engineer whose expertise is necessary to the interests of this great country. Such a defection would be against the national interest; so, to ensure his continued voluntary residence and employment here, you, Stella Goldman, will work for our great government in Berlin where you have been assessed as ideal material to serve as a secretary and translator. And so, to that end, you will be going to Berlin to discharge those duties. Provided you undertake this work, and your parents continue theirs, all will be well. If either party fails to comply the other party will bear the consequences.

Go and dress and pack a suitcase with underwear and office work clothes. Be quick and do not think of running away this officer will accompany you." He nodded at a spotty young man of about my age in a police uniform, who in his turn grinned at me.

My head was in turmoil but I went to do as I was bid whilst downstairs I could hear my parents being lectured by the officer in charge. I dressed in the bathroom, with the agreement of my sentry, after he had ensured that the window was a fixed one and he warned me not to lock the door. He hurried me along with the packing and said there was no need for me to brush my hair or get made up and within ten minutes we were going downstairs. I was led towards the door but broke away to embrace my mother, who had clearly been crying and then my father who hugged me tight and whispered to me.

"Remember these words, my darling Stella. Write always in English. Then, look out for idiosyncrasies and colloquial words in any letters I send to you."

I was grabbed roughly and led to the door where I collected my suitcase and was marched to one of the waiting cars. Daddy shouted.

"We will always love you and forever be sorry for our stupidity. For your sake and ours do whatever you must to survive."

These words, particularly the last six, were destined to become my creed for the rest of my life.

As the car drove off, I could see my father, with his arm around my distraught mother, waving. Framed in the window of her house next door, was Mrs Epstein, in her dressing gown, staring with her hand over her mouth in total, uncomprehending, distress.

I was taken first to the police station where I was put into a large holding cell. Then later in the morning a sour faced officer came to the cell and spoke to me.

"Just remember that the safety and welfare of your parents depends on your co-operation so do not be thinking of causing me any trouble. If you do, I will just shoot you and they will later suffer the consequences."

Two hours later we left and went to the railway station a short walk away. Sour face commandeered a six-seater compartment of the open carriage and ensured that nobody came near us. The train went via Duisburg and Dusseldorf to Cologne where, in the mid-afternoon, he delivered me to another police station and another cell. I spent several hours reflecting on the events of the day before at about six in the evening I was provided with my first sustenance since being unceremonially roused from my bed, it comprised a bowl of soup and a crust of bread to go with it. There was also a cup of water. It did not take much for me to realise that Mr Ulrich, the travel agent, had told the authorities of the nature of my enquiry about travel and as a result I had brought upon myself, and my parents' heads the wrath of our bigoted government. Father's skills were clearly too important for them to lose, and I was to be hostage to his continued work.

At about nine in the evening I was taken by two officers, together with my now much travelled suitcase, to the station where I was put aboard an overnight sleeper train bound, according to the station announcements, for Berlin. I was told that the door would be bolted from the outside and the windows were fixed, there would be a call at five in the morning as the train was due in shortly after six. My sleep was fitful, and I cursed

79

myself for my own innocent stupidity. At my morning call I was told that food was outside, and the door was opened long enough for me to collect a stale croissant and an unsweetened, un-milked and lukewarm cup of coffee. I ate ravenously then washed and dressed using the small basin, which distressingly, and with difficulty, I had had to use as a toilet in the night.

From the station at Lehrter Bahnhof a new guard took me to a waiting car, and we drove for about twenty minutes until we came to an old mansion in a suburb set in its own well-kept grounds, but obviously guarded, as there was a checkpoint at the gate. By now it was a little after seven in the morning and with my suitcase I was shown through a portico and large main hall, then taken down a corridor to a waiting room with one small, barred window. I was feeling weak from the shock of the events of the last twenty-six hours, together with the lack of sustenance and the uncertainty of what lay ahead.

As I sat there, I forced myself to think how I should conduct myself. There was no doubt that I was a hostage for my father's good behaviour and continued work. Therefore, so long as I co-operated my parents would, I had to assume, be safe. Accordingly, I decided that my only option was to comply with all I was required to do. Yet underneath this level-headed and sensible decision I was absolutely seething that a state or government could possibly restrict or control its citizens based solely upon their religion or ethnicity. But the more I sat and thought the more I came to realise that indeed that very issue ran through the history of civilisation.

After about half an hour I heard footsteps approaching and a smart Schutzstaffel officer appeared and beckoned me to follow him into an office that led off my waiting area. I followed in great trepidation, and he moved round a large desk and indicated that I should sit on the chair in front of it. He spoke to me in clear but heavily accented English.

"Your records say you have lived in England as a child and you are competent in English, so tell me, in English, why you think you are here."

I was determined not to be cowed by this man, on the one hand, but I realised that just the same I needed to be careful to say something of what he wanted to hear as well as to challenge.

"I was forcibly taken from my parent's home without warning and chance to say a proper goodbye and it has been made clear to me that I am a hostage to their, and especially my father's, continued work. Also, I assume that they are equally obliged to do as they are told for fear of something happening to me."

He studied me in silence for a long while and then reverting to German.

"Excellent English and, unlike myself, I do not hear any accent. I will need another opinion from a native English-speaking person in due course, but on the face of it you may be just the person we are looking out for. Now you are quite correct, your parents' current living arrangements depend on you. Your father's work is very useful but perhaps not absolutely crucial and of course as a Jew he is only tolerated because of his work. You, as with many like you, were destined for work as a servant to loyal officers like me, but we have need of people with your special language abilities. So, I am sending you to train for this special work, but in doing so there are some important rules. First, as well as learning new skills, you will also be assessed for your obedience to this country. Have no doubt that without passing on both these levels you will be sent off to work as a servant as I first indicated. Further, if you do well you will go on to learn secret things and once you start to learn these your situation will become even more serious, for if, after learning these things, we discover that you are not being loyal then you will most definitely be sent to service the soldiers, not the officers."

Although I did not know it at that time, and for some months to come, I was forcibly 'enlisted' into Abwehr, the newly formed German Intelligence Service and I was sent to another large country house to start my training. There I found myself amongst just a few young women, all but one of them were ideologues and followers of Hitler. None were Jewish and I was told to say nothing of my heritage, just to be quiet and learn my lessons. These mainly involved learning about coding and decoding communications, using short wave radio to send messages and some lessons in self-defence. The regime was strict; we were all discouraged from sharing personal information and indeed taught how to deflect such questions from strangers. It seemed that all the women had a second language, although I was the only English speaker.

One of the surprising elements of training was in how to deal with sexual advances and this was provided by a woman doctor. She covered the physiological issues and the history of contraception, both male and female. She explained the withdrawal method of contraception and the consequences of that not being used in unprotected sex. She then demonstrated how to use a douche kit after unprotected sex. Finally, we were supplied with a douche kit of our own and also with a supply of male condoms, referred to as 'rubbers', as they were made from latex, which we were encouraged to carry at all times. When one embarrassed student asked why we were being told this, she was told that we were to work in finding information from enemies of our great country and if that meant inducing men to talk by the uses of offering sex then we should do so. To say I was appalled and terrified does not even begin to capture my reaction. The girls at my finishing school were members of wealthy families and they had dreams of meeting a wonderful man from another wealthy family and living happily. I was now faced with the possibility that I would never have a happy relationship with a man and into the bargain I may even be required to prostitute myself.

After just five weeks I was driven back to see the original Schutzstaffel officer and this time he was accompanied by a woman, in her sixties, who spoke to me in a very plummy upper class English accent and engaged me in a long conversation about my childhood in England. At the end of this I was returned to my training centre. Several days later the Schutzstaffel officer arrived and interviewed me alone in the Commandant's office.

"Apparently you have studied hard and are considered efficient in much of your coding and signalling work. Your English is considered to be excellent and not able to be noticed as anything other than a native speaker. So now there comes the critical moment, for both you and your parents. We have arranged for you to travel to England later in the year where you will be taught to lead a normal life, until we have need for your services.

Now as promised to you when we first met, your first letter to your parents was hand delivered to them and it was explained that you were doing work of a secret nature and your letters would have no address on them, as I told you. They were told to not start their letters with an address and that they were to direct the letters to you at my address, for onward transmission, and that has been happening?"

He looked at me and I nodded. "So, all is well and will continue. They will be visited again and told that for operational reasons your letters will be less frequent, but they are not to worry. Your letters will go initially via our diplomatic correspondence route, but if it comes to any hostilities, then we will find alternative ways of dealing with that issue. Here is your latest letter from home dated only a few days ago." He said handing me an envelope.

"These letters will continue for so long as you do as you are told, but if the day ever comes when you fail to do as required then you will have whatever fate befalls your parents on your own conscience. After a few more weeks of final preparation, you will travel alone to England. This will be your first test and if you deviate from your itinerary your life will be over alongside that of your parents'."

After this I continued my spying education, until in September 1938, my British passport in my own name was restored to me. But I was not going return to my native land as I would have wished, as a free woman on holiday, instead I now had an enforced new role as a low-level spy for the Third Reich and it was in that capacity that I set off for England. My ticket took me via Hanover and Amsterdam to the Hook of Holland and the ferry to Harwich. The immigration officers welcomed me 'home' and I passed their scrutiny easily. From the Immigration Shed I crossed the rail lines, set in concrete to make an even walkway and then boarded the train to London's Liverpool Street station and a traitorous life.

Chapter 9

1997 Gareth – Porthcawl

Standing on the kerb outside my house I waved Rose and her family off that early September afternoon, waving and watching until the people carrier disappeared round the corner with two children's hands waving, one each side, out of opened rear windows. I lowered my hand, but for several seconds remained staring at the point where the vehicle had disappeared from view, before I turned and slowly made my way back into the bungalow.

I have always considered myself an honest man and broadly speaking a truthful one. I had not broken my rules of honesty and truthfulness that particular afternoon, but I had not been completely open either. What was that phrase I had recently seen in the newspaper a few days ago? It was used by a politician who had been caught out in some way or another, 'economical with the truth', he had said, and that is what I suppose I had been today.

In so many ways the afternoon had been a wonderful experience in my increasingly humdrum life. A very pleasant young woman had told me a most interesting tale, which I had thoroughly enjoyed hearing, until the point that realisation dawned that this, seemingly general historical personal story, actually might involve a moment in my own past that had, in its own way, haunted me through the years. The aftermath of that incident, whereby His Majesty's requisitioned tug *Loyalty* had effected an important rescue, was not entirely happy one for me. Fortunately, its negative effects were reduced over time and arguably actually led to my happy subsequent life in which I basically consigned the incident to my history thinking that it would never need to trouble me again.

Being a merchant seaman is an interesting role. When you are on a ship it becomes, for each trip, your world. Whatever your role your ship, and more properly your shipmates, need you to do your job. You are thrown together with a range of individuals with whom, for the most part, you have nothing in common save the fact that there is an interdependence of reliance upon one another properly discharging their respective duties. If the cook fails to prepare the food properly you all may get food poisoning. If the engineers do not care for the machinery, it may break down and the ship could be in danger, just like that American tanker. If the third mate does not ensure the lifeboat davits are in good working order they may not operate as they should and lower the lifeboat when you need it most.

However, your work-related interdependence is not matched by a requirement for social integration. But there is no way that you can avoid your workmates by, say, popping down the pub as you might do in a shore job in a factory, on a building site, in an office, or wherever. So, you learn to 'rub along' as best you can until you can pay off the ship or, if you remain, a different bunch of shipmates arrive to join you. As I moved up the ranks as a deck officer so the opportunity for developing friendships diminished. Crews were drawn from different shipping 'pools' so your 'crowd', as the crew were often known, might be Scousers from the Liverpool area, Jocks from Glasgow, Geordies from Tyneside, Cockneys from London and others, including Taffs like me from South Wales. In those circumstances many may have sailed together before and were known to one another and there may be a danger of cliques keeping non-members out.

My point is that your social contacts at sea are short lived and work related and often superficial. By this I am not suggesting that lasting friendships cannot be formed, it is just that they are the exception rather than the rule. You learn, I think, to live in the world of the moment and the ship, and once you pay off that ship it is consigned to history, and you look to the next one. When I became master it was worse because as a merchant ship's master, in my day, I occupied a very powerful role. Mine was the final say in how the ship was run and navigated, I was responsible for liaison with ports and loading authorities and of course I held a power to discipline any member of the crew who misbehaved, either by personal misconduct or failing to properly complete a duty.

A position of power like that sets you apart from your crew. Personally, I tried to be a humane and reasonable master and I would talk to officers and crew alike. Whereas I had known some masters who would not even give you the time of day for feeling a fear of losing their authority. But even in my sort of enlightened approach to man management, there being no women in the crew on my ships until the very end of my career, I was aware it was not just the way you behaved, but also how the crew members saw you. They saw a man of potential power and on that basis, they took it upon themselves to be polite and distant.

In all these circumstances I learned to become careful about indulging in anything other than superficial relationships. You might feel 'on a wavelength' with the attitudes or personality of one person but you might never see them again. So for me it was cheerful banter and work talk and that was it. Never revealing your personal feelings and keeping off religion and politics as topics. I suppose that you might say that all led to my developing a default position of reticence in my early contacts with people whom I had not previously encountered.

And, in one particular contact, namely today, then goodness I had been really reticent. What was it I had I said? 'Well, I have been thinking that somewhere in my attic I have boxes of notes and mementos from all my many years at sea'. Now that actually did go beyond the pale, so far as my desire to be honest and truthful is concerned and therefore it must have been a lie.

I know why I did it, but even that reason seems, in retrospect, to be unworthy. I wanted to buy myself time. I needed time to consider the possible implications of 'finding' and subsequently producing the papers for Rose. Of course, I knew Ordinary Wren Booth. I had in fact met her twice. Once when she came aboard *Loyalty* on that fateful day and on the second and slightly more prolonged occasion when we met ashore, on what also turned out to be another very fateful day. Although, I was not to discover how fateful a meeting, indeed how life changing a meeting, it would be until a few days thereafter.

With these thoughts in mind, I went to find my papers. Actually, that is not true either, for they were not in the loft amongst piles of things. They were on my desk in my second

86

bedroom, which I used as an office. And I did not have to 'find' them because that is to imply they were lost or hidden, whereas they were in a file which I could quickly locate.

Chapter 10

1942   Stella - Loch Ewe

My invitation to 'Taff' to go for a walk was both an emotional and spontaneous one. A more rational and unemotional decision was just to thank him for, what had turned out to be, an unexpectedly exciting day and wish him all the best for the future. The last thing I needed, just at this time, was any other contact to tie me to this place as I knew, in my heart of hearts, that I was done with this particular life of deceit. I was just awaiting my chance to make good my escape. A number of factors had eroded my willingness to continue to take the orders of that thug, Jack. First and foremost was my personal hatred of him and my London based spymasters, their attitudes to me, based solely on the religion into which I had been born, and their power over my life. Then, there had been no communication from my parents for months and in fact in the last letter from my father was the one handed to me by Jack, during that brief meeting at Euston station. In that missive the handwriting had been shaky and the note, in English, was brief.

"Darling daughter,

Mother and I are keeping well and we hope that you are too. Not much change to report here but we think of you always. If you are allowed any free time, do go and see our old friends in Marshalsea and take them some porky pies.

As stated, you are always with us in spirit and ever will be.

Your own ever-loving father"

My reading of this short letter was that it provided a very clear warning that things were not well for father and, I presumed, mother too.

Considering more closely what Daddy had written I realised that we had no friends in a place called Marshalsea. In fact, I had never heard of an actual town called by that name and the only context the name Marshalsea conjured up in my head was the name of the old debtors' prison in Southwark, London. My father's own interest in Charles Dickens meant that he had a collection of the author's works, and I had read a number of them including Little Dorrit which features the Marshalsea prison; indeed, my father had told me that Dickens' own father had been imprisoned there for debt when he, Charles, was only a boy. The reference to that, together with the reference to 'porky pies' which, so far as I knew, was the cockney rhyming slang for 'lies' was, I assumed, to alert me to the fact that my father was not telling me the truth and was possibly in prison or detention of some sort. If that was the case, then surely mother would be incarcerated as well. Daddy had said to me as we embraced for the last time to 'look out for idiosyncrasies and colloquial words' and of course the German censors would not have bothered to get out an atlas to look for a place called Marshalsea, just assuming it was a coastal town somewhere. Then again, they would not have understood the 'porky pies' reference and so let it go thinking it was alluding to the British love of the pork pie.

So, together with all I was hearing about the treatment of Jews in Germany, I had concluded that my beloved mummy and daddy were at best in prison or concentration camp, and quite possibly they were already dead. Also, my own spying role had been affected by my transfer to the distant and isolated Loch Ewe which meant that I was only able to pass information infrequently and by post and there was no easy way for Jack and the gang to meet me. About once a month we Wrens were allowed a trip out. Sometimes to Poolewe or occasionally Gairloch, and on those occasions I could post a coded letter to my 'uncle' in Molesey. The letter was actually addressed to a flat in Hammersmith which, in fact, was rented as a letter drop.

So gradually, I felt my ties to my spymasters loosening, and especially as the *raison d'etre* for my being a spy, namely the safety of my parents, was now in more than significant doubt. I began to turn my mind to my future, and I had begun to consider my options. At its simplest I could just present myself to the Commanding Officer and confess that I was a spy. I guessed that might result in just imprisonment; I say 'just' because the alternative punishment might have been more lethally severe. If

I decided to just run away instead, I realised that I would need to make some preparations, so as to be able to take any chance to disappear that may be afforded to me. Fortunately, in that regard, my training by my spymasters in Berlin had given me a firm head start.

When I had arrived at Liverpool Street from the Harwich ferry in September 1938, my theoretical, and as it turned out highly disciplined but relatively pleasant initial training was supplanted by a ruthless and aggressive induction to my new trade. I was travelling under my real name, Stella Goldman, on a real British passport but my instructions on arrival at the station were clear. I was to note the number of my arrival platform and then to leave the station and ask the way to Finsbury Circus. Then I had to walk there and do one lap of the circus and retrace my steps to Liverpool Street and stand opposite the ticket barrier of whatever platform my train had arrived at. This I assumed was to ensure that I was not being followed. I did as I was instructed and returning to my platform of arrival a man approached me and whilst apparently not looking at me, he told me to follow him at a distance till we reached a car. Once we arrived at the vehicle I was shown into a back seat and the man who had approached me sat in the front of the car with a driver and we travelled in silence for about twenty or more minutes. One of the lessons I had been taught, in Berlin, was to be observant at all times and so I noted that near the end of the journey we passed Hampton Court Palace which I had once visited with my dear old nanny, my long-lost auntie Bea. We went over the nearby bridge where I noted a shop sign advertising the East Molesey Post Office and we entered a road called Palace Road. This long road sported a number of large dwellings, some well set back from the road, and we turned into the driveway of one bearing the name Sefton Lodge.

The car drove round to a rear entrance, and I was hurried in, without my suitcase, to be greeted, well glared at, by a dour looking, dumpy, middle-aged matron who simply told me to follow her. I did so, noticing that the man who had met me at the station was close behind. I was taken to a first-floor room that seemed to be in the centre of the building with no natural light. Inside that room there was just a bed with a blanket. Matron and minder both left me, and the door was closed behind them, I heard it locked, and their footsteps retreated.

I sat on the bed wondering what this was all about and then, about twenty minutes later, the door was opened and a man entered together with the dumpy matron, whom I had seen when I arrived. He was in his fifties, short and his general ugliness was enhanced by a small but vivid strawberry mark beside his left eye.

"Why are you here?" He asked. Now this confused me. Had I been intercepted by British intelligence, I wondered? So, I thought I would be careful.

"I have come to visit friends in England." I replied.

He stepped forward and slapped my face hard.

"No!" He shouted. "You are a weak Jewish bitch who is here to save the lives of her stinking Jewish parents and in order to do that you are going to do exactly as you are told, because one word from me and your miserable parents will die. You have come from initial spy training in Berlin and they, living safely in the Fatherland, can afford to be nice and polite. But here, in the field of operations, we all risk our lives daily and cannot be too careful. So, we teach complete obedience and only when you can demonstrate it will you be put to work. If you are not obedient and you are not put to work then your parents will die and so will you."

"Get undressed." Said the matron, locking the door. "Oh. And by the way this room is soundproof."

And right there and then under the eye of matron I endured my first sexual experience as I was raped by the man I came to know as Jack, my spymaster. All the while he was abusing me, he was shouting that unless I showed my obedience my filthy parents would die.

So began the most awful month of my life. I was tested by short trips to the shops and back to see if I returned, always followed and always with the threat of what would happen to my parents if I failed to obey. I was taken to various locations and things were pointed out to me. I was told I was to have a new identity as Sheila Booth, and I had to learn her backstory by heart. I was frequently tested by Jack and errors were punished, sometimes by him forcing himself on me again. I was terrified but I eventually saw that he was testing me to be sure that before I was let loose on my own, that I was in no doubt that any failure on my part would be severely punished and that my parents would die as a result.

About a month later Jack presented me with new identity documents, passport included, with these I was now, to all intents and purposes, Sheila Booth. My story was that whilst I was born in England I had, at the age of two, gone with my mother to live with my plantation manager father in Malaya. Life had been comfortable, and I had been educated by a governess who was German by birth and through this I was fluent in the German language. In early 1938, following my father's death, my mother had returned home to England, but immediately upon return had suffered a heart attack and died. Whilst in Malaya we had been comfortably off because my father's salary was good, but he accrued no pension and, after paying for our travel together with mother's medical bills and her death expenses, I had just enough to secure a rented flat near Eaton Square, Victoria.

Then, a couple of weeks later and suitably word perfect on my back story and absolutely terrified of the consequences of my failure, I was given a job advert for a post as a translator for a business magazine, together with a typed application which had been submitted on my behalf. A week later, after interview, I was appointed and spent many happy months working at their offices in Shepherds Bush and renting an attic flat in Devonport Road just over half a mile away. Since Germany was a highly industrialised country, a lot of my translations were from German trade magazines. I made a precis of the articles and passed them to the editor. The office staff there, were few in number and I was by far the youngest, and all of us were preoccupied with the signs of coming war. Many colleagues worried about what impact war would have on their homes and their families, and I was no exception there. Nevertheless, the job was ideal for me as I had no need to fend off questions about my past. I was happy in my small flat and life was a lot easier, and the life of constant threat was somewhat temporarily eased.

Gradually the terror of my time with Jack began to wane and my link person was a tall slim man called Ralph. I met him once a month, at an appointed time, at one of four different meeting spots, all were in parks and our contact was always, as I had been taught, brief. Whoever arrived first would sit on an unoccupied bench. As the other approached the first would place an envelope with a coded message on the bench and then rise as if to leave the other approaching would call to indicate the apparently 'accidentally left' envelope and in picking it up would exchange it for an envelope they had brought. There would be nods of thanks and he would doff his hat, as though it had been a meeting of strangers. I was not required to provide any reports because there was nothing of interest to my masters, I was just building up my 'back story' as I later came to realise. So, the meetings every four to six weeks usually only involved receiving a letter from home and sending one back. Ralph was clearly under instructions to remind me that my continued co-operation was essential for their safety; and he did so without fail.

Then in September 1939 the war started, and I was informed that letters to and from my parents would become less frequent due to 'postal difficulties', but I was promised a letter at least every four or five months. There was little I could do to object given the circumstances. But in November Ralph told me that I was to meet him after work on the coming Friday for new orders. My heart sank when we headed to Molesey and turned into Sefton Lodge. However, Jack said that I had done well and now my real work was to start.

Apparently in September a Women's' Royal Naval Service had been re-formed, there had been one in the First World War, but it had been disbanded afterwards. Then in 1939, with war again with us, a formidable group of women led by Vera Matthews and Ethel Goodenough had been asked to recruit women to undertake work currently done by men so that they could be released for active service. There were some women still of active age who had been in the previous war, but more were needed. Apparently, preference was given, in those early days, to women with naval connections. Although in 1940 the application and interview process was now wider ranging it was decided that it would help if I was given a new relative, a Captain Rylance Smythe, a much decorated and recently deceased man who had been the naval attaché in Penang. He was to be my deceased mother's brother, my uncle, whom I had occasionally

93

met when with my father on business in Malaysia. Somehow, my spymasters had sneaked an application in on my behalf no doubt via some traitor working in the Navy or some related government department. However they managed it I was told that I was to attend for interview the following Wednesday afternoon at the Admiralty in London.

My current employers were suitably impressed when I told them the reason for needing Wednesday afternoon off. On the appointed day I went to the Admiralty building, together with my fake passport which confirmed me as Sheila Booth, as I had been instructed to bring it. The very beautiful and apparently accurate fake document bore the stamp of my pretend departure from Penang and arrival at Tilbury, early in the last year. I was shown to a waiting room and advised that the interviewing Committee were running late. Soon after my arrival a middle-aged woman came out of the room with a smile on her face and nodded to the young woman beside me. As she left the girl whispered that the woman leaving must have been accepted as she had told my fellow interviewee that she had been a Wren rating in the last war.

The girl beside me then went on with confidence to tell me that she had just left Cambridge University with a degree in German before she was called in to the interview room. Twenty minutes later she came out dabbing her eyes and left without a word. I realised that this was not going to be an easy interview, and failure may cause me trouble with Jack, so when I was called in I was already anxious.

Four women sat behind a huge old desk with one seat for the candidate in front. The Chairwoman introduced herself as the appointed chair of the panel and I think she may have been 'the' Vera Matthews; she then introduced the others whose names, like hers, did not percolate my anxiety. We then went through a lot of my background and my 'mothers' death, my knowledge of my 'uncle' and my current job. All of these I answered as confidently as I could manage.

"What would you bring to being in our service?" Asked one of the other members of the committee.

"Well, hard work and a willingness to serve. As you will see I have had a fairly unusual and sheltered upbringing, but I have had a wide education and my most telling attributes are my language skills, which may be useful in some of the work your service may be asked to do. I am fluent in German and Italian, as well as being passable in French. I currently work as a translator, so it is not just a theoretical or classroom understanding of language."

"Translation is not coping with spoken language though." The same woman said.

"No, but it means my language skills are current, and also I work with technical terms, and I understand colloquial German as well as school German."

"Not spoken language though." Persisted my tormentor and hers and another two heads went down.

The fourth woman member, who I think was called Nettlefield or fold stared at me.

"Colloquial? ...... explain."

"Yes, well because my mother was an ill woman my upbringing was by a German governess and that is a second language to me. So, if you listen to the English language we use colloquialisms things like 'peepers' for your eyes, 'long johns' for men's' underwear and 'best bib and tucker' for when people get dressed up for a special occasion. These terms do not come up in the schoolroom dictionaries for a German or French person learning English. What I am saying is that I understand the German colloquialisms as well as the language as a whole so I can better understand all that is being said."

Three heads had come up. The chairwoman looked at number four who nodded.

"Very well you are accepted. Go down the corridor to the second door on the left with this chitty and confirm your details so that arrangements can be made for your joining instructions. Subject to satisfactory references I am pleased to welcome you aboard Ordinary Wren Booth." She rose, smiled, handed me a piece of paper and I left in a daze.

Somehow, I know not how, Jack had given a referee in the application and again, somehow, that 'person' satisfied the authorities by providing a reference that must have been acceptable. Beast though he was, Jack and his gang were pretty resourceful.

Within ten days I was at a newly created establishment at Mill Hill, being trained in every aspect of service life, from whom to salute and how to march, and then being given a list of potential occupations within the Wrens. There were things like administration and typing, or maintenance of small harbour boats, or driving vehicles for officers or, the one I chose, which was as a radio operator. My German fluency I realised was where I would most likely be useful and when I mentioned this, I was allocated a post as a 'listener'. Jack had told me to try and get a post in the Government Code and Cypher school, but even if this was available, I did not ask as I did not want to be where I would really be of use to them. But I did get a posting to Abbots Cliff House a secret cliff top listening post near Folkestone. Whilst disappointed Jack was content enough that I was now part of the Navy and, if my current role was not all he would have wished, he no doubt hoped that after proving myself I may get a transfer to something more useful to him. He pressed me to seek a transfer as soon as possible to something involved in naval planning or deployment.

Abbots Cliff House was not big enough for all the listening staff required and eight of us Wrens were billeted in a large, requisitioned house in the nearby village of Capel le Ferne, within easy cycling distance. The job was to search the VHF frequencies for German transmissions. In those days the listening range was up to about 30 miles and was improved by our cliff top location. Bearings of the signals would be taken and passed to our local HQ in Dover along with a summary of what we heard being said. Our primary targets were aircraft and fast-moving E-boats operating in or over the English Channel. We worked eight-hour shifts, for six days and then had two days off.

The work was interesting, and I was very much thrown together with my small band of German speaking colleagues. Jack had warned me to avoid socialising with colleagues and suggested that I keep referring to the death of my fictitious mother as my reason for keeping a distance. He told me that understanding mental illness would be helpful if I ever had to use it as a ploy to get out of, at best, someone trying to get too close to me, or, at worst, if I was discovered and interrogated by the British Security Services. In the early days of my time in East

Molesey, when I was not allowed out much, he gave me books on mental illness and depression by Sigmund Freud, Kurt Schneider and Edward Mapother. I found them vaguely interesting, and, without any other reading material, I read them through, covering all types of mental illness, and noting particularly the symptoms of depression and schizophrenia. By remaining fairly self-contained, unemotional and making frequent reference to my deceased 'mother', I successfully set myself apart from the other girls who, after a while trying to draw me into their clique without success, basically ignored me.

My political masters did not get much of an initial return from their spy. Most of my reports were very general but I assumed that they were content for me to simply build up my reputation as a good worker and maybe I might be more useful later. No doubt they had many low-level personnel whom they hoped may eventually get an important position when they would become really useful. Just like planting seeds for food, some would produce a good crop, some just OK and some would fail. I tried hard to be the one that failed.

As well as any instructions in the envelope I received there was often, though not always, a letter from Daddy. In the years 1940 and early 1941 as the war developed and the German successes grew on all fronts and my father's few letters seemed normal and as happy as might be expected. But the frequency of letters had steadily reduced and towards the end of 1941 they had almost dried up. I was told that, due to the communication difficulties, letters were unlikely to be more frequent than one every six months. I was becoming less satisfied with the tone of letters from Daddy, whose writing had become more untidy and the content of them was much less normal, though I could not really put a finger on as to why that may be so. The statements along the lines of 'all being well' continued.

By the beginning of 1942 I had been working at the same place for nearly a couple of years without a break except for a few days leave here and there. I was content enough as I was doing no harm to the British cause by reporting such low level and time limited information. My reports to my superiors were either instantly useful or not and were immediately superseded by the next intercept. Due to the costal defence restricted area arrangements, it would have been much harder and more suspicious to meet my spy contact, Ralph, at Folkestone or Dover so about monthly, to coincide with my day off, I travelled to Canterbury to meet Ralph. The message from Jack was always 'keep trying to get to the Government Code and Cypher school now operating at a place called Bletchley Park'. I pretended by saying that I was trying but so far no success. I was just stringing them along.

At that time early in 1942 a new young Lieutenant-Commander came to take charge of our section replacing a much older man who had left on health grounds. The new man instituted a review of the work of stations like ours. As a result, he decided to shake up the postings and as I had by then been the longest there, I was informed that I would be transferred to HMS Helicon in Scotland. This I learned was in fact far out on the north-west coast at a place called Loch Ewe. Fortunately, I was given a fortnight's notice and the next week, when I met Ralph, I passed the information and the fact that I would be travelling the following Wednesday and would be catching a train from Euston to Inverness at two in the afternoon. Ralph told me that someone would be there to meet me and give me fresh orders. Whoever appeared, probably him, I was to act as though it was a chance meeting with a relative or old friend.

All packed, with my kit bag, I set off the following Wednesday to travel to London by train, alighting at Waterloo I decided to walk up to Euston, as I had plenty of time and it gave me chance to stop for a cup of tea and a bun at a Lyons Corner House on the way. I arrived at Euston not long after one in the afternoon and about fifteen minutes later, having established which platform my train would depart from, I stood near the ticket barrier waiting. My heart fell as I saw Jack coming towards me and completely out of character he boomed out.

"Sheila my dear! What a stroke of luck seeing you here" He advanced and held out his hand and then pumped mine vigorously. Having made clear to any interested watcher that this was a chance meeting he lowered his voice.

"Wonderful posting! Well done! Convoys to Murmansk are leaving from your new location. I cannot get Ralph to come and see you however as it is in a huge rural restricted area. Write to me with information. Go out of camp and post your letters in a letter box. I will hand you an envelope and it has the new communication address as well as the latest from your father"

Then, raising his voice again he said. "So lovely to see you again my dear, please do keep in touch. Here is my new address." And with that he gave me an envelope and walked off.

The train north was overcrowded, as so many were in those days, I decided that there was no point in trying to read Daddy's letter till I arrived at my destination. During the journey the only matter of significance was that, nearly three hours after leaving London, we arrived in York. There was shouting from station staff walking up the platform informing us that there was a twenty-minute delay, as the engine had developed a fault and they had to get steam up in a replacement. I was delighted as getting to the toilet down the crowded corridor looked to be a nightmare, so I went and sought out the women's toilets in the station building and walked around to stretch my legs. Then I managed to get a cup of tea and a sandwich from a WRVS stall.

After a refreshment stop at Edinburgh Waverley station, we spent an interminable journey through the night, until, at first light, the edge of a misty Cairngorm Mountain was fading behind me, on the right of the train, as we turned to begin the descent down towards Inverness. Then, on arrival, I was directed to another train which was advertised as heading for Kyle of Lochalsh. This one included some military ticket inspectors who told me to disembark at a place called Achnasheen, which was, when we arrived, apparently in the middle of nowhere. About twenty of us disembarked, mainly sailors but also another Wren and we were all called over to two waiting canvas clad lorries with bench seats either side of the rear area stretching back behind the driver's cab. I got to sit second from the back and after passing through a checkpoint into the restricted area I kept getting glimpses of a glorious Loch, which we passed to our right. Eventually after the best part of a jerky and noisy hour's journey we came to a place I came to know was Gairloch and then twenty minutes later Poolewe and ten minutes after that, Aultbea, followed shortly by HMS Helicon.

We weary travellers disembarked and a Leading Wren shouted to me to follow her, and she took me and the fellow

Wren, whom I had not encountered on the journey and must have been in the other lorry, into the Wrenery. It was there after unpacking that I opened Daddy's letter, the one which Jack had handed me at Euston, and which had indicated that he was no longer free, and I should assume that he was writing under duress. So, I realised that it seemed that I could safely assume that I was no longer a hostage to my parents' safety and as a result could begin considering my options for extricating myself from my predicament.

Thanks to the Third Reich I had been 'selected' for some up to date and very helpful training in espionage and when I reflected upon it I realised that it had given me quite a number of useful new skills. There was my ability to act a role which I had successfully done now for upwards of two years. I was able to learn a back story and then to act it out. Keeping sufficient distance from other people so that they did not get to discover anything of the real me was something at which I was now adept. Also, there was my enforced 'education' in mental illness, although I had only been required to use the symptom of depression; there were other illnesses and symptoms with which I was broadly familiar from all the reading in East Molesey. Aside from all this I had learned a good range of skills, like my ability to type. Finally, I was, after the teaching of my finishing school seamstress tutor, together with what I discovered to be a personal aptitude, a competent needle worker and might even be able to make a living from that. So, if I was to find myself free, I could probably make a living, one way or another, if I had to.

If I ruled out the option of a confession to all my spying, I made up my mind to look for a means of leaving and going underground and surviving as best as possible until I could start a new life. Surely the disruption of war would provide sufficient cover for that to be possible? Every day people were being bombed out of their homes in which all their possessions and documentation might have been destroyed and I could use that to my advantage. So, I determined to work towards taking an opportunity of applying for leave, or even being sent urgently on draft somewhere, and using it as an opportunity to disappear. If it all failed and I was unable to 're-invent' myself then the confession route could be used when I was left without any alternative. This then became the outline basis of my plan. Disappear when an opportunity to leave the district's restricted area arose or make an application for leave.

Whatever way I contrived to be able to disappear it was quite clear that I would by sought by two different groups, one would be the Navy and through them the general arms of law enforcement, the other group would be Jack and his organisation. To disappear for a long time until the heat died down would demand that I created a new role of a displaced person, perhaps appearing to be of limited intelligence or even mild depression or psychiatric illness. I would probably need to live rough at times and therefore I needed to make up a survival kit of some sort. The first thing I would need would be something to hold some essentials. I could not disappear with all my things in my Navy issue kit bag.

On my local walks, which were my main recreation because I could do this on my own, I had got into general conversation with an old fisherman who had been mending nets and had enjoyed a long chat with him about his work. I was interested in his net mending and conversation turned to my needlework and he told me how he used to be a sailmaker in his youth. He talked about the difficulty of stitching thick canvas and the need to use a needle and leather palm, a piece of leather fastened onto the hand and used to push the large canvas sewing needles through the tough material. On a second visit he demonstrated this technique for me and I told him that when I got some leave that I would love to go hiking and would like to make myself a knapsack. I omitted to tell him that the knapsack I had in mind would most usually have been seen in parts of Switzerland or Germany. On a visit to Gairloch I went to a shop which sold all sorts of hardware and ships chandlery and purchased some strong canvas and some thin leather webbing. I cut out and stitched the canvas into a simple knapsack or backpack, with a flap over top. Then with the help of the fisherman and his palm and twine, we stitched the leather webbing to make the straps, though the back of the canvas onto to some more webbing inside making a strong joint and trapping the canvas between. I paid him two pounds for his effort which he said was far too much. A few days later, when I saw him, he presented me with a lovely leather purse, which fastened with a toggle, made from our knapsack webbing offcuts.

My pay had been virtually untouched and had been accruing in my Post Office savings account. I had drawn ten pounds in one-pound notes before leaving Folkestone, because I knew my destination was a rural one, but so far, I had not spent it all. So now I turned to more needle work to help support my potential escape. Tightly rolling bank notes into tiny cylinders I sewed them beside the waistbands of two pairs of old, for emergency use only, raggy knickers. Then, every time I went to one of the nearby villages I went to the post office and drew a few pounds to sew into waistbands. I also learned that postal orders were valid for six months. So, I started getting one for £5 on the pretext of sending it home to support my family. These I kept in my new leather purse which, I reasoned, would be broadly weatherproof. This purse I hid in a false bottom I had sewn inside my rucksack. By the time I was told that I was to have a day at sea on the *Loyalty* I was ready for any chance of leave or transfer providing me with the opportunity to disappear, with over forty pounds to support me. Half the funds were sewn into my old underwear seams and the other half in postal orders in the purse.

Loch Ewe was at the centre of a vast restricted area, entry to which was monitored for train travellers as far away as Inverness. For road traffic there were checkpoints at Acnasheen to the south and Laide to the north. Even local residents had to carry identification. It was sometimes referred to as Port 'A' and had become one of the gathering points for merchant convoys and at this point of the war, many of the merchant ships bound for what became known as the 'Arctic Convoys' would assemble there. These convoys were to sail to Murmansk and Archangel to provide vital supplies to the Russians who had become part of the allied fight against the Nazi's, who had themselves invaded Russia. Thus, Jack's pleasure at my posting would no doubt have been because I would be ideally placed to send information about these convoys.

And I did. But I contrived to always send information of a general kind along the lines that a convoy was beginning to assemble and that I would confirm dates of departure when known. Then after it left, and I knew the journey would take between two and three weeks, I would wait before posting details, on the pretext that I had been unable to leave the camp, until I judged it should have arrived. I knew that Jack would not be happy, but he was a long way off in London and increasingly I felt safe and ready to escape to a new life, just as soon as I was granted leave.

If ever I had been in any doubt about my need to get away from this place the news about Arctic Convoy PQ 17 in early July – and about which I had failed to inform Jack of its departure - brought home to me the need to get away, as all bar two of the original ships had been sunk.

It was at this juncture that I was informed that I was to have one of these days of experience at sea in the local tug the *Loyalty*. It somewhat put off the day when I was building up to applying for a period of leave during which I intended to make a run for it and disappear.

If ever an incident was likely to confirm my decision to abandon my spying, however low level and unimportant, then witnessing the skill and bravery of the crew of the *Loyalty*, and in particular of the captain, Taff, was it. How could I in all conscience continue to work, however half-heartedly, for the enemy of these men, especially an enemy whom I now believed had at best imprisoned, or at worst, and most likely, killed my parents?

It was therefore these thoughts and emotions, driven by the elation of being part of such an event, and in the knowledge that soon I would shed this awful double life that had led me to spontaneously suggest to Taff a 'date' for a walk together and he had agreed.

After all it was just a walk by the sea.

But what life changing consequences there would be; for the both of us.

Chapter 11

1997 Rose – Otley

By the beginning of October, a month had passed since my visit to Porthcawl and I was beginning to wonder if I needed to make contact with Gareth. He had seemed such an efficient and honest man that I had assumed that I would have had contact from him, within a week or at best a fortnight, about whether or not his search for papers had been successful. Obviously I did not want to pressure him, but I had made up my mind to send him a letter if I had heard nothing by mid-October. I was delighted to get home in the early evening of Friday 10th October to find an answer-phone message from him. When I listened to that message he sounded much less like the man I remembered from that afternoon in Porthcawl, the voice was strained and much less confident than I recalled.

"Err….. Hello Rose. Its Gareth here. I hope I have the correct number. I hate these recorded message things. Anyway, if I have reached you then please call me at your convenience."

Despite being ready for something to eat I rang him before bothering with any tea. He answered very promptly and very formally.

"Hello, Gareth speaking. Who's calling?"

"Gareth. It's me Rose. You left me a message earlier."

"Oh Rose! Thank you so much for ringing and I am so sorry I have not been in touch before, but I am afraid I have not been too well, indeed, if truth be known, not too well at all."

"Oh dear. Whatever has been the matter?"

"I've had what I call an ague, probably influenza or some such virus, you know the shivering and shaking and the hot and cold and it laid me low, in fact as low as I can recall for many years, and I am only just beginning to come around. I am afraid that it's rather left me a bit weak."

"Oh! Poor you. How have you managed?"

"Not entirely well, to be honest with you. Oh, I have had these things before in life, from time to time, like everyone else and sometimes at sea a steward would ensure that you were fed and watered, and of course when Dyllis was alive she would do all the looking after. But this time I was really on my own. The neighbours did fetch me some bread and milk, when I asked but I must confess it has made me realise that I have not got a lot of local support. No matter, I have survived and now I am on the mend."

"Did you call the doctor; they could have arranged help if nobody else is available?"

"No, they are busy enough and we would never call the doctor for something as straightforward as the ague."

"Gareth, you should have done. It's not like your childhood days where the doctor is to be paid for. The NHS would have helped you if you were alone and ill. I see so many older people who are reluctant to seek help. Why should you not have some payback for all the taxes you have paid, certainly those you paid since 1946 when the NHS started?"

"Well, you are probably right, but we were brought up to get on with things and not to be forever running to somebody else for help. Anyway, as I say, I am on the mend. Although it is now nearly three weeks since I started feeling unwell and that is the trouble as you get older, things take that much longer to get better. Why, when I was a boy if you had a bruise playing out then within the week it was gone. Nowadays if I bang myself and get a bruise it takes me three or more weeks for it to begin to improve. But the point is, that I am now feeling more mentally able to get back to the issues raised by your visit."

"Look you do not need to worry about that. It has, as I told you, been an issue that has been running for many years, and indeed seventeen years with me, so a few more weeks is of no great shakes. The main point is for you to be well."

"Yes Rose, and thank you, but I found what I was looking for soon after you left and I had planned to just leave it a week or so, for you to settle back home and then I was going to ring. But then this wretched ague intervened, and I am sorry."

"Apology not required."

"Well, the point is this; as I said I have found what I was looking for and I have it with me but I had decided, before I got ill, that it was not something I could either just post to you or even telephone you about. For my part, I feel it needs some personal explanation along with your seeing the paperwork; therefore, the purpose of my call was to see if we could arrange to meet?"

"Of course we can, but there is a small problem. We are very short staffed here at present and I do not think I can get away before the end of November. Unless you think you might feel able to travel up here when you are properly better. I have plenty of room for you to stay and I would love to have you."

"I am much improved already, but it may be prudent to give myself a couple more weeks to build up strength. And yes, a break away from here would be most welcome. If you are sure, but I may need advice from you about appropriate local Bed and Breakfast or a hotel."

"If you do not stay here with me I will be most disappointed. I told you that things are very quiet in my life since Sally and company moved away. Oh. And by the way, Michael has got a job back up here and they are hoping to come back early in the New Year, and I am really looking forward to it."

"I am so pleased for you Rose, it will be nice to have your family nearby you again. As to my possible trip, well alright then I will be happy to stay with you and thank you very much. I am just looking at the calendar and Tuesday 4th November suggests itself as a good day to travel. By the way I will come on the train as I do not fancy driving all that way in November."

"Of course, but just to warn you that I will have to work some of the time you are here but it's a nice big house and in a semi-rural setting and I am sure that you will find it a nice change."

"You need not worry about me because I am used to amusing myself."

"Good. That date is fine. If you check the train times I can arrange to meet you in Leeds, because I can be flexible with my work. Also, you can get a through train from Bristol to Leeds and I guess Cardiff to Bristol has plenty of trains too. Unfortunately, Dr Beeching stopped the trains to Otley many years ago and our nearest station is Menston and I don't want you having to do all that changing and getting busses at the end of a long trip. So, I will park at Guiseley and come to Leeds on the train to meet you and take you back to Guiseley and we can drive home from there."

"Well, that is very kind. I will be in touch when I have found out about the train times."

"Fine. But can I just ask if you have made any connection for me from the papers you have found?"

There was a pause.

"Rose. Will you trust and bear with me for just these next couple of weeks. I prefer to tell you a full and whole story and to pick up on the many questions that I know that you will want to ask, as a result of what I have to tell you."

I was disappointed but, as I had told him, I had sat on things long enough and another fortnight was neither here nor there. But clearly he had something for me; that was the thing.

"Well, I must be honest and say that I am itching to hear your news, but I will try to be patient Gareth. Thank you so much for getting in touch."

Chapter 12

1942 Gareth - Loch Ewe

Saturday dawned with a light wind and blue sky. It had the promise of a beautiful summer day, in fact after the gale during the last week the weather had been settled, dry and warm. We were busy in the morning with a number of duties, but unless there was an emergency or a lot of ships were gathered, prior to forming a convoy, we were usually granted our allotted time off on a Saturday and the tug was allowed to tie up alongside the jetty, or at least alongside another vessel that was already moored to the jetty. On these days the crew was allowed ashore for the afternoon for relaxation and refreshment. Young Hopkins my second in command, who had really begun to develop well in terms of his ship handling, was always keen to have the Saturday ashore. Nominally we operated on the basis of half the crew off and half on, although I had only once taken my scheduled day off to wander round the area. This was because, in any event, I occasionally had the opportunity to go ashore as part of my duties, to report to the base commander, and other superiors, during the week. So, as young Hopkins was always keen to have a run ashore I usually stayed aboard and he usually went ashore on a Saturday. This week it was my turn on board, but I pulled rank and, much to his disappointment, said I needed to go ashore this week and reminded him that he had already had more than his fair share.

So it was, with a strong sunlight on my back, which had soon made me remove my sweater and tie it round my waist, that I arrived outside the Wren's quarters over ten minutes before the appointed hour of 1300. Sheila was there waiting for me and walked to meet me, looking very relaxed in civvy clothes, as of course, like me, she was off duty.

"In here I have some food." She said indicating the canvas haversack she had slung over her shoulder, "I thought that you might like to have a walk as the weather is so nice, and that we might have a picnic."

"That would be fine," I said, "but maybe not too far because if there is an emergency we are all supposed to be within striking distance of the jetty, if we hear the emergency signal on the ship's whistle."

"How will you know there is an emergency?" She asked.

"We have an emergency signal which is sounded by the ships air horn. So, if we hear seven short blasts followed by one long one then, I am afraid, that I will be off at the run."

"Will you know that it is your ship? There are lots of them in the loch just at present."

"Well, I expect to be able to tell ours from another ship, but it doesn't matter either way. Given that *Loyalty* is one of the emergency vessels then if it's not our emergency then it will be on another ship and therefore I will need to go anyway."

"Let us hope for a quiet afternoon then and, as the Wrenery is, as you have discovered, part way up the hill, may I suggest that we just keep on going further up. Beyond the farmed land of the crofts, which you can see, there is what I might best describe as a sort of moor like area with rocky outcrops and we can get a good view of the loch to sit and contemplate whilst we sit and eat and if there is an emergency you will not be too far away."

I agreed that this sounded a very acceptable plan and we set off without much conversation, as there were fields of livestock to negotiate, and the land grew steeper the higher we went meaning that conservation of breath superseded conversation. Quite quickly the arable land gave way to the rocky area she had described which appeared to be home to a flock of sheep, who were disturbed by our appearance and quickly moved away before they carried on feeding on the grass between the rocks. In a while we found a lovely vantage point with Loch Ewe and its island spread out before us shimmering in the sun. There was a cleft between a couple of rocks which provided a breeze free suntrap for us to sit and take in the wonderful view.

Recovering our breath she said. "After making the sandwiches I did wonder if you would be able to make it today, Taff." She said, smiling.

"Actually, I must confess that I did pull rank to get off duty, and my second in command is a little miffed. But he will get over it and also, he has had the bulk of the Saturday runs ashore, including many that were 'my turn' and so he could not argue too much. Oh. By the way, although I am a proud Welshman and therefore content to be Taffy in the naval setting, please call me Gareth."

"Alright Gareth, but seriously I do hope it will not cause you problems with your crew." She said, looking at me with some anxiety.

"Oh! No." I replied. "We all work very well together."

"Yes, you do and I was very privileged to see that in action last week. Only a set of men who were a good team could possibly have saved that tanker. From what I could see they all worked so well together because of their trust in one another and also with the trust that comes from a shared respect to the person in charge."

"Hey, steady on, flattery and sandwiches combined are a heady mix for a poor, simple lad from the valleys like me."

"You will not be a poor chap for long. Surely such a feat as you personally achieved, aided by your crew, will not go unrecognised. It is the talk of the base and everyone says there must be a gong in it for you. In fact, my Petty Officer required me to write a report on what I saw of the operation so that there was independent testimony as well as your official report."

"Oh dear." I said. "I do hope that you did not over egg the pudding because I do not want there to be a fuss. That said, from my perspective and that of the crew, we were just like any sailors responding to the plight of brother sailors in trouble. And, as you say, the well drilled unit that is currently this little ship all pulled together to achieve that outcome."

"Yes. There were men all working well together but one man actually risked his life to enter those fearsome cold waters, and I was not the only one aboard who were convinced that you would never make it to that tanker and back again, never mind manage to get a line aboard her."

110

"To start with and in retrospect what I did was really foolhardy, and I was extremely lucky to get away with it. That said I was brought up on tales of sea rescues and my early mentor, he was a Bristol Channel Pilot, had been involved in the Mumbles lifeboat disaster of 1903 when he went to try and aid the stricken lifeboat men whose vessel had overturned or been swamped; he even gave evidence at the subsequent Inquiry into it. Together with that, you should understand that everyone else at sea has a great respect for the lives of their fellow mariners and almost without exception will always help another seaman in difficulty. That is not to say that we are all that respectful of one another if we are not in trouble. We Brits tend to have a rather superior view of the capabilities, or rather lack thereof, of other races to be good seamen. We respect the 'Norskies', as we usually call the Norwegians, and the Dutch but we do not think highly of the French or Spaniards or any of the Mediterranean sailors, especially the Greeks. And the Yanks, of course, are always too full of themselves. But put any of them in trouble and we will help one another on the *quid pro quo* basis that you never know when you might need somebody to help you if you are in distress."

"So; how do you come to be the captain of this tug?" She asked.

And for a long time thereafter she teased out of me my life story. She was interested and attentive and I found a great relief in being able to talk to somebody in this way. I suppose that I had not realised that, despite the easy-going nature of my command, I still felt it was not the right thing to be over familiar with any member of the crew. So, after months of being the one person aboard who held constant responsibility with limited chance to relax, I found there was such a release in talking to somebody who was not involved in that self-contained world of mine.

"Sorry. I have rabbited on for ages, so, enough of me, what about you?" I asked after I had realised how long I must have been rambling, prompted by her occasional comments.

"I am hungry." She replied reaching for the haversack and proceeding to share out our food wrapped in greaseproof paper. We ate in companionable silence for a while and then I tried again.

"Is your present work interesting?"

She finished chewing and said.

"Yes, it is interesting and a bit hush hush and so, if I was to tell you anything, I would have to kill you!" She said grinning.

"And if accidentally you did tell me, would you feel able to carry out that threat?"

"Oh. What a question. I do not really know if I would be able to actually take a life. I do not know what some of our soldiers go through, fighting the enemy hand to hand and how they feel about having to pull a trigger with an enemy in sight. In theory I think I would find it hard. But I guess that given extreme circumstances, especially when it is kill or be killed, we are all able to suspend our normal beliefs about the sanctity of life and do what is driven by those circumstances."

"So, is there a real you under all this prevarication? I do not mean to pry but you seem a very nice person and I have enjoyed talking to you, but it's all been about me and you have carefully avoided letting anything slip about yourself. And to be honest I find myself interested in this young woman I am walking out with today, to the extent that it would be nice to think we might do something together again. But if you do not want to say anything about yourself it may be because you made a spur of the moment decision to suggest this date and now you regret it and so the best way to stop the possibility of another meeting is to give nothing of yourself away. Maybe you have a boyfriend already and you are just being polite and getting through the afternoon until you can leave me at the Wrenery and politely make it clear that you do not wish to see me again?"

There was a long silence whilst she stared out into the sunny vista before us. Then, without looking at me she said.

"You have had a life of freedom of choice, which is of course why this country is fighting this dreadful war, so as to ensure that freedom of choice will continue for its citizens. But mine has been a life where circumstances have dictated my choices. Ironically, I am approaching a moment when, for the first time, in a long time, I hope that the power to choose my life path may be restored, even though that may just be a pipe dream."

She lapsed into silence and even though I could not really make sense of what she was saying I felt that she had, for her, said something profound and so I decided to ride out the silence to see if anything more was to come. She turned to me.

"You have a home? Parents? A base that you can go to if you get leave from your ship? And when all this rotten war is over?"

I nodded, and she looked back at the view.

"Things have been very different for me since I lost my parents about four years ago. I was an only child and for over a couple of years before that I was away at a boarding school a very long way from home. Indeed, I did not get home for the whole time I was at that school. I did have friends at school, but we have not been in touch since. So effectively I have been very much alone, and I miss the thoughts of having a home to go to and so I suppose I envy you in that regard."

"Don't you have other extended family to take care of you?"

"No. As I say I am an only child, so no siblings. My parents had no contact with their respective families and their parents, my grandparents, were dead and added to that we moved about with my father's work. Looking back I had a very insular childhood, short term friendships at different schools and, to be fair, I was happy with my own company. Either I was happy or else got used to being a loner. I suppose that I still am. I keep myself to myself and I am sure that my colleagues have me down as a 'stuck up bitch'. But it's not that I am stuck up it's just that I am surviving this life the best way I can and the best way for me to do that is for me to keep my own counsel. That in turn means not engaging too closely with others."

I said nothing and allowed another silence until she, still staring at the view, said.

"After I lost my parents I stayed with, let me call him my 'uncle', Jack. He was not a nice man, in fact he took advantage of me, but he nevertheless had a hold over me because he knew, what I will call, a family secret which he knew I would not wish to be made public. For the last three years I have remained under his threats but recently I have begun to realise that it is time I challenged his hold over me and I have been making plans to do that when the chance presents itself. Over the last few years I have been too scared to take a chance but after I saw you plunge into those wild, awful seas it confirmed my recent conclusion that if you want to achieve a goal you sometimes need to take a big risk. Your actions led to a successful outcome, but you could have as easily been killed. I have determined that, whatever the outcome, I am going to be like you and take the risk."

She turned to me.

"It is so nice to sit and talk to you and I am sure that you will not understand one little bit of what I am going on about. However, for the first time in years I am having a real, personal conversation with somebody. I have felt so terribly alone, and I am afraid that might be my destiny."

There were tears trickling down her cheeks and on impulse I put my arm around her shoulders and she clung to me and sobbed for several minutes. I was uncomprehending of what was happening, of what all this was about. Her story had been enigmatic, to say the least, yet clearly she was in a highly emotional state. As the sobs subsided she said.

"Thank you for holding me. This is the first hug of comfort I have experience in years, since the last one I had from my father."

We sat in silence for a long time because I felt that she was still in a state of high emotion, and I did not want to pressurise her at all. I could not entirely make sense of what she had been saying but clearly telling her story had led to some sort of cathartic release. Without any warning she reached up and kissed me. I was taken aback, but the urgency of her kisses grew, and I began to respond and within a short while we were both so aroused that I doubt if even the sounding of the tug's whistle to summon me to an emergency would have interrupted our coming together. It was a gentle, natural and amazing experience for me, and she seemed to want to be loved and held in the fullest sense.

We lay together for a long time after our exertions finished and eventually she moved away and said.

"Gareth, please do not think me a monster. I told you that I am a person alone and loneliness means missing human contact. I have felt so safe with you, and I guess I just wanted, for the first time in my life, to make love to a person who was nice instead of being forced by someone with power over me."

"Sheila, that was so wonderful, and I will never forget this afternoon as long as I live and dare I hope that there might be other times that we can meet and get to know one another better?"

"Well, Gareth, I would like to meet you again and next week would be good but remember that I warned you that I am looking for a chance to move away from here and these chances come out of the blue and who knows I could be drafted before the end of the week, or you could have to go out to sea and find me gone when you get back. But I do wish to think that, if either of those things happened, I could contact you in the future, so maybe if you gave me an address then if things happen sooner than I expect I can write to you."

"Absolutely; that would be great." I said and she rummaged in her haversack and produced a pencil and a small piece of paper and passed them to me.

"This is my parent's home in Penarth." I said writing, "You can always get me through them. So, what is your address?"

"Well, I really am a loner and you can write to me here addressed to Ordinary WRNS Sheila Booth and I guess it will be forwarded because I do not have a fixed address in Civvy Street at the moment."

I made a note of her rank, name and number on the bottom of the page and then tore that bit off and put it in my pocket. We spent a little time coming round from our exertions and what turned out to be not long after three o'clock we collected our things together and began to make out way down to the Wrenery. We were both light-hearted and smiling and just chatting; occasionally, when the terrain allowed, we held hands. The Wrenery was the highest building on that bit of the hill and as we climbed into the last field before the building some one hundred yards or so away, she stopped suddenly.

"Gareth!" She said in a voice that was no longer light but instead it was insistent and serious. "Please point at something, anything, out in the Loch as though you were trying to explain something going on out there and then just listen to me. If you keep pointing out but glance down the hill you will see a staff car outside the Wrenery."

I glanced and noted the car with an Officer and rating standing beside it obviously waiting and obviously looking up towards us.

"Well, before I came here, I worked in a very hush hush operation and I hated every minute of it and when my Commanding Officer was seconded for a couple of months I

115

managed to swing a transfer up here from his temporary replacement. But I was always sure that when he came back my old Commanding Officer would want to have me back and now it looks as though my holiday here might be over. I need you to do something quite important for me. I am due on duty at 1000 tomorrow and it would be helpful of you could ring the base communications office tomorrow morning and leave the message that you had just called to see me and I was feeling ill and might be late getting in. Will you do that? It is really important to me."

"Of course I will, but why…… ."

"Please trust me Taff. You can be my lifesaver, and I promise to write and explain as soon as I can. Now let's go down and get this over with."

We continued down the hill and on arrival at the Wrenery the Officer wearing the rings of a Royal Navy Captain greeted Sheila.

"Ah. Booth. We again have need of your excellent services. Go and change into uniform and get your things. Time is short."

"I had better inform my Leading Wren." Said Sheila.

"No need, I have already been in touch with the Officer Commanding and he is aware of the urgent need for your services." Replied the Captain.

Then turning to me he said. "Thank you, Lieutenant. That will be all."

I hesitated, staring at this rather puffed up little man who stared back at me unblinking from steely blue eyes. I noticed, however, that to the side of the left eye was a small but vivid strawberry mark which gave him a slightly lopsided looking face.

"I said that will be all. Lieutenant."

"Yes. Sir." I said, saluting.

As I wandered away I felt to be really confused. I looked back a couple of times to see the car still waiting and then as I got to the jetty, about ten minutes later, I saw what I assumed to be the same car heading away from the base.

During the evening I reviewed the afternoon with its extreme high of our love making and then the unexpected deflation at the end whereby she was clearly scared to be apparently summoned to go back to a former job, to which she had no desire to return. I pulled the paper from my pocket and studied her name. Well, I would leave things a week and then, if I heard nothing I would write to her.

The following day I was left with a slightly guilty feeling as I was faced with making the call she had requested to say she was sick. It made no sense because surely if the Captain had informed the Base Commander as he had indicated her section would know already. But, I reasoned, this woman could become the love of my life and I had made her a promise so, admittedly against my better judgement, I contacted Sheila's Leading Wren to say I had seen her and she had not been well and may not be able to report for duty. I was thanked for the call and assured that they would send someone to check on her later in the afternoon.

But the implications of that previous afternoon and my telephone call would be far reaching, as I would find out.

Some implications would come to light much sooner than others.

Chapter 13

1943 Solly – Leeds, Yorkshire

Our legal practice is in Park Square Leeds and is a well-established firm founded by my aunt's husband and therefore, by marriage, my uncle, Paul Winterstein and my father Aaron Hoffman and we trade as Hoffstein, a combination of the two names. When I say 'our' and 'we' I hope that in due course I might become a partner but, as it stands, I am an articled clerk but one who, having reached the age of eighteen is about to face being called up. I am truly looking forward to it all as it must be much more exciting than the study of the law and the paper shuffling that my father and uncle say I need to master before I can be of real use to the firm. Also, over the year or so since the Americans came into the war on our side and their troops here had been building up, there had been talk of a possible assault on German occupied France. So, not unlike many young men of my age I wanted to be involved in this attempt to defeat that awful mad man Hitler who is doing so much to harm to Jewish people. Of course, what was happening to Jewish people in German occupied areas might have become the fate of me and my family if we had lived in Europe.

So, whilst I was engaged ostensibly on some boring house conveyancing relating to a property in Hunslet, my mind kept wandering away to think about what my life was going to be like in just two weeks from next Tuesday. That was when I was due to leave home and start my Army enlistment and training. So, I was rather startled out of my reverie when the door flew open and Uncle Paul stood there.

"Solly," he started, "there is a scruffy looking woman in reception who does not have an appointment and who says she needs to talk to somebody urgently and will not be fobbed off with an appointment for next week. I am busy with an important client and your father is, as you know, in the Magistrates Court this morning. So put on your jacket and go down and talk to her and see what she wants. Just make some notes and if its business we can deal with then sign her up and get a fee if possible." And with that he left.

Never mind the issue, Uncle Paul will deal with anything for which he can charge a fee, usually he needs some money up front to start anything. Money is everything to my uncle. Scruffy clients do not auger well for business in his view. Normally I am not allowed to get near clients, so this was a nice change for me and so after putting on my jacket and running my hands through my hair, I took the stairs, two at a time, down to our reception area.

"I have put the woman in the waiting room." Said Sue, our very attractive and efficient receptionist. "Mr. Paul says do not forget to be taking a fee if at all possible."

"Yes." I replied, grinning at Sue, "I have already been given that message by the man himself. I fully understand that my stock of usefulness to the firm will only improve, in my uncle's eyes, if I return to you with coin of the realm in exchange for which you will give me a receipt and put the money in the safe." Sue smiled; she knew my uncle well.

I went into the interview room via the rear door and put down my pad and pen before moving to open the door which led to the waiting room area and inviting its only occupant to join me in the interview room. As befits good treatment of a prospective client I held the door open and allowed her to precede me into the room. The lady was much younger than I had been expecting, plainly dressed, though not unkempt or unclean but as she passed close by me as I held the door I noted an odour, not unpleasant in the way of unwashed bodies or clothes, but that smell of institutional cooking, if you will, a boiled cabbage sort of smell that reminded me of school dinners. She hesitated as she got a couple of paces into the room and I moved ahead and indicated where she should sit before I moved to go round to my seat behind the desk, but before I could get there she spoke.

"So, as the receptionist said, you are Mr. Solly eh? Are you Jewish?"

Now, of course I am, and I am perfectly proud of it, but I am not silly enough to think that everybody is kindly disposed towards people of my race. Accordingly, I have learned that it is better to equivocate since to simply say yes may result in the person asking the question getting up and leaving.

"Is that an important issue for you?" I asked.

"No. But it might be extra nice for me if you were, I have walked around this square looking at name plates and Hoffstein & Co seemed as though it may be Jewish, but I have never heard it before."

I explained the derivation of the firm's name and I also confirmed my own status as a Jewish person. She showed interest and also appeared satisfied with the information. She opened a large handbag and drew out a small package which was heavily sealed with Sellotape, that wonderful product, which had been invented only two years before the war began and which was used for all sorts of purposes from household fixing to the sealing of ammunition boxes.

"Can you arrange to keep these papers for me?"

"What are they?" I asked, again being cautious before I committed myself.

"Personal papers that I wish to know are kept safe."

"I see. But you may find it more convenient and less expensive to leave them at your home or in the bank or with a friend?"

"Well not really. You see, I have been moving around and may still have to do so again and I want to make sure that if I, or any person I authorise, need to consult these papers then you could make them available."

I was a little uncertain and she saw that.

"Of course, there would be a fee attached and the papers may have to be held a long time so I would pay upfront." She rummaged in her bag and produced two five pound notes.

"Shall we say ten pounds."

I was astounded, but, thinking of Uncle Paul, and recovering, I said.

"I think that will pay for a few years' worth of our storage. But are you really sure that it is that important? It is not a confession to a murder or something." I said joking. She looked at me coldly and said in a measured tone.

"Why do you ask?"

"Well," I replied becoming a little more professional and serious, "in the unlikely event that there was information in the papers about a very serious crime, say murder for example, then, if I, as a prospective Officer of the Court, which is what a solicitor is, has knowledge of a serious crime then I think that might actually trump client confidentiality. I am not absolutely sure on that yet as I am only learning my profession and I am not yet a solicitor." She looked at me and smiled and said.

"So, if you are not yet a solicitor with this need to behave like the Court Officer you describe then it would not matter if my papers referred to murder?"

"Oh no. In that case you would be talking to me as a citizen and there would be no requirement for me, as a citizen, to keep your confidence. But taking that argument forward, if I was acting as a citizen and if I was given information about such a crime as a murder then as a public minded person I think I would still probably have a duty to report it to the police."

She looked me fully and steadily in the eyes.

"I can assure you Mr Solly, and, if necessary, I will swear on oath, that I have not killed one single person, and the papers have nothing to do with anything like that."

"Right then Mrs……..?" I realised that I had not yet established her identity.

"Horowitz. Sonia Horowitz. And yes, I am of the Jewish faith – though really badly lapsed"

I wrote her name on my notepad.

"May I have your date and place of birth, please?"

"Fifth June 1920. Woking Surrey" So she was a lot younger than I had guessed even when I first saw her.

"And your address, Mrs Horowitz……..?"

"Part of the reason for my wishing to lodge these papers with someone like you, rather than a bank, is because, as I said earlier, I move around a lot, so my present address is immaterial, it may not be my address tomorrow. Aside from that, shall we say, my health is somewhat precarious and the reason for lodging the

121

papers with you is so that they are available to any relatives or friends that may need to consult them in the future."

"But how will I be able to contact you if somebody contacts us seeking permission to access the papers?"

"Well, I wish you, as part of the fee on the table to draw up a simple document which you keep with the papers, which acknowledges that your firm will hold the papers unopened until they are redeemed by me or a holder of an authority which I will give to them."

"But, Mrs Horowitz, how can we release them to anybody including even yourself, assuming that I am not available to confirm your identity."

She did not reply directly but instead rummaged in her bag and brought out two one pound notes and in my full view she proceeded to tear them each in half. She handed me one half of each of the notes.

"Mr Solly, the document I am asking you to prepare for our immediate joint signature should confirm that neither you nor any employee of your company will open the sealed paper package and that it is only to be handed over to the bearer of one half of either of the notes I have given you. Is that satisfactory and agreed?"

Well of course it was most irregular. But wartime is a time for expedience and irregularities and so I agreed. I left her for a while and went to consult Uncle Paul, who was now free of his first appointment reading some papers relating to his next one. I briefly explained the situation and that she wanted us to hold some papers pending contact from a relative or friend.

"And she is offering us ten pounds cash, now?"

"Yes"

"Solly, my boy, just do it. That is at least your wage till you go to the army."

Upon which he waved me off and went back to reading his papers. Money talks with Uncle Paul.

I drew up a document which I took back to the interview room and in the presence of Sue, as a witness, Mrs Horowitz and I both signed it and Sue endorsed it. Whereupon, 'Mrs Horowitz', for even then I could see that this was probably a pseudonym, thanked us and left.

Two and a bit weeks later I joined the army and the fight against the Nazi's.

Chapter 14

1942   Stella – Yorkshire

"Darl'n't'n, Darl'n't'n, this is Darl'n't'n. Next stop York." Shouted the elderly porter as he passed my compartment window. Roused from a fitful slumber and remembering with horror why I was sitting on that overcrowded train, I went back to considering the remaining options that had been running through my mind before the exhaustion of the events of the past twelve or so hours overcame me.

In all my planning for escape I had used as the premise of my position the fact that I was a spy, albeit a reluctant one operating under duress. But the question was, would I be able to prove that? Even if I did, it would not necessarily exonerate me, after all, at any time from when I was released by Jack to work at being a translator and then at Cliff Hill House, I could simply have told the authorities, and I did not. Yes, back then I was fearful for my parents, and that was my reason for not doing so, but balancing that against the fact that Allied lives were being lost by the hundreds just so that I could protect two people, did not seem to me would be enough to save me from many years in prison, or worse.

So as soon as I began to believe that my status as a hostage was no longer necessary as a safeguard to my parents, I began to realise that I had two enemies from whom I needed to escape. First there was the cruel organisation that I had been forced to work for to try and protect my parents. Then there were the British Authorities who would see me as an enemy of their state. I felt that I was between the Devil and the Deep Blue Sea, as the saying goes. One thing paramount in my mind was that I felt that I could not face years in a prison. I was still young, in my mid-twenties and, aside from the pampered time in Switzerland, I had not experienced a real life as a normal person of my age might have expected. Suppose I got ten years in jail, I reasoned, I would be middle to late thirties having spent the rest of my youthful years locked up, and I did not want that. It also assumed that the British would win the war, if not and I was identified as an escaped traitor to the German cause, then there would certainly be no hope.

What could I do?

It had struck me that the destruction from bombing and the other chaos that this war had created, even in as regulated a country as England, had left room for people to disappear and perhaps re-emerge as someone else. I could see that I could use that to my advantage, especially in the short term, yet how that might play out in the longer term I was not sure. But it was the start of a broad-brush plan at least. My main stumbling block seemed to be the lack of identification, as my real proof of identity as Stella Goldman was contained in papers confiscated by Jack. The current false ones related to me as a serving Ordinary WRNS Sheila Booth and were not of any use, especially now that I was in the process of thinking about deserting or at least being absent without leave. I had no idea as to how to overcome the identity problem other than to play dumb and say that I had lost my papers as a result of being bombed out. I did feel that, even if finally, the authorities did catch up with me, it would be good to try and see if I could survive by my own endeavours. This had been my plan to try to put into effect, whenever I was able to slip away during transfer to another post or if I could apply for and be granted leave.

Exactly how might I survive and even re-invent myself was a leading question. But I did believe that I did have some attributes that might help. For example, I did have that aptitude and skills in terms of needlework and of course I was young and fit and willing and felt able to turn my hand to anything. By keeping my ear to the ground when my Wren compatriots were talking, it did seem as though there was a great shortage of labour in the country and women were able to work in factories and elsewhere. These thoughts had been exercising my mind for many weeks and long before coming down the hillside with Gareth, towards the Wrenery, and seeing the staff car and the figures beside it. One of which I immediately recognised as the slightly hunched Jack, apparently in uniform, pacing about and, as it transpired, I rightly assumed the man smoking on the other side of the car would be, Ralph.

I initially thought they would take me back to London and that would be a long journey and there would be a point where I could escape, but I needed to buy as much time before the military authorities started looking for me, as being absent without leave or AWOL as it was called. So, on the spur of the moment, and with the pretence of getting Gareth to point out to sea, I asked him to report me as sick before my next scheduled duty. In the event I think that it was helpful to me in terms of what happened, but thereafter I felt very guilty when I considered that, if he did do what I had asked, then he would probably get into trouble himself.

Jack played the part of the forceful Captain very well and with my mind racing I went off to change into uniform. Of course, they could not enter the Wrenery and so I had a short time to think and act. Once in uniform I stuffed into my knapsack a couple of pairs of civilian slacks, some blouses and jumpers together with all my underwear and some toiletries. This I placed at the bottom of my Navy issue kit bag and on top I put some spare bits of uniform. I did a mental check that all my underwear with my savings sewn into them were in the rucksack together with the purse in the false bottom. Now, if I could engineer a chance, I was ready to escape. In all I guess that I was about fifteen minutes and Jack was not best pleased when I returned. I was ordered into the back of the staff car behind the driver, who indeed turned out to be Ralph dressed as rating. Jack got in the passenger side at the rear beside me. Ralph threw my kit bag in the boot and then got onto the car.

"Get going." Ordered Jack to Ralph. "Remember nice and slowly we are on official business."

Ralph turned the ignition and pressed a starter. Nothing happened. He tried again to the same effect. He leapt out and came to the back door of the car behind the driver's seat where I was sitting and he collected a crank handle. He inserted this in the front of the car and at the second try he got the engine running. He came back to my door and threw the handle back into the foot well from whence he had collected it.

Jack had clearly been exasperated by the delay but had remained silent, but as we got going he then turned to me and said.

"We have come here to help you back to Germany. We think our security has been breached and a number of our operatives have been betrayed. We are heading to a deserted place called Sandwood Bay, which is a long walk from any road, where arrangements have been made for us to be picked up by a small boat from a submarine and we will return to that vessel for our escape to Germany."

"Have you a letter from my parents?" I asked him and it was clearly not a question he had anticipated and his reply, when it came was hesitant and clearly made up.

"We have been dealing with a crisis; I have not had time to worry about your domestic concerns."

We left Aultbea and turned right at the main road and travelled on through Poolewe and continued on in the direction that would take us to the Achnasheen check point.

Right away I knew that this meant that I was not being rescued at all. I was to be eliminated from the organisation because they had detected, rightly, that I was no longer being a good girl and bearing that mind I knew too much, I was therefore a threat to them. Clearly Jack had not even thought to have a story about my parents prepared in advance. He might have arranged a replica staff car, uniforms and papers to get through check points and the base gate, but he had not thought about what would placate me. As well as that mistake and for all the undoubted planning that must have gone into this operation, Jack had assumed that I, a mere woman after all, would have no idea of the geography of this part of Scotland and he had made a mistake in selecting the place where he had told me we were going.

I am not a fool, and I had studied maps of the area in which I had been stationed when I first considered trying to run away. Sandwood Bay was indeed a remote bay well north of our base at Loch Ewe and not far below Cape Wrath, the most north westerly point of the British mainland. Indeed, it is not serviced by a road and it would be an excellent place for a pick up in a small boat, launched from a submarine. But, with Sandwood Bay being located north of Aultbea the most direct route would normally involve going through the northern checkpoint to the restricted area at Laide. We, however, were going south via Gairloch and towards Achnasheen.

"Why are we heading south?" I asked. And almost at once realised that was not a sensible question for me to have posed.

"I told you we are heading to the remote Sandwood Bay for an evacuation by submarine tonight, hence the haste." Said Jack.

Jack was silent for a while. He had obviously felt under pressure whilst coming up to and entering the base and no doubt the fact that he had got me and we had passed out of the base entrance had lulled him briefly into a sense of security. But he was by no means a fool and my comment obviously made him realise that he may have let his guard down too far. Perhaps it suddenly occurred to him that my question meant that I realised that we were not heading for the place he had mentioned. He turned to me and reaching into his jacket produced a handgun.

"You will behave yourself. Please be aware that it has taken a lot of hard work to plan this operation, so I do not want you shouting when we are having our papers inspected at the Achnasheen checkpoint."

There it was confirmed. This was an operation to catch and silence me and I thought that I was already living on borrowed time. The base would have telephoned Achnasheen to advise them of the departure of a staff car, containing a driver, a Captain and a Wren. Therefore, until we passed that checkpoint, I was safe, but that was quite a long way and that meant I had a little time to think. If I was to misbehave at Achnasheen then maybe Jack and Ralph might be captured, but the guards at the checkpoint would be older men who were not suitable for front line combat and would not be ready to face the prepared wrath that I knew Jack could inflict. Some of them would die and Jack may escape. If he did not, he would probably kill me and even if he failed, I would be captured. I decided that I would wait and still see if, after the checkpoint, I could contrive an escape.

As predicted the checkpoint was manned by some older men whose rifles were casually slung by the straps over their shoulders. They paid attention as our car approached but remained unprepared for a sudden attack. A younger corporal was in charge and came out of the hut adjacent to the barrier that was across the road. He inspected the papers passed to him by Ralph and, after studying Jack and I, he nodded and one of the older privates lifted the barrier and we were under way again within just a minute of our arrival. Our way was now clear on the road to Inverness and the south. As we left the checkpoint behind the road ran along beside the river Bran but separated from it by the train line from Inverness to the Lyle of Lochalsh. That very railway line I had arrived on when I came to this posting from the south.

"In about five miles there is the side road to the deserted farmhouse where you remember we stopped to get into uniform on the way here." Jack told Ralph. "Turn off there and we can all change into civvies and paint over the markings on the car." Ralph nodded his understanding. Sure enough after a few miles the open land to our right, with a view across the railway and the river, gave way to a wooded area. Shortly after that Ralph slowed and turned onto a rough track into the trees and in a while we crossed the single-track railway line, at a farm crossing made of old sleepers and went further into the trees to a small clearing where we stopped.

"I need to go to the toilet." Said Ralph and got out and began to march off into the trees and I watched him go only to realise when I turned that this must have been a prearranged plan as I saw that Jack had exited the car and was standing pointing the gun at me.

"Get out and take off your uniform." He ordered, and when I did not immediately comply, he put his other hand to the gun and there was a distinct click. I presumed this was the release of a safety catch.

"For your information Ralph will be communing with nature for some time and will only return to a pre-arranged signal. You will do as I say and if you do then all may yet be well."

I did not doubt for one moment that all would most certainly not be well, but as he was standing some feet from me I had no way of trying to rush the gun, so I shuffled across the back seat, got out of the car and began to remove my uniform, slowly.

"And now the underwear." Said Jack, and as I did so I looked at him and I could see from his perspiring face that he was getting sexually aroused. He was clearly planning to assault me before he killed me and I was terrified that the certainty of my death was imminent. However, this certainty allowed me to remain calm, as I realised that to rape me he would have to come close and as long as he did there might be some chance to effect injury on him.

"Lay on the back seat there." he instructed. I moved to the seat and lay back to await my fate.

He did force himself on me, whilst maintaining a grip on his gun and between exertions I heard him muttering that this was my punishment for being a traitor to the cause. As I submitted myself, laying there across the back seat, with his and my feet protruding from the open nearside back door, my arm flopped down into the foot well and came to rest on a metal object. The car crank handle which Ralph had used to get the car started back at base. I closed my hand around it and waited until Jack had satisfied himself and pulled away. As he did so he pushed my feet down into the footwell so that he could sit on the seat beside me to recover his breath and then he began to adjust his dress. Having never let go of the crank handle and having sat crouched forward so he did not notice it in my hand, I sat up quickly and bringing my right arm forward, swinging over the top of the front seats, I smashed the crank handle right in the middle of his face.

At the last minute he must have sensed my movement and gripped his gun because it went off and the bullet must have missed me by millimetres and there was a metal twang as it hit, and passed through, the offside rear door. I whacked again with the crank handle, again aiming at and striking his head and he put his hands to his face screaming and in doing so dropped the gun. I scrambled backwards towards the offside door behind me and exited the car naked, thinking to just run. Unfortunately, the signal for Ralph to return must have been the gunshot because, at that same moment, he appeared out of the trees. No doubt the gun shot was to have advised him that I had been eliminated.

For a fraction of a second there was inaction on the part of both Ralph and me as we both tried to make sense of the unexpected situation in which each of us found ourselves. He was expecting to stroll back and help Jack to dispose of my dead body. I, on the other hand, had completely forgotten that 'not so dear' Ralph was around. Fortunately for me he was in a relaxed state expecting everything to be under the control of Jack and came fractionally slower to the realisation that it was not, whilst I was still in fight or flight mode. So, it was me that moved first. Jack was screaming still and had collapsed forward onto the very back seat where just a few moments ago he had been on a gratuitous high. Now he was blinded by two blows to the face with a heavy metal starting crank handle. Quickly I realised that I needed to defend myself against Ralph and I rushed round the back of the car to grab that crank.

By the time I arrived at the other side of the car Ralph had already covered half the distance that there had been between us when we first saw one another. As I arrived at the far door there was no crank handle laying there on the ground. It must have been still in the car where I dropped it after hitting Jack. With no crank handle was available to me for self-defence I was in trouble. But lying there was Jack's gun. I glanced up and Ralph was just a few yards away. I bent down grabbed the gun and, as I stood up with it, Ralph was almost on me, and I just had enough time to put my finger on the trigger as he arrived at me and made a grab. I had been intending to raise the gun and threaten Ralph but just as my arm came level with my waist, he grabbed me and the pressure of his body against me caused my finger on the trigger to fire the gun, from a point blank range, into his midriff.

He half released me in shock then came at me again and this time I aimed at him in the head. He staggered back for a couple of paces before collapsing backwards, his torso half disappearing into the grass surrounding the edge of the clearing. The immediate silence was broken by a screaming Jack, and I turned back to my erstwhile tormentor. I realised that I had probably just killed a man whom I knew to be a henchman of Jack and I had not intended, or wanted to harm him, for he had never harmed me. But Jack was another proposition altogether. He had violated me on several occasions, and I was convinced that his mission here today, taking all the risks that must have been involved, was to silence me and so prevent me from compromising his operation. If I had not struck him as I had, it would be me lying in the undergrowth instead of Ralph. In that instant I hated Jack and I hated the regime he stood for and who undoubtedly had killed my parents. In a mood of calm fury I walked to the car where he was still moaning and I put the gun to his head and shot him.

I stood there naked, actually I think I was still wearing socks and shoes, and for a long few minutes I stared at Jack's body. Then the sound of a vehicle could be heard approaching on the road. It broke into my reverie, and I listened as it came closer. I held my breath and waited, but the engine noise did not change and it passed on and the sound diminished. Suddenly I felt cold. It was not warm on this late summer evening, but part of the cold was shock. I looked down at my bare breasts and belly to find I was bespattered with blood. Jack? Ralph? Both? I could hear the tinkle of a nearby stream and I went to it to quickly wash myself then returned to the car and grabbed a travel rug that had been over the passenger seat in order to dry myself off.

It had always been possible that in taking any escape opportunity that presented itself, ad hoc, that I would have to be ready to think and improvise. I had thought through a number of scenarios but none so bizarre as the one in which I now found myself. I put on my underwear and then went to Ralph. He had fallen partly into some undergrowth and I managed to roll his body a couple of times so that he was further into the long grass and then I looked for bits of fallen branches to cover him. As I was doing so I thought that I had better remove any identification. He had a wallet with identity and ration cards and some cash. I took that to the passenger seat of the car before returning and covering him as best I could.

Now Ralph was tall and lean, but Jack was a fat man and I soon realised that there was no way I could lift his body from the back seat of the car let alone lug his body across to the undergrowth. He was collapsed face down on the back seat and so I rolled him into the foot well of the rear seat, stuffing his legs up to be able to shut that nearside rear door. Then, before I covered him with the travel rug, I searched him and removed his wallet with identification and money and a bunch of keys and put these with Ralph's things on the front passenger seat. I then dressed back into my uniform and considered my options. I would not be missed until ten tomorrow at the earliest, longer if Gareth was as good as his word and reported me sick. So, I must get as far away as possible before noon tomorrow. Wearing uniform I could go to the road and hitch a lift but using the car I could be sure to get to Inverness and a train before the last one of the evening if I drove, whereas relying on a lift would be much more hit and miss, not to say risky.

Next, I looked in the boot of the car and found Jack and Ralphs's change of clothes and then I checked my own hasty packing of just an hour or so ago. All my spare uniform I moved to the bottom of my kit bag making sure my knapsack was on top. This way I could ditch the main of the kitbag and go off with the smaller bag, containing all my essentials at the drop of a hat. The car was marked as a Royal Navy staff car, so I dressed in uniform again. I found a road atlas and memorised the route via Muir of Ord and Beauly to Inverness. Then I was ready to go. Now fortunately I had been taught to drive at finishing school but the last time I had driven was in Daddy's car that last weekend in Essen. Fortunately, the engine was still quite warm and started at my turn of the ignition switch and with a clattering of gears I turned and drove back to the main road and turned right heading eastwards.

It was now approaching five thirty in the afternoon and I knew that sunset was after eight in the evening as we were in July. I had no idea how long the journey to Inverness would take but I thought that it might not be much more than an hour and a half. In the event I was approaching Inverness long before seven. I was in a dilemma. Here I was in what was made to look like a staff car, and whilst I was driving in a Wren's uniform that would be fine but once I left it then would somebody wonder why it had been left unattended. If it was daylight would they look at it more closely or call the police? On the other hand, if I did not abandon it until dark then might I miss the last train out and so be trapped until the following morning. In the event I decided that I could not remain a minute longer than I had to in that horrible vehicle, so I decided that leaving a staff car unattended might put off local people from interfering with it, as most folk respected official property and vehicles and would assume, at least to start with, that there was a reason for its being there.

The approach to Inverness was along the only road into that city from the north, beside the Beauly Firth. As I approached the beginning of the houses the road turned sharply to the right and after a while I crossed a bridge over a canal. Proceeding another quarter of a mile I saw that I was approaching a river bridge and the main of the town rose up beyond it. Not wanting to be too close to prying eyes I swung sharp right before the bridge onto a street running beside the river. Shortly after that on my left I passed a footbridge over the river and just before and beyond that footbridge I noticed several cars parked at the roadside beside the river. The occupants, perhaps being workers or shoppers or others doing business in the town, I thought that they had probably left their cars there and walked across the bridge. I pulled into a parking space and sat to take stock once again.

I needed a train south as soon as possible, so checking that nobody was in sight I got out and went to the car boot for my kitbag and placed it on the passenger seat. Then I locked the boot with Jack and Ralph's suitcases still there. Returning to the driver's seat I looked at the personal possessions from the pockets of the two men which I had placed on the passenger seat before leaving the clearing. Ralph had only possessed a small amount of cash, but Jack had well over twenty pounds and so in all, including change, I was able to pocket nearly twenty-six pounds. I was thinking to throw their identity cards into the river but, on second thoughts, I dropped them beside Jack's body. Hopefully the authorities would find this imposter of a naval Captain dead in this pretend staff car, and they might pay a visit to Sefton Lodge. I very much hoped so. The road atlas was on the seat and it was a hardback book, but I tore out some middle pages which showed roads in an area between the Scottish Borders and the Midlands and stuffed them into my knapsack.

A quick look in the mirror revealed some blood on my right ear, which I must have missed when I washed myself in the stream. My handkerchief wetted with a little spittle did the trick and I thought I was presentable enough as a Wren who may have been jolted about in the back of a military truck on the first part of her journey. Checking again that the coast was clear I got out of the car, retrieved my kitbag checked that all the doors were locked then turned as though I wanted to look at the river. Placing my hands on the railing with the keys in my right hand I allowed them to fall into the water.

Then I was off, over the footbridge and, with one stop to ask directions, I was at the station in a little over five minutes. I passed a large station hotel and made my way to a fairly busy concourse and joined a queue for tickets.

"Return to Liverpool, please." I asked as I got to the front of the queue. I had already decided that although it would cost money it would have looked more suspicious, given the story I was planning on telling, if I only bought a single.

"Where is your travel warrant young lassie?" Replied the clerk, almost as I had anticipated.

"Oh. I do not have one but let me explain. A telegram was sent to my C.O. to say that my mother is very ill and asking that I be allowed some compassionate leave for a few days. He agreed and left things to his administration staff as there was some big operation just starting. They could not find the warrants so they gave me some money from the petty cash and told me to use that, then keep the tickets and then when I got back they would sort out the paperwork and put things in order."

"Most irregular." He replied and stared at me obviously noting my uniform, the anxious look on my face and the notes in my hand he looked down and said "That is nine shillings and nine pence....... each way." I handed him a one pound note and accepted the sixpence in change. He passed me my tickets and explained that my best route was to change at Edinburgh Waverly for Glasgow, then a train south to Manchester and thence to Liverpool. I had chosen this destination because it seemed a big city where, if the authorities were to look for me, they may spend a lot of time before realising that I had not gone there at all. London held the possibility of being more amorphous and therefore more easy for a single displaced woman to hide, but against that it held the base of the spy ring, which, even without Jack, might find it easier to locate me.

"To get your connection to Glasgow from Edinburgh, you will need to catch the London bound train which is supposed to leave at eight fifteen but if I were you I would be in the queue by seven thirty if you want to get a seat."

A glance up at the station clock told me that I had three quarters of an hour till I needed to queue, so I asked. "Is there anywhere to get a cuppa?"

"See the goods yards over there." He said pointing across the concourse. "Well, the WRVS ladies offer refreshment to military personnel and if I were you I would try there 'cos the station buffet will be full of 'Tommies' getting liquid refreshment and no place for a lassie like you."

I moved across in the direction he had indicated and came face to face with two Redcaps as they were known, but more formally, Military Police. Both were older men on what was probably pretty much an easy posting, unless the 'Tommies' took too much drink and started fighting. They smiled as I passed them, and I managed a tight smile back and as I did so I experienced a huge sense of relief that they had no interest in me. What a feather in their respective caps had they nabbed this deserting double murderer.

Joining the short WRVS queue I was lost in thought, standing behind a painfully thin girl in a WAAF uniform. A large WRVS lady came up and said "Now you two girls. Take that table over there and leave your things and collect your food from the serving table."

We did as bid and when I approached the serving table I realised that apart from breakfast in the mess I had only just had the picnic with Gareth and otherwise I had not eaten, and I was famished. For the sixpence in change I had received from the ticket purchase I came back to my allocated table with a half pint mug of vegetable soup, a hunk of bread, a doorstep size cheese sandwich, an oatcake and a cup of tea. These I started to devour but my table mate just had a sandwich and pot of tea.

"Don't they feed you in the Navy?" She asked and I shook my head and carried on eating. "You should have joined our lot we get well treated, much better in fact than when I was in civvy street trying to make a living as a typist and support my old Mum. I love it even though I have been posted to the ends of the earth. I am Vera, by the way."

"Sheila." I replied, fervently hoping that by being monosyllabic she would leave me in peace, for the last thing I needed was having to say anything about myself just at this juncture. Vera, however, was clearly an inveterate talker, but fortunately by dint of occasionally looking at her and smiling and offering the occasional nod as I ate, she was as happy to indulge in one sided chatting as I was in remaining almost silent and filling my tummy. I learned that she came from Bradford and was stationed at an airfield north of Inverness. Today she was embarking on her first week of leave in a year and had walked the three miles from her airfield to Tain railway station where she caught a train to Inverness. She was looking forward to her trip home, as during her week she would attend the wedding of her brother. But inevitably she paused and asked about me and as I had finished all but the last of my tea, I had little excuse to avoid saying something.

"Had a telegram to say that my mother is dying and I am off to Liverpool to see her." I hoped that this downbeat news would be an indicator to Vera that I was not up to talking more about myself but, just to ensure a change of focus, I asked her what Bradford was like as I had never been. Straight away she was off. It's the textile capital of the world, she told me, a very important centre for the weaving of cloth. At this my ears pricked up and I enquired if there were many seamstresses there. She replied in the negative but fed the helpful information that Leeds was big in the making of garments and it was only about ten miles to the east of Bradford. This seemed a useful piece of information, so I made a mental note of it in case it would prove useful in the future.

I made my excuses, saying I needed to go to the toilet and was then able to join the queue for the train at a different point to Vera. I managed to get into a compartment and find a window seat in the corner where I was joined, to start with, by some sailors on leave from Scappa Flow and after some low-level exchanges and telling them quite clearly that I was from HMS Helicon, as I thought that if my journey was traced, I wanted them to remember me on that south bound train.

It took till midnight to get to Waverley Station, in Edinburgh, where I disobeyed the suggestions of the ticket clerk, knowing that if later challenged I could always say I had missed my stop as I was asleep and so I was going to York to then cross by way of Leeds and Manchester to Liverpool. If the car and its cargo had been found and I was traced to the station then, after my train left Waverley, the authorities would initially be looking for me on the route to Liverpool via Glasgow and Manchester.

137

Arrival at Darlington was not long after four in the morning, and the next stop would be York. As we departed I was aware that all the choices which I had been mulling over now needed a final decision. So as the train pulled into York, as the clocks were striking five, I had made up my mind.

York and Yorkshire it would be.

Chapter 15

1942 Gareth - Loch Ewe

Having been dismissed by the visiting Captain who had come for Sheila, I had moved reluctantly away. But once out of sight behind a building I stopped and loitered and kept a covert watch for a long while, until I saw Sheila come out, now dressed in uniform. The driver took her kit bag and she got into the car which, after starting trouble, requiring the driver to use a starting handle, drove off. I turned and went off down to the pier trying to make sense of it all. My mind was in turmoil as I returned to the *Loyalty*. What I had anticipated as a pleasant afternoon of meeting and talking to a nice, but apparently reserved, young woman had become a couple of hours of wild emotion, followed by complete incomprehension.

As a merchant seaman for many years I had seen right from the start that some men, taken from their homes and communities, were able to feel that they could do as they liked abroad as because neither their community nor, in the case of married men, their wives, would know what they were up to. Many is the man I have seen, both lower deck and officers, kiss their wives as we left home port only to see them entering the nearest dockside brothel in the first foreign port of call. Now yes. I did have a chapel upbringing, and I am mighty glad of it too, but I was never prim about the sexual behaviour of others. Just that my upbringing had perhaps made me a bit straight laced and in addition to that I was also dissuaded from promiscuity by seeing the frequent outcome of some of these activities, in my crew mates. Especially when those exploits subsequently required a course of medical treatment. Unlike the passenger liners of my day, merchant cargo ships of my experience had no doctors and such medical duties as were required were the responsibility of the Chief Officer. No training was given to us

Deck Officers in relation to medical issues, but we were provided with a medical manual which, in relation to venereal diseases contained this wonderful diagram of a human posterior with a dotted cross on one cheek to show where the officer should administer the injection of penicillin.

Anyway, my sexual experiences up to that point were limited, to say the least. Not surprisingly then, when I found myself out on a walk with a good looking, but apparently reserved, young woman I was out to enjoy a complete change of atmosphere from the all-male camaraderie of interaction on *Loyalty* with some different conversation and a pleasant walk. As things had gone on, I began to realise that this was a very personable young woman in whom I could easily become emotionally interested. Then we had this long conversation where I told her about myself and eventually she said some very enigmatic, but obviously personal, things about herself, leading to her shedding tears.

I remember comforting her and that turned unexpectedly into deep emotional connection, first on a human comforting level and very quickly it turned into sexual arousal and engagement. Being inexperienced as a lover, her vigour in our love making went far beyond anything I had experienced before and was something I will never forget. But whilst I was a willing participant and enjoyed every second, I realised that I had not exactly been the leader in taking things as far as they went. It seemed that her desire was such that, even if I had wanted to, it would have been hard for me to stop things taking the course they did. There was, in what she said and, in her action, something that cried of an expression of loneliness and desire for positive human contact. It was almost as though she were starved of care from any other human being.

Then there was the shattering of, what for me was, a great contentment and hope of a real developing loving relationship, which came about as we came into sight of the Wrenery. When she had asked me to point out to sea, to mask the fact that she wanted to tell me about a Captain who she feared had come to take her back to some previous posting and the fact that she obviously did not want that to happen. This led to her request to ring her in 'sick', as it were, the following day. And it all happened so quickly and there was no time to think or ask questions because so quickly we were face to face with the Captain, who, in his turn, dismissed me out of hand.

But I am a man of my word and so the following morning, as she had requested, I made contact with her Leading Wren and told the white lie that she was feeling unwell. And then life went on.

We were busy all week, as a convoy was beginning to assemble and I thought little more about it until several days later, when, on the Friday, we were instructed to go alongside the pier and await orders. It was an unusual directive, but we headed in and as we approached the pier, I could see the base Captain there along with a couple of Red Caps, or Military Police. Perhaps they had come to be taken out to some ship where there was trouble.

Once we alongside the Red Caps came aboard and straight up to the bridge and the Sergeant came to me and asked.

"Lieutenant O'Shaughnessy?" And when I nodded. "Do you know this woman?" and he showed me a picture that clearly was Sheila.

"Yes." I replied. "That looks like a Wren called Sheila Booth."

"And when did you last see this woman?"

"Last Saturday." He nodded and said.

"Very Good. Will you please come with us; we need to ask you some more questions."

"Well can it not wait we are very busy just now."

"No Sir. It is an urgent matter and your superior officer," he said nodding in the direction of the base commander who was walking back up the jetty, "has authorised your second in command to take over for the time being. Just bring your cap and coat."

"Am I under arrest or something?"

"Not at this point. But you are at least a witness in a matter, and we believe that you may be able to help us in our enquiries about the disappearance of the Wren you just identified. We can discuss this further ashore."

I gathered up my cap and the short bolero jacket of my Number Three uniform and we left the bridge and as we descended to the main deck, I could see both Hopkins and the Chief Engineer were hovering.

"Number One." I said to Hopkins. "I am required to answer some questions ashore and I understand that you are to take charge in my absence. Until you receive orders from someone above me, like the base commander, you stay alongside." He nodded.

"Do youse need a Mackenzie Friend with youse at all?" Said the Chief Engineer. "Where I come from ye cannae trust the polis not to turn your words about."

"Thanks for the offer, Chief, but I have nothing to hide so the sooner I go and find out what they want to know the sooner I will be back."

As I left the ship and walked up to a waiting car, I could not help but see my whole crew gathering and looking astonished to see me being led off by the Red Caps. I reflected that the conversation over the next meal would have been rife with speculation about why I had been 'arrested'.

A short drive took us to the Commanding Officer's house where a room had been vacated for the purpose of my being interviewed. The Sergeant bid me take a seat and he sat behind a desk and a corporal took another desk and made ready to take notes.

"Sir." Began the Sergeant. "Tell me how you know this Wren Booth."

"Well just over a week ago she came aboard my ship *Loyalty* as part of the Commanding Officer's project to enable a range of Wrens to experience ship handling in the safe environment of the Loch, she was just one in a line of one day visits made by a number of Wrens. That was the first day I set eyes on her."

"So, you had never seen or had contact with her before that?"
"No."

"Was that the only time you saw her?"

"No. She and I went for a walk and had a picnic last Saturday."

"Tell me all you can remember about that afternoon."

"Well like I said we met............ look, perhaps I can explain the context of all this. All the women who came aboard as part of the programme to give the Wren a day's experience at sea were probably aboard for maximum six, say seven hours. My contact with them was very limited and indeed if you ask me to describe

142

them now the best I could do was to say the first one was fat and jolly and I could not tell you anything about at all about the rest. I can tell you more about Booth, or Sheila as I came to know her. Whilst she was on *Loyalty,* we unexpectedly were called upon to leave the Loch and to perform a rescue of a disabled ship in a storm. Because it was an emergency, I was unable to land her because of the urgency to proceed on the rescue mission and so inadvertently she became part of that operation. It turned out to be a very scary episode and it really bonded my crew. Because of that unusual episode where she was on the bridge for the whole of the rescue, I got to know her better than the other Wrens and she was with us for much longer than the others had been. The whole episode was very emotional for me, the crew and her because we had been into danger and yet come our pretty much unscathed.

So, whilst we were both in that state of some euphoria, we fixed a date for a walk last Saturday. It was a fine day, and we walked and talked, and I will be honest and say that, by the end of it all I was beginning to have some hope that it could become a serious friendship. But just when I thought that might be the case, we returned to find her former commander, a Captain in the Royal Navy by his uniform, waiting in a staff car to take her back to what she said was her old posting, at a moment's notice. And that is the sum total of my contact with her"

"But it is not the last contact you had about her, is it? You subsequently made a telephone call to her supervisor did you not?"

"Yes."

"What was that call and why?"

"Well, as we approached the Wrenery, at the end of the walk, she saw the staff car and told me that she recognised her old Captain, from what she said he was from some hush hush unit, and she did not want to go back to it, for a reason she did not have time fully explain, but she asked me to report her as being sick the following day. She gave me no fuller reason as to why and, when I think about it in retrospect, I should not have made that call, but I can only say in my defence that I was doing a small service for somebody I hoped to keep in contact with and I realise now that I did wrong."

"Have you heard from this woman since, or do you have any address for her?"

"No and no"

"Do you know anything about where she comes from?"

"Not really. She may have said something about Surrey."

"Not Liverpool?"

"No, I am pretty sure that she never mentioned Liverpool"

"Describe the 'former Captain'."

"Well, he was a chubby white man, short with dark hair and with some sort of birth mark on his face beside his eye, small but obvious."

"And the driver?"

"Cannot remember really. Tall, maybe fair. Not sure."

He produced a photograph and showed it to me. It was clearly taken postmortem and showed a dark-haired man with an awful wound, right in the middle of his face and it would be hard for me to identify him other than the fact that the small vivid strawberry mark beside his left eye was clearly visible.

"Yes." I said somewhat shocked. "That seems to be the man I saw."

"Sir, I have heard what you have to say, and I am satisfied that you have told me the truth. I must warn you that, sadly for you, the fact that you made that phone call was wrong, and I must inform your Commanding Officer and there may be consequences, but otherwise I believe you were inadvertently used to facilitate the escape of a spy."

I sat for a moment in silence, and he went on.

"On Sunday morning last, in the early hours, a car marked as a Royal Navy staff car, but actually it was not one of ours, was found in Inverness and in it the body of a man, the man you identify as the 'former Captain' was found in the back seat well, dressed in a Captains uniform. It might have made sense more quickly if we had realised that Wren Booth was missing but what we went on to discover was this.

At some point after leaving here, with apparently two imposters posing as a Captain and his driver, they passed the southern checkpoint. The car was later abandoned in Inverness and a Wren, matching the description of Booth, paid for a return ticket to Liverpool, giving some cock and bull story about how her Commanding Officer could not find the travel warrants and had given her the cash. She had boarded the overnight train south and should have changed at Edinburgh but apparently did not but went on to York where some of her belongings were later found. From there she could have gone across to Liverpool or more likely, we suspect, continued south to London.

But now sir, you should stay here with my corporal whilst I speak to your commanding officer."

Chapter 16

1943   Doll – Leeds, Yorkshire

Do not let anybody tell you they know about the hard side of life unless they, like me, have had what you might call a career in prostitution. Me dad was a lazy, violent useless slob who failed to even have the decency to bugger off and leave us. Mum, whom, God rest her soul, I loved dearly, was probably only nine pence to the shilling and of course that was not her fault. Then dad made her into a downtrodden whipping girl, both literally and metaphorically and she never had much of a life, and it was probably a relief to her when she died at 35, when I was just sixteen. My childhood was spent in a succession of awful lodgings, mainly around the areas of Armley, Hunslet and Beeston south of the centre of Leeds, which meant that such schooling as I got was frequently interrupted as I changed from one school to another. I would have run away before I was sixteen but for some sense of pitying loyalty to Mum. But her untimely death gave me the reason to go.

Understanding of the proverbial birds and bees was one of the early lessons taught to me practically, but unwillingly on my part, by my father. I knew that women could sell themselves for money and it seemed preferable to me to do that, for my own gain, than be abused at home for no benefit. So straight after Mum's funeral I was off to Chapletown where I knew the Leeds 'ladies of the night' mainly operated. Fresh meat on the street would have been very popular with punters but I was naïve enough to think I could just turn up and sell myself and keep the money. As soon as I was seen by the other girls they realised that I would be a threat to their living and reported me to their pimp as I was likely to spoil their business. Now there were many pimps around, but if my life had to that point been unlucky, then that very day my luck changed because the first to be notified of my presence was Billy. A big man in every way, I can tell you.

Billy must then have been mid-forties but took me off and bought me a meal and got me to tell him all about myself. Innocent as I was, I told him everything, including my real age to which he instructed me to never reveal, but that I was only to say I was twenty-one but looked younger. When he heard about my father's misuse of me, he took notice and questioned me about where we lived. In all innocence I told him everything and two weeks later he told me that he had sorted my dad out for me. This, I was told, involved his involuntary eviction from his then lodgings, given a good kicking, especially below the waist and dumped in the guard's van of a train to Hull and told never to come to Leeds ever again on pain of death. Many years later a prison warder client of mine, from Armley jail, told me that even thieves and pimps have 'rules' and men who abuse their daughters break one of those rules and are dealt with by summary justice such as my dad received.

Whilst Billy did look after me he was a business man and he explained the facts of a prostitute's life, whilst moving up and down on top of me. The short version was that given my age he could sell me up market rather than have me tramp the streets. He bought me some smart underwear and clothes, told me his rules and said, if I stuck to them, he would see me right. Amazingly it turned out that he did see me all right, which many others of his kind would not have done. Given the nature of the trade he was a very humane 'employer' and for whatever reason he took a shine to me. Oh; I worked for him for years but for a long time not on the streets but instead I would be sent on business on the bus to a hotel, from the poorer end hotels right up to the Queens in City Square. Or else I would be sent in a taxi to some posh house up Alwoodly.

I worked hard for Billy and, as I have said, he saw me right. For example, he saw me through two back street abortions and then, after the second of those and before I was ready to resume work I started helping him with the newer girls. Getting them clothes and teaching them the tricks of the trade and ensuring they knew Billy's rules. Throughout the time he would occasionally want me for a 'free do' as he called it, and he was

147

basically quite a gentle man in bed. I was christened Dorothy, but he renamed me Doll, because he said that is what I looked like when he first saw me. Then one day he asked me to help him run a better operation by ensuring that we had the best girls and that they were all able to perform in the higher end trade. What he proposed was to buy a house, not to run as a brothel but as a place for a few of his 'high end' girls to live, so that they could have their clothes kept well and they could get a reasonable diet. He would have the attic room converted for himself. My job was to, as it were, manage this 'hostel' and keep the girls in line. Of course I worked as well occasionally, but I spent a lot more time cooking and cleaning for the others.

All went along for over twenty years and then Billy became unwell with what turned out to be a terminal stomach cancer. The diagnosis was, it transpired, quite late and the first I knew he had to go for an 'exploratory' operation in 1938 and he realised that he would need nursing after his discharge. The operation was apparently unsuccessful, in that when they opened him up they found the cancer was too widespread to do anything about it, and so they stitched him up and sent him home. Looking back that operation probably shortened his life and also took away a lot of his energy, which he never recovered. He died seven months later aged just fifty-seven. Whilst he was in hospital I got things rearranged and had his bed moved into the front room so that I could nurse him.

On discharge from hospital he told me he thought his days were numbered and he wanted me to set about sorting his business out. Billy had a sort of minder called Mick and through him he got into negotiations with a nasty pimp called Jimmy and arranged to sell him some of his high-end clients. The deal was that Jimmy would bring a large sum of money to the house and when it was in Billy's hand Mick would take it to pay into the bank and then phone to say it was done and then Billy would hand over the information. This was done and then Billy set about getting me to help him put his affairs in order, which I did whilst nursing him.

As I have said Billy was into an awful trade, but he was essentially an honest rogue. We had been together, in a very loose sense, for a long time and he had come to trust and rely on

148

me more and more over the years. He knew that I looked after our girls and that at heart, because I had been in their shoes myself, I had sympathy for them and tried to help them as best I could. But I had no claim on him, and I was concerned about what would happen if he did die, as now seemed quite likely. In the event I need not have worried, because he told me one day that before the operation, he had thought that as he was getting fed up with the business, and the increasing number of aggressive pimps around, he was thinking of suggesting that he would retire. He said he wanted to buy a house and get me to be his housekeeper. I nearly fell off me buffet when I heard that.

Anyway, that was obviously not going to be, but he gets me to arrange for his solicitor to come and see him and afterwards he told me he had made a will. He was leaving everything to his sister who was widowed and lived in Sheffield with two little boys; their daddy had been killed in an accident at a foundry where he had worked, but the firm had not paid much in compensation. Apparently, he had been sending her money regularly, ever since her husband died and he had arranged for that to continue until his own time came. However, he said he owed me a lot and he also realised that he had misused some girls in the past and he had been pleased that he had enabled me to help and support some of the lasses who had worked for us over the years. So, before he died, he was going to buy a small shop on Chapeltown Road in my name. It was to be a café which I would run and, through which, I could use my understanding of being on the game to advise lasses who worked the streets. He would give me a small sum to buy equipment for the café but then I would be on my own in terms of income from that and from short-term letting some of the bedrooms above the café.

In 1939 he died, and I found myself a café owner and manager. I suppose my own awful childhood and my own childlessness had made me into a bit of a broody hen who was happy to give help and advice to girls on the streets. The local coppers came in for a cuppa and even pointed new girls in the area in my direction. By late 1942 I was very settled doing work that I liked and I was well known and accepted in the locality. By this time I had been able to help directly, or else advise, many girls who came into the café and I was used to recognising a lass in trouble. I ran the café to suit my clientele, so I opened for dinner and stayed open into the evening, closing when I felt like it, somewhere between eight and ten, as the spirit moved.

One late autumn evening in 1942 I was not busy and a girl I had never seen before came in and ordered a tea and dripping sandwich. I told her to have a seat. As was my wont I looked at her whilst I was preparing her order. With my experience I could usually have a guess at the category a new face fitted into, but not this one. Medium height, mousy and unkempt hair and crumpled clothing and the hand which had passed me the money for her order was a calloused one. She was to my mind, clearly not on the game. Yet.

But a lone lass in Chapeltown at this hour of the evening may be thinking about it as a last resort. So, as I would not wish that life on anyone who had a chance to avoid it, I thought I would have a word with her. I noticed that she had arrived with some unusual canvas rucksack, and she was careful when she took it off, to put her foot through the strap of it before she sat down at an empty table. She obviously knew how to avoid someone nicking her prize possession. I took her order over and watched as she cupped her hands round the mug of tea and then to take slow careful bites from her bread, chewing slowly to make it last. Two of my regular working girls that had finished their tea left, and were careful to ensure that the blackout on the inside of the doorway was closed before opening the blacked outside door itself. The new girl was still deep in thought and savouring the last of her bread and I went over and drew out a chair. She flinched and drew back.

"Sorry love." I said "Me name's Doll and for me sins, of which there are quite a few, I run this café. And I am guessing that you are new to the area and may not know that this part of Leeds is where girls offer their services to men who can't get it at home or want something more or something different. Now so long as you know that you can make a decision about how to go on."

She looked at me, obviously considering what I had said before replying.

"I have just come to Leeds. They said at the Crypt that there may be seamstress jobs up Burmantofts way, but I tried a load and had no luck and that's how I ended up here."

"You a seamstress?" I said looking at her hands.

"Once. Been on the road a while and last got farm work, but now with the winter......"

"Where you from then, obviously not round here?"

"South London. A long time ago."

"Family?" I asked and she shook her head. Her answers had been delivered slowly and carefully and she was obviously wary of me and of revealing anything too much. Despite the hesitant speech and limited answers those eyes of hers radiated intelligence. This girl was clearly intent on keeping her situation close to her chest. So I changed tack.

"So, you off to the Crypt again tonight?" She shrugged, so I continued. "Well one alternative for you is to go on the game and there will be plenty of business for you, out on Chapeltown Road tonight, if that is what you want."

This provoked a reaction, and she stared at me, pushed back her chair and started to rise.

"Sit down silly cow." I said. "I used to help a man who pimped a load of girls and I was on the streets myself and it 'aint a nice place for a lass like you."

"You don't know me."

"No I don't, but you have just told me, by your reaction, that you are not a tart. However, you obviously are in a dark place if you were in the Crypt last night and were unable to get a job today. Now it just so happens that I help girls who are on the game, but I also try to help those thinking about whether there is another way they can sort themselves out, so let me see what I can do. At this time I am guessing you are in some trouble, running away from family, a fella or some other big problem and that you do not want to talk about it. That is fine with me; I do not need to know. But tell me; when you got to Leeds what was the plan? And don't tell me there was none because despite you trying to show me that you are a lost soul, I think you are better than that."

She stared at me for a while, obviously still weighing all I had said and thinking carefully before she spoke, and this time it was less stilted and hesitant.

"You're right, there are things I am trying to leave behind. I was trained in needlework a long time ago, but I am very rusty. But sewing in a factory would give me work where I could keep myself to myself and I could rent a room and try to settle."

"Right, now we are getting somewhere………what did you say your name was?

"Sarah."

"OK Sarah. First off I have an attic room, and you can kip there tonight. Then tomorrow I know a Jewish man who has a small tailoring business who has helped me in the past. Sarah could be a Jewish name, and I am not asking, but if I was lost in London and looking for help, I would be more likely to get it if I asked a Yorkshire person because we are the same clan and the same is true with Jewish folk."

"Yes, well I am Jewish and many of the employers I saw today were probably Jewish as well, but my problem is that I have no address, references or papers and ration cards. I am not easily going to be able to overcome those issues."

"In a place like Chapeltown lots of things are possible if you know where to look and have the right connections and a bit of money. But first things first, tomorrow morning I will take you round to see Paul and if you can satisfy him that you are able to stitch neatly he will take you on. He will probably pay you half the going rate because of your situation, but it will enable you to afford to rent one of my rooms and to save to buy yourself some forged papers from one of the local folk I can put you in touch with. Is that OK?"

Her nodding head dislodged a tear that had formed in her eye which she hastily brushed away with a sleeve and said.

"Thank you for your kindness. It is not something I have experienced a lot of in recent years."

So began what would become a long-term relationship with 'Sarah', because I was sure that was not her name and I also realised that she held a past which she did not wish to discuss. But many girls on the game are running away from a past, just like I had done. But I had struck lucky with Billy and that had let me be a friend to other girls in a difficult situation. I was happy to help and I had no need or right to ask girls for their reasons for being here and in need of some friendly advice or direct help. My motto was start where they were at and help them to either cope with their lot, or to move forward, and if they wanted to tell me about their past I would listen and if they did not want to then that was fine.

In Sarah's case I took her to see Paul in his little run-down sweat shop and he gave her a lapel to stitch which she did very slowly but neatly. He told her that her work was neat but far too slow, but she could start tomorrow, and he would give her half pay until she could get up to a good speed. He later told me that she was the best girl he had for intricate and neat work. She was happy for about a month and then one evening after work she came to me.

"Doll. I think I am going to have to think about moving on."

"Why? Don't think that I am going to be bothered about having an unmarried mother in the house. But I was wondering when you were going to talk to me about how to manage when the baby comes."

"How...... ." She started and then looked at me unable to finish her sentence.

"In my experience there are two 'p's' which go together, prostitution and pregnancy. For girls on the game it is an occupational hazard and although I have no children I have been pregnant myself a couple of times and I have dealt with countless lasses who get left with 'a bun in the oven'. As a result I am well aware of the signs and I even thought that was the reason for you turning up here in the first place, that you were escaping a life where you did not want a person, or persons, to know of your so called 'condition'.

I am guessing that you fully realise that you have left it too late for an abortion, so what's it to be? Keep the child or adoption? Either way I can probably help you"

She began to cry and for a while I let her and then she looked at me and, after a long pause, said.

"I loved my mother, but I cannot begin to imagine how she would have faced my telling her my situation and she certainly would not have been able to be so calm and practical as you, Doll."

Over the next few months we continued our time together. I got her a false Identity and ration card under the name Sarah Simpson, for which she paid me back, as I financed it originally myself. She kept on working as a seamstress, renting a room from me and over the next few weeks she decided that she would have the baby but not keep it. We were agreed that it would not be easy to approach the authorities, in relation to having the child adopted, as they would want to know all about her background.

We made a plan which involved one of my 'old girls' who had herself had a child and come off the game and gone to live with a brother in Otley. This brother was now in the forces, and she lived alone in his two bedroomed flat. It was agreed that all being well she would work as long as possible then go to stay with Mary in Otley. With it being a first child, the likelihood was it would not be a quick labour and the flat in Otley was just half a mile from the local hospital. Once her waters broke, she would turn up at the hospital and give a false name. After the baby was born then she could find a way to slip out before the end of the normal seven-day post-natal care most hospitals provided. She would leave the baby and go back to Mary until she had recovered enough to come back to me.

Chapter 17

1943 Stella – Leeds

My night had been interrupted twice but just the same I was wide awake at just after five in the morning, according to the clock above the nurse's station in the hospital ward. Blinking, I remained perfectly still to let the fog of sleep clear and to give chance for thought, before I faced another watershed moment.

My life had become a metaphorical tramp across mountains with a succession of watershed moments as I moved from one unwanted situation to another. Such as my parent's foolish decision to return to Germany, my spontaneous visit to Mr. Ulrich the travel agent, the unplanned murder of Jack and Ralph and the decision to leave the southbound train in York. I could still have continued southwards to London and perhaps gone back to the familiar area around my first home in Surrey, but I was clear that I felt that a new area would be better, and so I had been ready to get out and go when the train arrived in York.

Some of the intervening time between then and now I remembered vividly, like that arrival in York. Leaving my seat, I had carried my kit bag to where, during the enforced stop north I had been afforded enough time to get to know the station layout and as part of that had learned where the women's toilets were located. I waited a while until the rush of the few women on the train, who like me, had not wished to risk the trip to the train toilets past the sleeping servicemen in the corridors, had subsided. I went into a corner cubicle which I was glad to find was partitioned in brick and tiled, floor to ceiling. Here I changed into one of my pairs of slacks and a blouse and sweater. I retrieved my knapsack from the bottom of the kit bag and checked everything was in place adding all of the other non-uniform items. Then I re-stowed all my uniform in the kit bag. Waiting till there seemed no other occupants in the general wash basin area I exited the cubicle and facing me was the row of hand basins. I quickly washed and then left with my knapsack temporarily in the top of my kit bag. Instead of returning through an archway, to the platform, I exited to the outside and turned left into what turned out to be the goods yard. Even at this early hour there were men at work pushing milk churns and moving post bags. I walked on to a dark corner and there, out of sight, I removed my knapsack from my kit bag which I stuffed into a recess in the hope that, for a while, someone would think it had been stored whilst the owner walked into the city. Then hopefully, it may not be drawn to the notice of the station staff till I was long gone.

There was a moment of panic as I left the goods yard because I had no detailed idea of the geography of the York area. In my mind I knew from a general map of the country that York lay a little north of a line of cities that ran from Hull in the east, through Leeds, Bradford and Manchester to Liverpool. Anyone knowing that I had a ticket to Liverpool might think that I could have travelled from York to Leeds on route to Liverpool, so that seemed best avoided. But where to go? I pulled out of my knapsack the pages I had torn from the large scale road atlas that Ralph and Jack had used in their car. It showed, spread over two facing pages, the breadth of the country from the east coast, including Hull and Scarborough, right across to the west including Liverpool and Preston; but only the major roads were marked. I noticed that a road to Harrogate would lead me away from the conurbations around the Leeds and Bradford areas and to start with that sounded like a reasonable choice.

Now all across the country signposts had been removed to disorientate any invaders and I guess maps should have disappeared too, but perhaps a map showing how to walk around York was not felt important in that regard. By great good fortune there was one near the station entrance which I noticed as I returned from depositing my kit bag. In one in one corner was an index explaining the symbols on the map, like a cross on a circle to represent the York Minster. There were also different symbols for each of the City Gates or 'Bars', the nearest being Micklegate Bar. Then, in the other corner, there was a thumbnail depiction of the county of Yorkshire and its three 'Ridings'. From this and the car map I was able to discern that along the Harrogate road there were other small towns, well north of the big cities of Leeds and Bradford and my eye was captured by the town of Skipton which seemed to be out in a part of the country where there were few roads marked and so I thought that might be a good objective. To reach that there were other significant places between, namely Knaresborough and Harrogate. Looking again at the York City map I saw that the Poppleton Road ended with an arrow marked "To Harrogate". I mentally noted in detail my route from the station to the Poppleton Road as I was loathe to ask for directions as that might jog someone's memory if the police started asking about a missing woman in the area around the station.

Following what I had seen on the city map I left the station and soon arrived at Micklegate Bar on my left. I turned to the right and after a hundred or so yards to the right again. I headed out past a big yard full of railway waggons and rolling stock. After less than a couple of miles, the buildings were beginning to thin out and I came across a bakery and the lights were on as it was nearing six. I went in to buy some bread or a roll and the baker, a man in his sixties I guess, whilst friendly said he could not help me without a ration card, which I professed to have mislaid on my journey. I took out my wallet and he still shook his head but as I turned to go, he said that he did have half a small loaf from yesterday and it cost me sixpence. That loaf, wrapped in a paper bag, was my main sustenance for quite a while.

That first encounter was my warning that without papers I was going to struggle to get a new life and that very soon I would have to face questions about whom I was and where I was from. So after a short nibble at my bread, I trudged on considering my options. It was clear that I presented as intelligent and articulate and, because of this, somebody presenting that way would be expected to explain themselves. So, in order to avoid that sort of enquiry I needed to reposition myself as someone who was less able. There was that slogan which reminded people not to give away potential secrets to an enemy "Loose Talk Costs Lives". In my case I revised that to something like 'too much talk will give you away'.

I invented a new story for myself, after all I had done it once when I moved from being Stella to Sheila, and so I would become

157

Sarah. Sarah would be shy, cowering almost, and would approach but not directly speak to people but wait for them to engage her. She would be terse and limited in any replies. She would be a lost soul, unable to remember where she was from and very vague, but occasionally talking about bombs in London and giving the appearance of some person suffering from shell shock or a mild mental illness or handicap. All those books that Jack left me to read would come in handy and particularly depressive symptoms would be displayed, so far as I could possibly remember them.

The first day was taxing as I was not used to walking long distances. I got to the village of Kirk Hammerton about lunch time, having taken several rests and there I struck lucky when I knocked on a door and a kind old lady, seeing this cowering girl asking for a drink of water actually gave me the remnants of her lunchtime pot of tea and watched me drink it and nibble my loaf. She presented me with a bottle full of water, secured by a wire fastened stopper, which I gladly took together with half a scone. My planning, I then realised, had omitted the acquisition of a water carrier so I really struck lucky there. It began to rain as I crossed a big arterial road, late in the afternoon and I surmised from Ralph's atlas that this was the main north road to Scotland from London, the A1. Not long after this I saw an isolated barn across a field and I made my way there to avoid the rain and to sleep for the night, as by now, with all the exploits of the past twenty-four hours, I was feeling exhausted.

The following day I passed through Knaresborough, first climbing up to the town, hurrying along the main street and then descending and down to the bridge over the river Nidd. To my left I saw an amazing railway viaduct and was even treated to the vision of a train puffing across. As I approached Harrogate from the village of Starbeck, a couple of hours later, houses ended and a wide area of what may well have previously been a park had been turned to an area for the growing of vegetables. I skirted this area and then as I got into the centre I became completely lost. My previous easy to follow road became less clear to me as I got closer to the town centre and, without signposts and not wanting to ask, I took the turn that I thought was my main road. However, after a couple of miles the road left the houses behind and became little more than a country lane which was not so well maintained and far less busy than the main road I had been following since leaving York. Considering my options, and wondering whether to retrace my steps, I could hear a farm cart on the road behind me and it was going slightly faster than I was walking. I decided that I would not turn round until after the cart had passed me and so I plodded on slowly and kept my head down hoping to avoid any conversation. The cart slowly caught, and then passed me, without a word from the driver and I slowed my pace to let the get cart well in front before I turned to retrace my steps and try again to find the Skipton Road. Just as I was about to stop, the cart itself stopped and the driver, a sour faced woman turned on the driving bench looked back at me and shouted at me gruffly.

"Oi! Girl! Come along 'ere."

Reluctantly and slowly I walked to the side of the cart and looked up at the weathered, pinched and grumpy face of the woman.

"What you doing round here." Even though in fairness she remained seated on the cart she was, in any event, obviously not one for standing on ceremony.

Mumbling and not looking directly at her but over her shoulder I played my planned part.

"Just walking, Missus."

"Where you from?" She asked.

"London."

"What you doing round here."

"Got bombed out. Mum got killed. Left on me own. Came to find me brother in 'arrogate but he must 'ave moved. Goin' to Leeds, to see if I can find 'im."

No doubt looking at my crumpled clothing emanating from the previous night's barn stopover she asked, but in such a way as though it sounded if she were making a statement.

"You're looking for work."

Now I was, and I was not, doing what she said. Ultimately, I wanted a job, though now was not the plan I had for the type of work I was seeking, nor the location. As against that, last night's accommodation had not been the best and maybe, if the work was right, it may solve the issue of where to live in the short term. What is more out here, miles from anywhere, I would not be

159

noticed at the time when I was most likely to be sought. So, continuing my contrived simple person persona, I equivocated.

"Dunno what to do missus."

"You lazy girl?"

"No, missus."

"Well, this ain't the road to Leeds. I got work on the farm. Nice little corner you can bed in the barn. I can feed you and you can work for me this harvest time for bed and board and paid at the end of harvest."

To be frank I could see at the outset that this woman was seeing me as a person she could manipulate. In an ideal situation I would dearly have loved to tell her I could see what a sour faced, exploitative person she was in taking advantage of the simple-minded lost soul that I was portraying. But instead, I appeared to consider the offer before replying.

"Alright, missus."

"Hop up on the cart and I will give you a couple of days' trial to see if you are up to the work."

I sat in the rear of the cart for about three miles before we turned off onto a farm track which led to a run-down farmyard. The house was in a poor state of repair and the barn was worse, chickens ran about the yard, and I could hear the grunting of some pigs, which I could not see, but most certainly could smell. She took me to the barn and showed me a ladder to the loft and we went up to look and there was one side of the barn open to the weather but the other had a wooden side to it and in the corner she indicated a crude wooden bed frame. She showed me some hessian sacks and said that she would let me have a needle and thread and I could fashion myself a mattress from the straw left from the previous harvest. She said I could leave my knapsack, but I held tight to it saying I would put it there when I had, literally, made my bedding. I did not trust this woman one bit.

After she had given me the wherewithal to make my bed mattress and handed me what had probably been a horse blanket for cover I began to fashion a mattress. I then found some loose bricks in one of the supports to the barn and carefully secreted my purse and some of my money knickers as I was quite sure that this woman would go through my things as soon as she got chance. Then I went to be given my orders.

160

It was an odd set up which I never managed to figure out. It was a working farm, but sour face must have inherited it. She was clearly in charge and she gave orders to her husband as well as me. He was clearly required to do the farming whilst she went off to different markets every few days. On these trips she took some of our limited supply of produce, but I noticed that the farm cart had a storage area under the driver's seat, the access door to which was padlocked. All very strange, until one day a lorry arrived, and I was sent off on some errand in the further fields, but on one glance back I could see that boxes were being unloaded to another padlocked store next to the house. The proverbial two plus two led me to the conclusion that, as well as farming, she was into some black-market trading as well.

And so I passed what remained of the summer and early autumn, cutting, turning, stacking and collecting corn, feeding pigs, digging potatoes and carrots. She was a hard taskmaster both to me and her docile, henpecked husband, but it bought me time to let any hue and cry continue to calm down and I stayed there until I had got their harvest home, by the end of October. At that point I was glad when it became clear that my useful time there was up, as far as 'sour face' was concerned, and I asked if she might give me a lift to a market and it was agreed that two days later I would ride to market with her husband. I was expecting to be taken to Harrogate but in fact he was off to Otley.

We started before dawn and, as the area was very hilly, we were often walking as the horse drew the farm cart up or down steep hills, but we descended our last hill into the market town of Otley at about five past nine. Our entry into the town started as we approached Otley Cottage Hospital, which the farmer told me had originally been a workhouse and then in the early years of the century an infirmary had been added. We crossed a river and climbed a gentle hill to a crossroads and the market was there just beside a clock tower built, farmer told me, in 1877, the year of Queen Victoria's Golden Jubilee. Farmer, as that was all I had ever called him, passed me a bag which contained some bread and cheese and he added, I am sure from his own meagre allowance, two pounds. A pound a month for two months work! And they say the Scots are skinflints.

161

Nevertheless, the sojourn working on the farm had done several positive things. It had allowed any possible hue and cry to subside, and it had allowed me plenty of time to make some plans as to how I might go forward. I knew that I could not eke out a living trying for farm work and living in barns for a whole winter. Added to that I had been lucky here in that the farmer and his wife were real loners, but other farmers might always be off to markets and the like and may mention my existence. I knew my recent landlady was just exploiting me, but at least in doing so she was keeping me a secret as otherwise she herself may be in trouble.

I had come to the conclusion, almost contra to logic, that rather than hide myself in a small town like, say, Skipton as I had first intended and where I would have been a good candidate as a discussion topic, I would instead go and hide myself amongst the throngs of people in either Bradford or Leeds.

Another conclusion that I had also recently come to was that being lost amongst the crowds in a larger place might also be an advantage related to a change in my physical state. Whilst, in many ways, the Stella from Essen was a simple and unworldly girl, nevertheless her expensive education had also provided her with an opportunity to live with a lot of other girls from different backgrounds. Despite the fact that my horrific first experience of being intimate with a man was a shock, in both the physical and the emotional sense, my time in Geneva had led to informal sex education. Not in the classroom but acquired by late night dormitory discussions of sexual activities and also of issues relating to reproduction and the signs of pregnancy. So, I was aware from bouts of sickness and the absence of my last couple of monthlies, that I was likely to be pregnant.

Not long before ten in the morning I walked out of Otley on the road which took me to either of those two cities that I had in mind. After about three miles I passed a huge building set back from the road which styled itself as the West Riding Mental Hospital, Menston. A couple of hundred yards later I came to a tram terminus and discovered that although Bradford was only eight miles distant, and Leeds ten, the tram went to Leeds and I thought that an hour on a tram versus three hours of walking would get me to a city centre in time to make some arrangements before it became too late, as darkness now fell by about five in the afternoon.

So, I took the tram and that was how I came to Leeds.

The tram arrived in Leeds in a storm of lashing rain, and the ancient gabardine that 'sour face' the farmer's wife, had got for me to work in was soaked in just a few minutes. I took shelter in doorways and arcades but there was no let up and I was stopped from making any real enquiries before it was dark. I asked a scruffy girl where I could stay the night and she suggested I try St Georges Crypt just off the Headrow, the main street. I presented myself there at about seven in the evening and putting on my now well-rehearsed act I told the staff that I was lost and homeless. I was given soup and tea and a mattress for the night.

In the morning there was tea and bread and margarine and then I was told to see a man called Dan who was in charge. He told me he was not interested in why I was there, only that he wanted to point me in the right direction because I could not stay permanently in the Crypt. During a very short conversation, using my put-on persona of being simple and possibly mentally ill or backward, I mentioned my seamstress skills. He told me of the Burton's factory in Burmantofts but agreed that without papers they would not take me on but suggested that between there and Chapletown I might find some other tailors who may need my skills and who may be less formal in their recruitment arrangements than Burtons.

I spent a depressing day traipsing from big factories to small ones and getting nowhere and eventually when it was coming dark found myself tired and hungry on Chapletown Road. Because of tiredness I suppose that I did not notice that there were a lot of differently dressed women loitering on the pavements and it was not until one told me to 'sling my hook' because this was her patch, that I realised this was an area for prostitutes. Just as I was wondering what to do and which way to go, I saw a café and decided that I needed something to eat before I fainted. I went in and fate once more took a hand, because I met Doll.

Through Doll I found happiness, or at least contentment, in a cocoon of support that never, in my wildest dreams, could I have expected to have materialised whilst sitting on that train south to

York. A ready acceptance had been extended to me without any questions from those around me; Doll, her friends, Paul my employer and my workmates. I was happy that I had occupation for the mind as well as the hands as I re-learned and then developed even further my seamstress skills.

No sign of repercussions of my flight from Scotland had yet appeared. I had obtained sufficient forged papers to allow me to have an identity and ration card. Living day to day, concentrating on the here and now, I was enjoying this hiatus in my recent adventurous exploits in avoiding my past.

But I was sitting on a time bomb.

Well, that is not strictly true, because the time bomb was within me, and inexorably it would interrupt this moment of calm in my life.

Chapter 18

1949   Gareth - Penarth, South Wales

I should have come to my parents' home before, but life had become complicated after I was relieved of my command of the *Loyalty*. First, I was turned overnight from hero to villain and the latter trumped any possibility of a gong for me or the crew in relation to the rescue of the tanker. I was paraded before the commanding officer, not long after my interview with the Red Caps, who were also present when he spoke to me.

"O'Shaughnessy you have been a damned fool. Some woman flutters her eyes at you and all the good reputation you have built for yourself is lost in the twinkling of those eyes. The facts are that this Booth woman may have been a spy, because it appears that the man she has apparently killed was himself a spy with a big operation in south London which, by the way, appears to have been dismantled by our people down there. Now the overall role this woman played is not known but several things are now clear. She is not Sheila Booth, that we have established, but who she actually is remains a mystery. She worked before in a listening station on the south coast, for a couple of years and what intelligences she passed on down there we will never know, and whether she has been able to get information out from here we do not know either. But damn it man, she could have sent Jerry the information on the departure of convoys. Imagine she might have told them about PQ 17 and that would have been awful.

Why suddenly was she being spirited away? Why did these two men come here to collect her? It is not clear, but we know that three people left in a car made to look like a staff car. Within hours it is found three hours' drive away with one man dead and one missing, but the dead man's papers were in the car and one possible reading of that is that she killed him first. The Wren 'Booth' is then known to have boarded a train south from

165

Inverness and she has been traced to York where she abandoned her uniform in a kit bag in the goods yard, but from there she disappears. We cannot establish if she made it to her stated destination of Liverpool, or, as the powers that be expect, is she in London and did she get there just in time to close their operation down before we were alerted to the existence of this den of thieves, or rather spies?

But what is clear is that you, albeit apparently innocently, bought this woman time by making the telephone call to say she was ill, just as she must have hoped you would. And for this you must face some consequences. After a long discussion with the Admiralty, we have accepted that there is nothing to suppose that you were in any way complicit with this woman's activities, you were merely a pawn she used to her advantage. However, it is deemed best if you are no longer active in this country in the fight against Hitler and so you will proceed forthwith to Portsmouth where in two days' time you will join a ship which is due to sail to the Far East, and you can have a go at the Japs instead of Jerry. Sadly therefore, it is my duty to relieve you of command of the *Loyalty* and you will go with these Military Police officers and collect your belongings and they will take you to Inverness for a train south. Please inform young Hopkins that he will take temporary charge and ask him to report to me forthwith.

Very good. That is all. Carry on."

And so I was escorted back to the ship and told I was to pack my kit and talk to nobody. When we arrived at the jetty there had been somebody on watch and by the time our jeep drew up all hands were waiting to greet me. The Red Cap sergeant approached the gangway and said.

"Make way for this officer who has been relieved of command and who is ordered not to speak to you and just to collect his belongings."

"Of course he's gonnae talk tae us." Said the Chief Engineer. "Cos I dinnae see any one present whose gonnae stop him."

The sergeant drew back his shoulders ready to respond and I quickly intervened.

"Sarge, let's all be sensible here. There is no way I want any of these guys to be in trouble, but they are my crew, and a very close crew at that, and they have not got the foggiest as to what

166

has happened, so let's be fair to them and let them know what is happening and why. You can tell them if you like, it's just they need to know."

The sergeant looked at the crew and then at me and realised that perhaps discretion was the better part of valour, or mutiny in this case, and he jerked his head to one side to indicate I could continue.

"You will all remember the Wren that was with us the day of the tanker rescue. Well, she invited me on a walk last weekend and we had a nice time. On the way back she got upset about seeing what she told me was her former Captain, with whom she said she worked with previously on some hush hush job, and he was waiting outside the Wrenery with a naval rating driver. She told me she had left that former job whilst he was on leave, because she did not like him or the work. But here he was, and she immediately thought he was coming to take her back onto his staff and she was very unhappy about leaving and did not want to go. So, she asks me to ring in sick for her, for reasons I did not, and still don't, understand and she did not explain more fully because it all happened so quickly. However, because I had come to like and respect her and wanted to keep seeing her, I wanted to keep in her good books; so, I did as she asked. Turns out she has disappeared and the Captain who came for her is dead. The other man, the driver, who was with him, is missing and this missing one and the dead one may well have been spies. The powers that be have determined that, albeit inadvertently, I aided her escape and so I have to be punished. Reading between the lines they believe this lot were Jerry spies and so they want to be sure that I was not involved with her or them and so I am being sent off to the Far East.

Now let's not have any trouble, I may have been misguided but it is not the end of the world and, for what it's worth, I do not actually believe that Wren was a spy buy clearly there was something funny going on. Obviously, it's a mess but I can see that something beyond my comprehension must have been behind it all and I should not have made the phone call and said something which I knew to be untrue. I have accepted that I did wrong and deserve to get punished, and let's face it the punishment could have been worse. Just let me get my gear and go off with these men and you give your support to Mr Hopkins, who is to take temporary command and, by the way Hopkins, you are to report to the Base Commander pronto."

"So youse gets the peddler for one phone call to say some bugger's gonnae be late on watch. Is that what you are tellin' us?" Asked the Chief Engineer.

"Chief. I did not think things through. Albeit at the time she did not give me enough time to ask why I should do this. I had plenty of time afterwards to consider what was asked of me and to see that it was an irrational request. She had left, it seemed as though she been officially transferred if a Captain, car and driver had come for her. So surely, I should have had no reason to make the call. To be honest I really fancied her, and I suppose that clouded my judgement."

"Aye, the power of the old John Thomas." Said the Chief. "There is many a good man had his downfall because he was ruled by his dick not his head. But I can see that you know that what you did was stupid and as you have said that you also see the need for punishment and have accepted it." I nodded.

"Well, you silly old bugger...... Sir, thanks for explaining it all and at least we can understand why we are to lose one of the best skippers one is likely to get."

And so I left the *Loyalty* with the good wishes of the crew to begin a new experience in a big navy ship bound for action in the war with the Japanese.

Seven years later and my life had changed beyond recognition by the time I returned home to the United Kingdom and shortly afterwards travelled to Penarth to my parent's home. I had seen out the war as a junior member of the wardroom on a big cruiser where I was a very small cog in a rather huge wheel. When the war ended I sought discharge from the RNVR and building on the contacts I had made out there I got a job as a master of a little trading ship, owned by a local company and running around ports close to Singapore and never going further than places like Penang. This suited me very well because, after the war and before my discharge from the navy, I had met a nurse in Singapore and after a brief engagement I married Dyllis out there and we were both very happy working abroad. It was a good life for a young couple and we quickly built up savings. Neither of us were close to our respective parents, and both of us had siblings who were offering any necessary support to our folks, back home.

Then, in 1949, we decided that maybe it was time to go home, as her parents were unwell and my father had died the previous year, and neither of us had seen family since the end of the war, indeed I had not seen my parents for nearly ten years. We went initially to Cardiff where her parents lived. It had been cheap living in post war Singapore and both my and Dyllis' pay had been good, and we had plenty of savings, so we were able to arrange to buy a house in Lisvane, but immediately on return we lodged with Dyllis' parents. The very first weekend I took her to Penarth to meet my mother and I was shocked at the state she was in when we arrived. She looked unkempt, which was unlike her, and the house was a mess. She was somewhat uncomprehending of me, though recognition did eventually occur, but even when it did her emotion remained quite flat and matter of fact. Despite my many letters she appeared to have no idea that I was married and kept asking Dyllis if she was here to make her tea. I felt so guilty that I had not realised my mother was in such a state. Dyllis told me that she thought my mother was suffering from one of the age-related mental illnesses which lead to either memory loss or confusion, or both. After some time when she had accepted who I was she did seem to warm to me and seemed very happy discussing the old days when I lived at home and when my dad had been alive, but she seemed to have no understanding of current affairs.

Dyllis and I quickly saw that she needed help but at the same time we had also to consider the needs of Dyllis' parents, both of whom had suffered mild strokes and had lost some mobility, though they were able to, between themselves, prepare meals and generally manage. On that first visit to my mother's home we made her a meal, in which she took little interest, and we agreed that we needed to regularise the situation in one way or another. Having agreed to purchase a house our savings were much reduced, and we both needed to get jobs. Fortunately, we both had skills that were in demand. There was a grave shortage of experienced nurses, and the war had decimated the ranks of merchant navy masters, and the shipping industry was booming in the UK.

For my part I quickly secured a post with Eagle Oil Tankers and had one week to put my affairs in order before I set off on what would probably be up to a year away from home. My post was well paid, and I would remit most of my pay home each month and so we decided that finding a nursing home or the like would be best for my mum, my sister was no longer able to help as she had moved to Toronto with a former Canadian airman whom she had married. We got mum a place at a local old folk's home who were able to take her and deal with her needs and Dyllis would visit from time to time to check up that things were alright. Provided she settled then we would sell her home in a few months' time to pay for her ongoing care. So just two days before I went back to sea I travelled alone, Dyllis had started work by this time, for a final visit to our old family home in Penarth to put it into mothballs pending sale as it were, ensuring all windows were secured and turning the electric and water off. I did all the tasks I had set myself and was having a last look around when I noticed that behind the large clock on the bookshelf were a number of letters which I had previously not seen.

There were various bills and demands which I or, given my imminent departure, Dyllis would have to sort out and several letters from me to Mum, which had remained unopened and then a few letters addressed to me. Most of these turned out to be unimportant when I opened them, but one was clearly a personal letter written in a hand which I did not recognise. I opened it and the single sheet inside contained within it one half of a one-pound note. How extraordinary I thought and turned to the letter itself which contained no sender's address.

"Dear Gareth,

This is a heartfelt apology as I am guessing that subsequent to our parting after that lovely afternoon together, I may well have left you in some difficulty. It was spur of the moment panic on my part, but on mature reflection I should not have asked you to make the telephone call, which, knowing the honourable man you are, I expect that you made. Inevitably in doing so you would, I now realise, have probably become embroiled in an event which in no way concerned you. If you did become collateral damage then I am truly, truly, sorry.

I am sure that you will have heard of my disappearance and undoubtedly also the accusations against me of heinous crimes. I can only say, in my defence that things are not as they seem. If they allege I am a spy, then I am not. If they say I am a murderer, then I would say there is another side to that accusation. But your intervention did enable me to disappear, and I am now living a very simple life, grateful to you for the fact that I am not dead and that I escaped from the shackles that were around me at that time. I cannot say I am, or ever will be, happy, but I am content and making the best of a very bad lot.

You may never know what the humanity of that afternoon meant, and still means, to me and if on receipt of this letter you would like to talk to me then you can contact me through Hoffsteins Solicitors, Park Square, Leeds. The enclosed half bank note will be your passport to contact with me. Of course, if you think badly of me and believe the narrative that will probably have been created around my disappearance then you may think of going to the authorities. There is nothing I can do to stop you.

I can only ask that before you consider reporting me and presumably providing them with an opportunity to apprehend me that you talk to me first. Every story has two sides, and I would ask you to consider my side before you take that decision.

Truly and sincerely yours,
Sheila Booth"

The postmark was Leeds.

Nearly six years ago.

The letter was intriguing and one part of me wished that I could hear Sheila's side of the story but, in the event, I decided not to make any contact for a number of reasons. First, six years had passed since the letter was written and Sheila's situation may well have changed. Then, my own circumstances were changed also and whilst Dyllis had heard the story that led to my banishment to the Far East, during the war I had made little of the actual time that I had spent with Sheila. I had decided that perhaps that was a chapter of my life which Dyllis had no need to know anything further about and there seemed little point in having to revisit that time in detail, given that we were happily

171

married. Finally, there was only two days to go before I went to sea.

So, I put the letter away amongst some old papers.

Chapter 19

1946   Solly – Leeds

Just a week after demobilisation I was back in the office. My dad, and amazingly also, the hard taskmaster that was Uncle Paul, had told me to take a month off but within a couple of days of being home I was bored with it. I was not just three years older than the idealistic youth of eighteen who had been keen to get into the fight; I was eons older in terms of my understanding of life and for the first time in three years my days were not structured for me. Structured! Ha! That's a laugh. I had been trained and prepared for the Normandy landings. No, I was not one of those wading ashore through German machine gun fire, because I only arrived three days later dry-shod after disembarking on some rickety jetty thing. But I was part of the incessant fight up through Belgium, Holland and Germany and I saw sights that completely eradicated my idealistic zeal.

Until then I had never seen a dead body, but during that period I saw countless. In some ways I became inured to death and actually the sights that affected me most were the living wounded. Men with awful burns, missing limbs and even men pleading with me to put them out of their misery, as they clutched open wounds in their bellies and who knew there was little or no hope of their survival.

War will probably have a dictionary definition along the lines of armed conflict between countries or nations, but I have never, and will never, look it up because I have seen war, and I know it means something terrifyingly worse. And if what I saw happen in those three years was not bad enough, then the later news of what the Americans did to those poor people in Japan will make warfare in the future even worse. Terrifyingly worse.

So, to relieve the boredom of home as well as the need to have my mind occupied in order to begin to leave behind the vivid memories of the terror of what I had been through I was keen, no desperate, to get back to work and to try to recover just a little of what had passed as normality three years ago.

For some people I guess they work to live, but in my case, I sensed that I might only recover life by working. I realised that that there may be some solace in having some discipline in routine and also something which would focus my mind in a direction that avoided reflection upon my recent experiences. War does that, and not just to the fighters. Looking around I have seen everywhere the impact of war on society. Damaged buildings, not so bad here in Leeds compared to what I saw in London, which is going to take years to repair. But more significantly damaged lives. Families without a member lost in the war, and where that was the main breadwinner then the impact on children would be not just the absence of a parent, but also consignment to living on a limited income or even a descent into poverty.

But there are signs that the mood of the country has changed and Atlee's overwhelming victory over Churchill, in last year's general election, may signal a desire for all classes of society to work together to re-build the country with a more co-operative mind-set. Of course, that in turn builds on the working together that we wartime workers, both combatants and those at home, have experienced. During the war the vast majority of members of all creeds and classes in the country have set aside their old divisions and worked towards a common purpose. This seems to be leading towards developments which will benefit everyone; for example, there has been the Education Act of two years ago giving access to education for all children and this year sees the start of a National Health Service. These are clear signs that some good may come in uniting people which gives me hope for a future in which we may all work together and support those less able to support themselves.

So, here I am, at just before nine in the morning, walking with my father up the steps of the offices in Park Square. We have driven in from Alwoodly in his car and, despite his attempts at conversation I have been pre-occupied and quiet. I think it would be good for me to insist on some independence; at least I could travel in on the bus or may be even move to a flat in the city, as home feels to be smothering me. Mother cannot understand that I am not the teenager of three years ago who is delighted to have a fussy mother doing everything for him. I love her and I know she means well, but I fear that she may kill me with her kindness, and I must find some way of establishing my own space without upsetting her.

The office reception area is, to all intents and purposes, just as I left it three years ago; but there is one significant change. Gone is the delectable Sue. The woman, even then in her thirties, who was the focal point of the office. She was always dressed so smartly and with never a hair out of place. Sue was my first, if not exactly love, then a crush at least. But, of course, not an actually requited love, because apart from our office interaction I never ever saw her in a social setting. No, she was, to me, a sort of 'ideal' woman so slim and attractive, so competent and I suppose she was the only woman, apart from cousins, with whom I ever interacted, other than my mother and sister. But when my teenage mind became excited sexually Sue was my object of desire. I smile because that is the old me, and the old me is no more. No more a teenager, most definitely a man.

In place of the delectable Sue stands, or rather sits, an even more delectable ……who? Father introduces me to Gina, and maybe I am about to replace Sue as an object of my desire! Gina was smaller in height, I discover when she stands, as my father introduces us, but bigger in many other departments, and with the most gorgeous brown eyes. Uncle Paul must have excelled himself here. Uncle Paul is really disappointed that Solicitors are not permitted to advertise, since advertisement would attract more clients, and more clients means more money to Uncle Paul. So, he tries to advertise in other ways. He always tries to represent clients whose situation might end up being newsworthy and reported in the press and in such cases he always makes comments to reporters just to ensure that his name will appear in the paper. Where he has instructed Counsel in a serious case that has to be heard in the Assizes, he always attends himself and sits behind Counsel as instructing solicitor, to be sure to be seen. He dresses in very snappy handmade suits and to impress visitors he always requires a smart good-looking receptionist. In appointing Gina he has, in my opinion, excelled himself.

From father I learn that despite the fact that I still need to qualify as a solicitor I will no longer be used as a general dogsbody and indeed arrangements, including minor structural adaptations, have been put in place to provide me with my own office, even though it is on the second floor. He takes me to my new office, and I am suitably impressed and express my gratitude fulsomely. He outlines some of the work that has been allocated to me and provides some files for immediate attention and leaves me to my own devices. I look at the work scheduled for the forthcoming few days and read two of the files which have been left for me. A little later I notice that it is nearly half past ten and I descend to seek out a drink in the kitchen at the back of the reception area. The reception desk is vacant, but I hear cheerful voices in the kitchen, so I proceed there.

Upon opening the door, I am confronted with both the old and new 'delectables' who are in animated conversation which quickly ends upon my arrival but not before I notice that the original delectable is no longer her svelte self but is, as they say, large with child.

"Sue, how really lovely to see you! And may I say it seems as though congratulations may be in order."

"Thank you Mr. Solly but let us leave the congratulation bit until this part of the process is duly behind me and I am fully congratulatable......if that is a word."

"I suspend congratulations, but I am sure that I am right in thinking that you will soon reach that congratulatable position and when you do, I will most definitely be happy to say so again. And may I say you look in blooming good health and can I ask when my deferred congratulations are likely to be needed?"

"All will hopefully be revealed in about another two or so months' time, Mr. Solly. Oh! Can I say in return how delighted we all were that you came through the war unscathed, especially as you seem to have been in the thick of it from Normandy right until the end."

"Sue, 'scathing' comes in different forms and whilst I did not get so much as a splinter from a piece of wood in the physical sense, I think that I am some way off adjusting to all that has happened these last three years. You will be amazed to learn that even Uncle Paul offered me a month off, but I could not just sit at home for a month as I would have been bored out of my mind."

Turning to Gina, Sue said.

"Mr Solly was only a year or so younger than you, at the start of the war and he had only worked for about six months in the office here before he was called up and went off to join the Army."

From this I deduce that the delectable Gina may only be in her late teens' but she must be quite bright because Uncle Paul is not a just stickler for good looks alone. He wants real value for money so she must be first rate in typing and shorthand to even get on the shortlist for a job here.

"Yes, Gina. I arrived here straight from school and Sue here taught me all that I know about how to behave and work in an office."

"Of course I have previous experience in an office." Gina replied. "But this opportunity is a big step up for me and it really has been invaluable that Mr Paul allowed me two weeks overlap with Sue before she left."

"Well, knowing Mr Paul he will have worked out that it would be worth the extra expenditure to get somebody able to run the office as efficiently as Sue. And taking a leaf from her book you must remember that I really do not know the job very well yet and I can do with all the help I can get. In fact, the last thing Sue helped me with was that really funny case of the woman who came in off the street and tore up two one pound notes, keeping half of each for herself. All this in order to ensure that the papers she deposited with us may only be released to the bearer of one half of one of the notes, with an identical serial number. It was quite an unusual case, as far as I can see and one which we only took on as a result of a significant upfront fee. Which reminds me Sue, has Mrs....................?"

"Horowitz."

"Ah, yes, Mrs Horowitz. Has she been in touch in my absence?"

"Not for a long while. After you left, I got telephone calls every two or three months and then the intervals gradually increased and, I would have to check the file notes but, I do not think I have heard from her in well over a couple of years now."

Chapter 20

1997   Gareth – Leeds

Railway journeys have always been exciting to me. Of course the wonderful days of my youth with the steam trains have long gone, but with it too have gone the grimy carriages, which steam engines caused. Also departed is the serious risk of getting a smut in the eye if you dared use the leather strap to first lower, and then look out of, the window in the carriage door. Perhaps children these days are totally ignorant of the concept of a 'smut', and I am sure there is little point in educating them on the matter; indeed, most of today's trains are not fitted with lowering windows. But the excitement of a rail journey is a condition which should, as excitement often does, keep you awake; and yet I find train travel highly soporific. I managed to leave the Principality, from my starting point in Porthcawl, in a waken state' as I needed to remain alert in order to exit the London bound train at Bristol Temple Meads. A lovely name for a station; built in the middle of the 1800s on a meadow near to the Temple church; hence Temple Meads. But once I was aboard the cross-country service, bound for Leeds, the soporific effect of the clickety clack, of the wheels on the rail joints, soon had me in the 'land of nod'.

As a lifelong professional sailor one learns to sleep when one can. Sleep at sea can be interrupted by the system of watches, two four hour shifts twice a day. That is the merchant navy way, unlike the Royal Navy who use the so called two hour 'dog watches' to break up the routine. But in the merchant navy system the Master did not take watches but was always on the bridge when arriving at or leaving a port or in congested waters like the English Channel or Gibraltar Straits and the like. Then the watches were the four to eight, running from four in the morning till breakfast at eight and four in the afternoon till eight in the evening, and does not interrupt much sleep, and in my day, that watch was usually taken by the Mate as the senior officer under the Master. That watch like the eight to twelve, which was the province of the Third Mate, were not too disruptive to a sleep pattern. Finally, the twelve to four was the province of the Second Mate, and this did mean that your night was interrupted when you had to arise to go on watch at midnight.

But there again, and unlike shifts ashore which are all happening in the same country in the same time zone, at sea these routines are interrupted by the change in time required as a ship moves east or west. A fast ship travelling due east or west can require an hour's time change every day or two. If the landlubber complains about the inconvenience of the change to, and from, British Summer Time, give a thought to the sailor who has his time and body clock changed very frequently. Sailing south to Africa does not trouble you too much because you are broadly speaking going south but crossing either the Atlantic or Pacific can involve a change of up to an hour a day. On such voyages as those you find it hard to develop any pattern of sleeping, so the watchword is sleep when you can.

On my very first trip to sea we arrived off our second port of call at about ten in the evening. When coming into port all hands were called to assist with the process of coming alongside the berth allocated for our cargo to be discharged or loaded. On these occasions there was a working party on the foredeck with the Mate dealing with the head ropes and, if required to deploy the anchor and then they operated the windlass, and I was allocated to the stern party, under the direction of the Second Mate, to deploy the stern mooring ropes. The lights of the port of our destination twinkled close by and I was excited and in the belief that the pilot would soon be aboard and the ship would be entering harbour and all hands called to stand to, I decided not to turn in to my bunk. We entered harbour at six the following morning and it took me weeks to make up those lost hours of sleep. Thereafter it became a principle for me that in such circumstances I would always turn in to my bunk and try to sleep, even if I was called just five minutes later.

But sleep I did after the cross-country train left Temple Meads train and I missed the lovely Worcestershire countryside, which

I had been looking forward to seeing, and instead I was jolted from sleep in the subterranean depths of Birmingham New Street station. Upon departure from that station, I opened my sandwiches and purchased a cup of expensive tea from a passing railway refreshments trolley. Undoubtedly my ague had taken a lot out of me and that was why, perhaps, I had slept so long, but my sleep had most certainly not been that of the righteous, for I was not looking forward to confessing the knowledge which I had initially kept from Rose.

Dealing with crises and problems is part of life but I tend to the view that, by and large, dealing with issues becomes less all-consuming as you reach mature years. As a child facing your peers after you have made a silly inconsequential blunder in public, feels like the end of the world. As an adult, major problems of work or relationships come at you all the time, and some have a very debilitating impact on you. But in your mature years you are able to firstly draw on past experiences in dealing with difficult interpersonal situations, and then you are less fearful of causing upset because you know that, with patience, most problems can be sorted out. Finally, when you are as old as I now find myself, you know it will not ruin your life because you have had most of that life already.

Nevertheless, as the clickety clack miles drew me closer to Leeds, and to Rose, I did begin to wonder if, after all, she might think the less of me when she discovered that I had not told her all I knew on the first occasion of our meeting. Yet Rose seemed a very level headed and competent woman. From the story she had told me she had been interested to discover her origins, but it was more by way of the interest than an absolute necessity. I had seen occasions in other friends who, upon reaching that time of life when family pressures diminish, begin to consider their own family history. Ironically, as with Rose, those friends often come to the enquiry too late as their best sources of information, parents and aunts and uncles have either died or forgotten many of the details the seeker requires.

In this case I suppose that I will be able to add to the information Rose is seeking, but how will she react to the possibility of contact with the solicitors? Equally pertinently, how will I react if she does decide to pursue that contact?

Furthermore, that in itself is an uncertain enquiry because the firm may no longer exist, or even if it does will it have kept records that go back that far? It is not as though we are talking something that happened say twenty years ago where you might expect that somebody in the firm would have a memory of what must have been an unusual arrangement. We are talking fifty-two years ago and that is longer than the working life of many people, let alone a working life in the same firm.

Reflecting on that very belated letter which I discovered six years too late, and which I now carry with me, there was not a lot that I needed to be concerned about in terms of explanation to Rose. I could easily explain the rumours of the time about Sheila being a spy. In that letter she was clearly not wishing to go into details but there was an implication that if I contacted her she would tell me more. Or indeed if I had contacted the solicitors would there be something written about her and would that include more about our, albeit fleeting, liaison. Anyway, fifty-two years on, the firm was hopefully long out of business or else subsumed by some great big company who would not be able to find the papers and I would be let off the hook.

With these thoughts in mind, I dozed again waking to the conductor's tannoy that the next station would be Wakefield Westgate. Looking out from my seat which was towards the rear of the train I saw the front carriage snaking ahead of me over a long viaduct, as we approached the station. I tried to wake myself up because I was aware that the next stop thereafter was Leeds and I knew my arrival time was just five minutes from the time now showing on my watch, so we must be running a little late. When the train came to rest in the station I decided to get my small suitcase from the overhead rack so as to be ready for the off when we arrived at Leeds, as the train itself was ultimately bound for Edinburgh. But I was slow off the mark and before I could shuffle from my window seat to the aisle, several passengers were filing into the walkway from the nearby door. A man with a flat cap and brown raincoat with a small black rucksack took a vacant seat opposite me and when I moved to get my case the train started, and I momentarily lost balance. Seeing what I was attempting to retrieve from the rack the newcomer, in his fifties I guessed, leapt up and took the case down for me.

181

"Thank you, kind sir." I said to him as we both regained our respective seats. "Not as nimble as I used to be, and I have been sat down too long and the old legs had gone to sleep."

"Long journey up from Wales? I guess." Said my new acquaintance.

"Wales, eh. Next you will be telling me what part."

"Somewhere between Newport and Swansea is my guess."

"Cheat." I said. "I believe that a very sizeable proportion of the population of Wales lives between Newport and Swansea, especially if you include twenty miles inland from that coastline. Anyway, you are correct. But I do not detect a Welsh accent so how otherwise did you reach your conclusion."

"My dad was from Aberavon and we spent many a Christmas in Aberavon and later St. Brides Major where Dad's youngest sister lived."

"Ah, well I live in Porthcawl now. And you?"

"I live in Bradford, where I work."

"Not today though?"

"Oh! Today I have been to our Head Office in Wakefield for a meeting, and I am now going back to my base. In fact, I am willing this train to get a move on as I am due in Court at two fifteen and I am desperate to catch the thirteen forty Bradford to Forster Square train which will get me to Bradford for two, and I will just make it in time, as court starts at two fifteen. I should make it if they have scheduled this train to platform eight as usual as I will then not have to climb the stairs to get to my Bradford train which may cause me to miss it."

"You work in court, you say?"

"Yes. I am a Probation Officer working in what we call a Court Team."

"You spend a lot of time in court, then?"

"Yes, most days because we represent our Service to the court and act as the conduit between our colleagues who work in the district offices, dealing directly with the offenders in their local area and it saves them having to break off and come to court with their cases and reports. We also write reports on offenders for the Magistrates or Judges and finally we see people starting their sentences. All of this is done amongst a host of other administrative jobs."

182

"So, I would see you straight away if I was put on Probation?"

"Ah! Yes and no. A popular misconception, even in this day and age, is that because there is a Probation Service, well several and mine is the West Yorkshire Service, and there are Probation Officers that *ergo* and therefore there must be Probation Orders. Sadly, there is no such thing as a Probation Order anymore. Albeit they started in 1907, Probation Orders lasted until the beginning of this decade when the 1991 Criminal Justice Act abolished them; there are now Community Orders of various types. There are differences and the change is to the detriment of engaging with and trying to reform offenders, in my view. But I am amongst a dying breed of older officers who came into the job when caring for those who did not fit into society were felt to be deserving of help and that is less of a driver of policy these days."

"So how are you still a Probation Officer if there is no Probation?"

"An excellent question, and I am sorry, but it is not easy to give you a clear answer. You see when I was first in post in the 1960s, we were run by a committee of the local Magistrates. Gradually managerialism took hold, and managers did not like being beholden to amateurs like Magistrates, who in those days were mainly volunteers from local communities. Managers like concepts of power, large scale and centralisation. It started for us with a move from city services to bigger areas like mine and now the politicians in London want to call all the shots for our service on a national basis. Despite there being a big shake up in the ways offenders were dealt with and they got rid of Probation Orders they did not want to have to explain it too much, so the name stayed the same for the service and officers. Bet you wished you had never asked."

"Fascinating. But you do not like what the Government has done?"

"No because in my view local services of whatever ilk are best run by local folk. But, I had best get off my hobby horse as that over there..............," he said pointing to the right hand side of the train, "..........is Elland Road stadium, home of Leeds United and it means that we are only a couple of minutes out from the station and I must get to the door and be first off if possible. Nice to meet you."

He rose to go, but I raised my hand and asked, "And in your court work do you come across any solicitors from Leeds?"

"Yes. A few; do you have any firm in mind?"

"Hoffsteins?"

"Oh Yes! Mr Solly from Hoffsteins is a great act, although I think he may have just retired. He was a real character in court; his clients have never done anything wrong, but if they have then it must be due to their inadequate upbringing – so 'I beseech the Court to please be lenient with the defendant' was his usual defence. Oh! Here we are at Leeds. Been nice talking to you; must dash."

So Hoffsteins were still in business; what a disappointment.

Chapter 21

1943   Stella – Leeds

On the journey into Leeds, with my secretly written document, carefully and excessively sealed with Sellotape into a foolscap envelope, I am aware I need to move fast, or the hospital staff may discover my absence. If they do, then I could be circulated as missing and there is no way I want to become involved with the police again. The routine at High Royds Hospital is well known to me and with luck I will be back before they notice I am missing. They are used to me now, as I am apparently recovered from the more florid symptoms of my illness, so I am tolerated as this uncommunicative but compliant affectless patient often given to walking, in all weathers, in the extensive High Royds Hospital grounds, or even the nearby countryside, and because of this I sometimes miss meals but I always return by the end of the day, so they will not be worried if I miss lunch again.

If a fatalist is one who just tolerates or accepts what happens to them then I am a fatalist.

My parents were brought up in the Jewish faith, but I know that they themselves had lapsed and, in their turn, they did not indoctrinate me into that faith, so I suppose I never established a belief system, either faith based or of any other sort. Belief systems established in early life must be very useful in providing reasonable parameters; in particular they can helpfully guide a person's decisions at a time of turmoil. But a belief system can be too strictly observed resulting in slavish adherence to its tenets which may be counterproductive. And therein lie a number of the world's problems; there is no one faith based belief system universally accepted, though many claim to be the true faith. Arguably, many of the world's conflicts are generated by internecine disputes between the many versions of different faiths which exist on our diverse planet.

But ironically, at the point of leaving the Otley Hospital where I had just given birth I wished, in retrospect, that I had been given a faith or some entrenched value system that would guide me, because I was about to become lost, and my mind overburdened with options on how to proceed. Taken away from me had been the life position of middle class daughter of professionals, one who attended a finishing school, ostensibly destined to marry another middle class boy and raise three children in a settled home environment. Instead, that madman Hitler managed to control the mind-set of too many people and cause this terrible war. Also, he created a bigoted society which picked on a minority group, and it was because of that I was turned, first into a traitor to my country of birth, and subsequently into a fugitive.

But once a bad thing has happened it is disabling to dwell on what might have been. Also as destructive is surrender to the urge to apportion blame. I can reasonably blame Hitler and also the millions of his countrymen and women who allowed him to hi-jack their belief systems to the point that they were led into an unnecessary war. But more personally I can blame myself for foolishly going into Herr Ulrick's travel agency and possibly hastening the point at which my parents were earmarked for trouble. I could even have stayed in Switzerland and my parents might have been able to escape to me there.

If only.

Retrospection is a semantic occupation and there is rarely, in my experience, a positive outcome in going over what might have been. So, I had to play the hand which I had been dealt, although once again the dealer appeared to have had it in for me.

If only those dratted fates had again not taken it into their capricious minds to further complicate things, by the loss of my mentor and sounding board that was Doll, I would have had someone to help me focus and resume my re-invented life. But as I hurried away from the Otley Hospital that morning I was completely unaware that she was lost to me and that I was about to enter a state of directionless emotional turmoil. And in that state, and without the aforementioned personal belief system, I collapsed mentally. This was for real; no need for pretence or play acting.

Doll had helped me to become as emotionally prepared as was possible to face the ordeal of giving birth knowing that I would leave the infant as soon as possible after the event. Looking back it was amazing that I was able to stay at Mary's until my waters broke and then managed to get the short distance from her terrace house, across the river bridge and up to the hospital. On arrival my presenting problem was fairly obvious with contractions now coming fairly frequently and because of this I avoided any immediate questions, for which I was most grateful. I was also lucky that the process of giving birth to, what turned out to be, my little girl was fairly short in relation to stories I had heard before and from the experiences of other mothers in the ward around me. Also, I was lucky not to have medical requirements myself, like the need for stitches which would have hampered my early departure. Indeed, I was lucky not to have had a caesarean as that would have completely scuppered my early departure.

To start with the staff treated me well but as I played my intended role of a monosyllabic and mentally dull girl, they became a little less helpful and a lot more directive. Nevertheless, I managed to persuade them, not long after my baby's birth, that I needed to get some fresh air and when I had returned from the first supervised outside visit, they seemed to think that there was no likelihood of my absconding. I nearly managed to keep the other women in the ward at arm's length, though at one point I had to berate myself for saying a bit too much to the girl in the next bed. She seemed nice and in different circumstances, especially if I was resident in the locality, I could see that we may have become friends and watched our children grow up together. But I was not like any other mother there, I could not afford to contemplate rearing a child in the situation in which I found myself, so I was intent on maintaining my determination to not bond with this child. Indeed, I planned, as soon as practicable, to get away on my own, as to stay with the child would have led to questions and ultimately to my arrest and separation from the child in any event. I would have got out the day prior to the day I actually left, but I thought that as the Almoner was not due to see me till the next day, I would have one final night of peace, except for feeding baby.

And a final night of quasi peace of mind it proved.

On that Monday morning I fed the baby and then said I would go for a breather outside for half an hour and return for my meeting with the Almoner. This was wartime, they were short staffed in the hospital and there were new admissions and so the staff were rushed off their feet. As soon as the coast was clear I hurried off and within minutes I was crossing the bridge into Otley by which time I was feeling sore and very tired. I returned to Mary's flat in the terraced house. I knocked quietly on the door and Mary was there to let me in.

"Come in and sit down; you look awful." She said.

"I had to rush before they realised that I was gone." I said and she nodded. "I am so grateful to you for allowing me to stay and in a few days, I must telephone Doll who said she would fix with one of her contacts to come to take me back to Chapeltown."

Her eyes filled with tears, and she was quiet for a moment, and in the pause, I realised that she had news for me; news that I immediately sensed would not be of the sort I wished to hear.

"Oh!" She sobbed. "Doll is dead, and the café burned down. It happened on Friday night and the girls reckon that some of the pimps in the area got fed up with her helping girls and recently she had persuaded one really good-looking new girl to move away and get off the game. The street word is they got somebody to set the café alight to give her a scare, but it ended that the whole place burned down, and Doll and another girl died from getting choked by the smoke."

"Doll's dead?" I asked, and she nodded. "And the café and all of the rooms are gone?" She nodded again.

I sat in disbelief. But even if I lacked faith, or a belief system I did retain some innate reflex response, based I suppose on the instincts of a hunted animal, the basic instinct for survival. This was reflected in my next question.

"You still have my knapsack?" And when she nodded, I experienced a significant sense of relief.

Now the agreement planned by Doll was that I would stay with Mary at the inflated price of five pounds per week for up to a month. I had already been there for over three weeks, so I asked.

"Can I stay on for another week or two until I have sorted myself out?" Mary shook her head.

"The landlord has found out that I have had somebody staying here, it's the nosey bloody neighbours who will have told him just to get at me. It's against the rules to have lodgers who are not family and if the neighbours found out about you when you was pregnant and stayed in all the time, they are going to know even quicker if you start going out. I cannot afford to lose this place otherwise its back on the game for me and I don't want that. I told the landlord that you were my sister who had come from Leeds to stay with me because you needed support as your husband had just been killed. He obviously did not believe me, but he said that was alright for just a short time and he said he would tell the neighbours my tale but just the same I had to get you to go home by the end of this week. He said he would call round to do spot checks starting Friday so I have to make sure that you leave before then, cos there's no way we can prove you are family."

Of course, I was unable to be sure that Mary was telling the truth, or whether she had owed Doll a favour in agreeing to help me out in the first place and now that Doll was out of the picture she maybe wanted rid of me before it brought any trouble to her door. So, I spent a rather tense few days with Mary, as I knew that I had nowhere to go, and I needed to recover at least some strength after giving birth. Also, because I was well aware that it would have been difficult to manage living rough whilst battling to stop the flow of milk which had come into my breasts after a couple of days of feeding the baby. I was at a very low ebb but the underlying survival instincts in me remained strong.

My principles of avoiding the German spies, of whom the late Jack had been leader, and also of still being unwilling to risk the possibility of execution or long-term imprisonment, as a spy come murderess, left me determined to keep running. I reflected that there could not be another stroke of good luck like finding another Doll. A return to Leeds and my former job might not be sensible, as other women would have seen that I was pregnant, and it was just possible that the story of an abandoned child, less than ten miles away, might ring bells if I returned to work without any sign or mention of a child at home. But my dilemma was that I was tired of running, and at least I had some knowledge of Leeds, so maybe that is where I should go.

What is a mental breakdown? There must be an accepted definition. Whatever it is I doubt it would sufficiently describe the torture I experienced after leaving Mary's. I must have retained some sense of normality for a day or so, before leaving because I took some practical steps. First, I went carefully through all my things, especially the knapsack to ensure that nothing which might identify my former self and all that I kept were the hard-won Identity Card and Ration Books, in the name of Sarah Simpson and the address given on those was that of Doll's now burnt out café. Then as all my other possessions had presumably gone up in flames at the café, I realised that as a homeless person I was more liable to have the knapsack searched for clues about me. The false bottom would be discovered which might well give rise to some suspicion, so I unstitched it. By now most of my original stash of money and postal orders was long gone so I dispensed with the purse. I still had a few notes, rolled and stitched into some knicker waistbands and I then cut two old pieces of material from the detached false bottom and stitched one inside and one outside the side of the side of the knapsack, to look as though a hole had been mended with a patch. In fact, there was no hole and several banknotes were secreted inside the stitching.

This done I said goodbye to Mary, on the Friday morning, and I set off for Leeds and from what I later discovered I must have, after a few days sleeping rough, gradually become more and more disorientated over the next few weeks. Possibly at the start I developed a physical illness with poor diet and exhaustion from walking the streets. Gradually it became as though I suffered from a permanent mental haze or fever, where there were very occasional and fleeting moments of lucidity and a lot of the time I seemed to be stuck in a very confused kaleidoscopic world of coloured images. These sometimes took frightening forms as though coloured arachnids were stalking me and at these times I must have been terrified, and I remember several bouts of screaming.

Apparently, I was found, clutching the knapsack which I would surrender to nobody, sheltering in a derelict house in Hunslet. Attracted by my screams some children found me but were terrified by my appearance. The Police were summoned and as my behaviour was so irrational and I was making no sense, so they took me to the Police station There it was determined by a police doctor that I was physically emaciated and clearly behaving irrationally and he felt that I needed a period of psychiatric assessment and that was how I ended up at High Royds.

It was several weeks, well into summer, before I re-learned how to feed myself and for my mind to begin to reason again. I was clearly in hospital, and clearly a hospital of the mind, given the sometimes bizarre actions of my fellow ward mates. I think that whatever happened to me was an episode of mental breakdown that had a swift onset and a fairly slow recovery. Despite my readings on the illnesses of the mind, this episode was in no way feigned; it was real and scary. There were a couple of days when my mind cleared and the coloured lights and spiders, and the like, went away and I remembered who I was.

Sarah Simpson, in High Royds Hospital by my current papers (alias verbally Sheila Johnson for the short stay in the maternity hospital and soon to be Sonia Horowitz for the solicitor), nee Sheila Booth, nee Stella Goldman.

Piecing together what had brought me to this pretty pass was not easy. The staff were wary of Sarah as apparently, in the early days of my admission, I was clearly hallucinating and could thrash around and, inadvertently, I hurt one of the nursing staff by catching her with a backhander from a flailing arm. I was seen as confused, disorientated and apparently staff thought I was 'speaking in tongues', whereas I was possibly reverting to one of my several languages.

Over time, as it became accepted that my treatment with drugs and a course of Electroconvulsive Therapy had controlled my schizophrenic episode, and the old symptoms were relieved. Looking back, I did clearly suffer a brief psychotic episode, but once the worst symptoms were passed and, when I was again in control of my thinking, I did adopt the new persona of the mildly depressed, uncommunicative and dull patient. Gradually I was able to piece together what had happened to me to cause my admission.

Apparently, I had been living rough for some time in some derelict building in the south of Leeds. Local people had seen me scratching around for food, becoming more and more unkempt and finally I was reported to the police because I was shouting in the building where the children found me. The police were unable to make any sense of me and were worried about my unkempt state and unintelligible speech. Then there was also fact that I became aggressive when they tried to take my knapsack from me to try to establish my identity, as I seemed unable to give them clear answers myself. The police doctor was called and eventually I was sedated and then sent off to High Royds.

So, I became a long-term in-patient because I was still deemed depressed and ill and also because I was apparently rootless, having nowhere to go and no relatives that could be found. The Police had made enquiries at my former address on my identity card, which they found, burned out and even though they probably showed my picture to many of the street girls, none told them more than that they recognised my face and knew that I had lived with Doll but nothing more. My doctor questioned me quite a bit trying to establish some previous life or links to that, but I played the role of knowing nothing and also being hard to draw out. Eventually, as I was causing no problem his attention turned to sorting out the more difficult patients, and I crept along under the radar, so to speak.

Though my presentation was dull and uncommunicative I was not challenging as far as all the staff were concerned and after their first negative experience of me they came to accept me as a biddable patient and to leave me in peace, especially as I posed them no problems. Internally I was back on track, but I realised that I had suffered a chronic mental collapse, but by good fortune I was now in a safe place and this life even held a few parallels with my finishing school where I had boarded. I was housed in good conditions, had three meals a day, no worries about finance and did what I was told. The difference was that I did not have as much mental stimulation as I would have had in my Swiss school or, indeed, as much as I would like.

The absence of mental stimulation had made me think about the choices I had made after that car took me away from Loch Ewe and what choices lay ahead for me. Given that I remained steadfast in my determination not to surrender myself even though, provided I was not executed, my life in prison may not have been so very different to life at High Royds. Save in one particular. I could leave High Royds for short spells, and more significantly I could ultimately disappear from this place far easier than might be the case if I were imprisoned. So, I determined, for all these reasons, that for the time being I would stay.

But the future? Chance was most unlikely to bring me another Doll to ease my journeying so remaining here would be my future I decided; if……………….. if I just had one go of turning to the only other person who might possibly be the second Doll in my life. One of the few people who ever showed me any compassion after my departure from Essen.

Gareth.

I made up my mind to take just one chance to communicate with him, through some intermediary, in such a way as to let him consider whether he may be prepared to be my mentor. It was a risk, but the fates had been firmly against me these last few years, maybe, just maybe, he might help.

Somehow, I believed that even if he had been negatively affected by my request to him to phone me in sick, he might still be prepared to give me a chance and to hear my story. It was a big risk. After all he might be so angry with me that he just gave me up to the police. But if he did then so be it; after all I had been through I would accept my fate.

And this is why I am on my way to seek what I trust might be a friendly looking, ideally Jewish, solicitor in the centre of Leeds.

Chapter 22

1997   Rose – Otley

We are both companionably quiet as we travel silently together in the car, away from Otley and towards Guiseley station and the train to Leeds. The journey is in order to follow the next link in the chain of my lengthy investigations into my origins. The last two days have been, to say the least, interesting. My quest to identify my birth mother is still some way from reaching a conclusion. Nevertheless, my silent companion beside me has opened up a surprising new avenue of enquiry. In the short time since his arrival in my life I have come to respect, and like, this serious and honourable elderly man, and if nothing else he is a nice addition to my circle of friends.

Just two days ago the cross-country train had pulled into Leeds as I waited on platform eight and, looking along the train, I saw a middle-aged man in a brown raincoat and with a black rucksack come rushing out of one of the doors and shout a cheerio over his shoulder before dashing off. He was shortly followed by Gareth who stepped out and turned to retrieve his little case on wheels. I noticed that he was a lot thinner than when I had first met him, but he was still agile and, as I moved towards him, he caught sight of me and smiled broadly. On impulse I went right up to him and gave him a hug and a kiss on the cheek, but I sensed him tense a little as I did so.

Declining my offer of help, he trundled his case across to the Guiseley train with me and, it being the middle of the day well before the home time rush, we found an empty four seat section and sat opposite one another. Gradually I sensed Gareth relax a little as we set off and straight away he wanted to know about everything about our journey. I had to tell him that the line to Ilkley was only electrified a couple of years ago and that it was part of the electrification of the whole urban area to the north and west of the Leeds, Bradford sprawl. One terminus was at Bradford Forster Square, another Ilkley, where our current train was bound, and then Skipton was the third. I explained that actually you could travel beyond Skipton as there were trains to Morecambe and Carlisle going beyond that station, but not via the electric power our train used. The line to Ilkley was nevertheless dubbed the Wharfedale Line and it did indeed end up in the town of Ilkley, which is situated on the river Wharfe. On the other hand it travels a long way beside the river Aire before turning up to the higher ground at Guiseley and then running along the edge of Ilkley Moor, well above the Wharfe. A true Wharfedale Line, I told him, should have gone through Otley.

The Airedale line faithfully followed the river Aire and I explained the landmarks as our journey started following that river, first past Kirkstall Forge, which it appeared was being run down by its owners, then, after crossing the river again at Rodley, we soon branched off uphill to our destination at Guiseley. I had parked a little way from the station, down the cobbled road, so I insisted on carrying his case which did not cope with being bumped over the uneven surface. I then took the route over the Otley Chevin which would take us past the Royalty Pub and Gareth was so delighted, when I stopped the car, to be able to stand and look down on the runway at Yeadon Airport. I explained to him that it was now officially named Leeds Bradford Airport, but everyone locally still calls it Yeadon. I told him that I believed that it had operated as an airfield from the 1920s and became the Leeds Bradford Municipal airport in the early thirties and went on to become important in the War due to the large Avro factory built next door. The runway, I explained, had been extended over the main road in the middle 1980s and very recently the nighttime flying restrictions had been eased and that had made it become much busier.

On we went and soon reached our farm where Gareth commented what a beautiful job we had done of blending the new buildings in with the original farmhouse. I took him inside and showed him his room and the bathroom and told him to come to the kitchen as soon as he was unpacked and had freshened up after his long journey. I did hear the toilet flush but long before the tea was ready I sensed that Gareth was standing behind me.

"Rose." He said. "I have not unpacked for two reasons. First because I am feeling guilty that I could have told you what I will now tell you a lot earlier and secondly, as a result of what I have to say you may prefer I found somewhere else to stay."

I was taken aback but let him go on, as he clearly wanted to get something off his chest.

"You must understand that I have lived my life trying to be honest and straightforward and to care for my friends. But I am sure that every single person on God's earth has made an error of action or judgement which they either immediately, or subsequently, have regretted. For some people it may be a huge issue, like they failed to own up for something they had done wrong and another person got into serious bother as a result. In my case it was, I felt, a minor matter and one which I had long learned to live with and which rarely if ever, impinged on my day to day life. Until, that is, the day when you appeared at my door with your story.

As I recall it, you told me about the probability that the woman who bore you and almost immediately abandoned you remembered the incident of the rescue performed by the tug *Loyalty* off Loch Ewe. You asked me whether I knew her, and I prevaricated, claiming that I needed to locate old papers, but Rose those papers could easily have been accessed that day. But I chose not to do so because you had hit a nerve. I just hope you can forgive me."

"Gareth, I am sure there will be nothing to forgive." I replied, concerned about the fact that he was looking so anxious and I did not want him getting over emotional. "We are dealing with relatively ancient history as far as I am concerned, and I am sure that whatever reason you had for delaying telling me what you know has a perfectly understandable reason behind it."

"Rose, it was not that I wanted to delay telling you, it was rather that I needed to think before I said anything. You see I always harboured some guilt about the whole episode. Let me explain.

There was a plan, devised by the officer commanding the shore base to which my tug, the *Loyalty*, was attached to give

196

some sea experience to the shore-based Wrens under his command. Our tug never normally left the confines of the Loch, a large sea Loch called Loch Ewe up in the northwest of Scotland. The Wrens were allocated singly to this experience and observed our work on routine duties in the relative safety of this large, but well protected, body of sea water. However, on the fateful day this Wren, called Sheila Booth, although that may not have been her real name as I will come on to later, was, by chance, the one aboard when we got an emergency call to leave the loch and go out into a storm ravaged sea to try and rescue a drifting ship. We accomplished this and in doing so I took a foolhardy personal risk, which she clearly witnessed, before we returned to the loch all safe and sound. That Wren was present the whole time the rescue was being effected and right up until we brought the disabled tanker into the safety of the loch.

I must admit I found this young woman attractive and when she was leaving the tug we agreed to meet a few days later, which we did, and she made a picnic and we went for a walk. At that stage I had not had a girlfriend whom I felt had something about them intellectually, as it were. Sheila was different, she drew me out about myself and I felt very comfortable talking to her. On the other hand she was enigmatic in respect of herself but, after a while, she began to express a deep and sincere unhappiness for reasons, which did not then or ever since, become clear to me. I did however detect that she was under a lot of personal pressure, and she told me that she had come to a conclusion and that was that she was going to take some unspecified action to deal with that situation, in the near future.

Looking back, I had clearly and quickly become infatuated with her and I was considering how to fix another meeting as we walked back to the hostel where she was billeted. As we approached that building from afar, she was clearly shocked to see a man dressed, as I was to discover, as a Captain RN, waiting for her with a staff car and a driver. She told me that she had previously worked for this man, on some secret work and she had hated it and did not want to return to it and was fearful that was the reason he was here to collect her. She asked me to do her a favour and telephone her section leader, the following morning to say that she was ill. Of course I agreed, but it was an odd request, and I know that I should not have done it, but I did because I did not want to offend her.

Within a week I was relieved of my command and sent to join a ship bound for the Far East, with my copy book most egregiously blotted. Because it turned out that Sheila Booth was not her real name and she had got into the Wrens on false pretences."

"You mean she was a spy?" I asked.

"Well, that is what they thought and what is more when they questioned me they told me that the Captain who was waiting for her was dead. In fact, I saw a grisly picture of him as he was found in a car in Inverness with his face badly beaten and a bullet in his head. The only other thing was that this 'Sheila' was known to have obtained a train ticket to Liverpool and boarded a south bound train. In short, she and two men had left the base, one man was dead, she had caught a train and the other man remained unaccounted for. My action, though small was deemed to have provided extra time for her escape and, whilst in fairness, they accepted that I was not actively complicit with her in any way in facilitating in her departure, I had nevertheless inadvertently assisted her by marginally extending the time until her absence could have been noted. So as this fact was known to some amongst her section and, as the Commanding Officer felt some action should be seen to be taken on the basis of *pour encourager les autres*, I was banished, literally to the far side of the globe.

Obviously, I was shocked and disappointed and there the matter may well have rested because I got on with my life, saw out the war and met and wed a woman to whom I was happily married for the many years until she died. And back then it did rest for some six years as I worked on ships trading out of Singapore and my wife and I had a lovely home out there. Eventually we returned home to the UK and shortly after it became necessary to move my elderly mother to a care home due to failing health and I became responsible for clearing out her house. It appears that for many years she had suffered from memory loss and perhaps other mental challenges which can afflict the elderly. Obviously during her declining health a number of letters had arrived for me and she had put them away, no doubt meaning to let me have them when she saw me and then forgotten all about them. Amongst those letters was one marked 'personal' and I will show it to you shortly, but it was written by 'Sheila' about a year after the incident at Loch Ewe and in essence it was a letter seeking to explain that things were not necessarily as they may have been related to me and that there were genuine reasons behind her actions. I think she was seeking to apologise and ask forgiveness for the trouble she imagined, quite correctly, her request might have caused me.

Clearly, she was aware that I would assume that she had just used me and, in case I felt angry about that, she did not want to go into any detail in the letter. She implied there was another side to the story and set up some complicated arrangement whereby I could contact a Leeds solicitor if I wanted to be put in touch with her. On the face of it I took the view that she was in hiding and it must have taken a lot of courage for her to contact me and to trust me. After all I could have gone to the authorities and then, pretending that I wanted to meet her, I could have been in touch with the solicitors and through that, arranged a meeting where she could have been apprehended. Indeed, she hinted at that in her letter and even absolved me from guilt if I decided to take that course.

But through the passage of time since she had written the letter until I opened it, all those six years after it was sent, I had constructed a new and happy life. I had never mentioned my contact with 'Sheila' to my wife and I did not want to raise the matter at that point because it was a difficult time, with us trying to re-settle back in this country and, in any event, I was just about to depart for a long trip at sea. So, I made a considered decision to leave the matter and did not, then or subsequently, contact the solicitor. But on several occasions in my life, since that time, I have wondered about her motive in sending that letter. She must have been somewhat lonely or unsupported otherwise why, given the potential risk that I might compromise her whereabouts, did she reach out to me at all. Then, when I did not reply what did she think? That I did not care about her and how might that have made her feel given that she was apparently friendless? Did my rejection hurt her even more? Or possibly, after the passage of time, did she just assume that I had not survived the war?

But gradually, and perhaps irrationally, I began to feel guilty that I failed to acknowledge her in some way. For example, I could have written care of the solicitors, explaining the time gap in my receipt of the letter and explaining that my life had moved on. But I rationalised that in order to make that contact, I would need to make an explanation to my wife which might appear to her to imply that there was more to the relationship than was the case. So, I did nothing immediately because the letter was six years without response and I was shortly going away; and then later I did nothing for fear it might stir up unnecessary issues in my home life. But underlying it all there lay a guilt that I had let this woman down; that in some way I had failed to acknowledge her attempt to explain or apologise or whatever and perhaps that had in some way had compounded her loneliness or hurt.

It was that guilt which came back to me when our discussions about your quest took the form they did. As I say it was most probably an irrational guilt, but it was within me none the less. That said a quick review of the letter and a few minutes of thought led me to realise that I would only exacerbate my guilt or create another bit of guilt if I did not let you have the information and so I had decided to let you know within just a few hours of your departure. But I felt that it would look funny if I phoned you almost as soon as you got home so I planned to leave it a week and then of course I got my dose of ague and that delayed things even more.

So now you see why I was concerned and why I am so sorry that such a long time has elapsed in my bringing you information and I am also sorry for being so silly and having delayed your search and worst of all making you think I am a silly old man."

Sensing that he was sincerely upset and worried I said, "Oh. Gareth!" And on impulse I went to him and gave him a hug and this time he accepted it, and hesitantly reciprocated.

I had made a casserole earlier in the day and after he had gone upstairs, unpacked and had a wash, Gareth re-joined me for a small glass of wine before we enjoyed a companionable meal and I washed up and Gareth insisted on drying after which I made a coffee, which he took small, strong and black, and we moved through to the lounge.

"Well, Rose," said Gareth, taking some papers from his jacket pocket, "it is time for us to get down to business and I have here a photocopy, which I did in the library, of the letter which I received in 1949, some six years after it was posted. I have the original letter and envelope, but I thought you might like to start with the copy and it was easier for me to just keep it in my pocket. Perhaps you would like to take your time and just sit and read it."

The letter was written in a neat hand, and, whilst I may be wrong and there may be no difference in the gender of handwriting, it nevertheless looked to me like a woman's hand; I have often looked at envelopes and judged it to be a woman sender and often been right, though not always. I read the letter, then I read it again, conscious throughout that Gareth was watching me intently.

"Gareth, given all you said to me about your guilt I can understand that this letter is the foundation of that particular emotion for you. This is a heartstring tugging letter on so many levels. From what you said about her being regarded as a spy, and maybe even worse, she is telling you that there is another side to those allegations. But, having made good her escape she is in a very lonely place, as she says here '……..*I am now living a very simple life, grateful to you for the fact that I am not dead and that I escaped from the shackles that were around me at that time. I cannot say I am, or ever will be, happy, but I am content and making the best of a very bad lot.*'

And having escaped one set of shackles, that she says she has shed, I suspect that she is now shackled by her need to keep her own counsel and to live, possibly a false life, and this probably means she can neither trust nor rely on the people round her. But there was somebody who really made an impact on her, someone who, if they were willing, might be able to offer her some stability or love or something. '*You may never know what the humanity of that afternoon meant, and still means, to me….. .*' So, she obviously thought very highly of you and it seems to me she is reaching out to you in the hope that you may rescue her from some unsatisfactory situation."

"So you do think I let her down, then?"

"No! No! No! Gareth. YOU did not let her down. Fate intervened. Fate intervenes everywhere. I once went on a trip to

London with Walter my husband only the second time I have been there in my life. A colleague, where I worked at the hospital, who had moved to a different department and whom I had not seen for several months, bumped into us at Piccadilly Circus. That is inconsequential fate. But consequential fate can be where a healthy person contracts a non-hereditary illness, or a pedestrian in the wrong place at the wrong time is hit by a car mounting the pavement, whose driver has passed out, or you are the only one in a field at a summer fete who is struck by lightning.

The particular bit of fate in your case was meeting and marrying someone else in the Far East, leading to your non-return home for six years and having a mother with memory issues who forgot to forward you a letter. Then, when you did get the letter you are about to go to sea for months and in any case, as you rightly told me earlier, by the time you read the letter Sheila must have assumed that you were either killed in action or otherwise did not want to contact her. So, either way she knew, by the time you actually did open the letter, that you were not able, or were unwilling to contact her and therefore you were not going to be part of her life. Then that would have led her to have to move on. Perhaps she even found a new friend and, in that case, she may not have welcomed your contact after all."

Gareth sighed and said.

"You have put into words some of the thoughts, or are they excuses, which I have had when considering what might have happened if I had made contact, six years too late and that really helps a bit towards assuaging my guilt."

"Your time together must have made a very deep impression on her you know."

"Yes, and it did for me but I wondered, in retrospect, if it was the timing of our contact which raised the emotional levels, because immediately after a very pleasant afternoon things happened very fast for both of us in different and perhaps not positive, ways. Anyway, that is in the past, what do you want to do about the future? Are we going to see if we can redeem the half one pound note at the solicitors, whom, 1 learned from a young man on the train, still are in practice."

"Well from my point of view the answer is yes, but I must be guided by you because I sense that this may only add to the difficult emotions that impinge on you regarding this former part of your life. It could open a Pandora's Box of issues with which you would then have to deal."

"Do you not think that ever since you left my home, and all through the long hours of feeling ill, I did not think about what I should, and should not, do? Of course I did and it became clear to me that as a duty I should now revisit this matter and see what we can find; if anything is still there to be found. Do you remember the old television game with Michael Miles in the nineteen fifties 'Take Your Pick'?"

I nodded. "Do you mean the show which included the 'Yes, No interlude' with the gong? Where you were 'gonged out' if you answered a question with a nod or shake of the head or uttered the words 'Yes or 'No' to any question."

"That's the one." Said Gareth.

"Well as you remember contestants built up a sum of money by correctly answering questions and then they were offered the chance to take the money or 'Open the Box' which may contain a wonderful prize like a car, or a foreign holiday, or it might be a duff prize like a tin of baked beans. Well, I feel that I have been answering 'the questions' by living my life and that has been satisfactory enough, but now perhaps having always been the careful, prudent man for eighty odd years I ought to see if it is possible to 'Open the Box'. If there is no 'Box' to open that is the end of it. If there is then I will cope with whatever comes out. Let's face it I may not have to cope for that long, given my age."

So, it was agreed that we would just turn up at the Solicitors to at least see what the place looked like even if there was nothing else to be done. The following day, Wednesday, I had to work in the morning so we planned to go today, Thursday.

And here we are on the train to Leeds.

Chapter 23

1943   Maurice – London

As I contemplate signing off my final report on the Loch Ewe incident of last year, my mind goes back to a wonderful Proms concert in last year's first full Proms season at the Royal Albert Hall since the old Queens Hall was destroyed by bombs. I was entranced by the wonderful performance of Variations on an Original Theme, Opus 13, which was completed by Sir Edward Elgar in about 1899, and it has long been a great favourite of mine. One of its themes came to mind as, having read through the final copy of my report, I prepared to sign it. Actually, I had started humming the tune before I realised what I was doing and, having made the link, I realised that this was a subconscious transfer from what I had written for my superiors, and what my report had just, in effect, concluded.

Namely, that the whole episode, just like Elgar's Variations, remains an enigma.

I have been unable to solve the riddle and, I suspect that unless someone gets lucky or one of the participants was struck with a severe bout of conscience, I doubt that the truth will ever come to light.

Directorate of Military Intelligence: Section 5
Incident Report - HMS Helicon 11th July 1942

This report has been compiled by reference to the following. Study of all written reports of individual investigations and evidence from various sources including Military and local police covering Inverness and HMS Helicon; civilian police in York, Manchester, and

Liverpool; all are individually referenced in the appendix hereto. Furthermore, I have personally overseen operations in London and additionally I have visited Inverness, HMS Helicon and York, to make additional enquiries of the relevant reporting officers together with some of their witnesses and also to make enquiries of my own.

The presenting issue was the report, to the police in Inverness, by a member of the public on Sunday 12th July 1942 of a suspicious vehicle, apparently a Royal Navy staff car, parked on a road beside the River Ness. The report was received at 0941 and an officer attended at 1005. The reporting woman, a local resident, Mrs Brown, explained that she had been walking her dog the previous evening in the twilight, sometime after 2100, when her attention was drawn to the car by her dog, which showed particular interest in sniffing and whining at a rear door. In the fading light she could not make out much other than the car appeared to be unoccupied, but she was surprised by the unusual difficulty she experienced in dragging her dog away. On the following day, the Sunday morning she attended 0800 Mass at her church and subsequently took her dog for her usual walk beside the river. The same vehicle was still there and again the dog was unusually demanding to approach and Mrs Brown allowed this and studied the dog's interest in what looked like blood stains, round an area of the rear door. She felt that the vehicle was suspicious and contacted the police.

Constable Johnstone attended and examined the vehicle together with Mrs Brown and he concluded that it did appear to be blood on the car and in addition he observed what appeared to be a bullet hole in the opposite rear door. He attempted to open the vehicle, but it was locked. He took the particulars of Mrs Brown and dismissed her, after establishing that she had not seen the vehicle arrive but could affirm that it had not been there on the previous morning so must have arrived on Saturday in between approximately 0900 and 2100. Such were the constable's concerns that he cycled immediately to a police telephone box and summoned his sergeant.

Sergeant McCullum attended at 1040 and together the two officers further examined the vehicle. They determined that the naval markings, whilst serviceable, might not be genuine and this together with the blood and bullet hole led the Sergeant to decide to force entry. A window was broken and immediately a noxious odour was released and on further inspection they discovered a body in the foot well between the rear seats and the front seats. It was clear that the person was deceased but as he was wearing a uniform of a Captain in the Royal Navy the Military Police were summoned. Prior to their arrival the two policemen continued a search of the vehicle and discovered two sets of papers, the first appeared to relate to the Captain whose body was in the vehicle and the other to an Ordinary Seaman. In the boot of the car, together with some paint of the same colour as the car, were two holdalls one of which contained civilian clothes, some money and the papers belonging to one Jack Smithson, with an address in East Molesey, Surrey. The second identified a Ralph Sheridan whose residence was the same as Smithson.

The Military Police arrived at 1135 and were briefed by the civilian policemen. A guard was set on the car and the Sergeant, and the Military police went to Inverness Police Station to conduct telephone and other enquiries. In summary their findings may be expressed as follows.

A staff car containing a Royal Navy Captain and driven by an Ordinary Seaman had entered the restriction zone at Achnasheen at 1310 hours on Saturday 11 July. Papers appeared in order. It left again at 1705; on this return journey there was an additional passenger in the form of a member of the WRNS. This Wren was later identified as one Ordinary Wren 'Sheila Booth' she was off duty during this period and was not rostered for duty until 1000 the following day, Sunday. At 0850 on Sunday a Lieutenant G. O'Shaughnessy RNVR, then in command of His Majesty's requisitioned tug 'Loyalty', telephoned 'Booth's' section duty officer to state she was unwell and would be late at work. Later that day at 1215 the Officer Commanding HMS Helicon received a telephone call from the Military Police in Inverness concerning the incident and he caused various enquiries to be put in hand and it was quickly discovered 'Booth' was the missing person.

Later in the week the Military Police officers attended HMS Helicon and as part of their enquiries interviewed Lieutenant O'Shaughnessy RNVR. It appeared that it was only his second meeting with 'Booth', the first had been a few days earlier, when by chance she was taking part in a programme of allowing all WRNS staff on the base to get some sea experience, on the tug 'Loyalty' in the Loch area. On the Saturday it appears that this was the first social meeting between the two and they went for a walk. The officers were satisfied that the Lieutenant was not complicit in the activities of 'Booth', and they were also clear that his evidence suggested that she had appeared shocked and disappointed at the arrival of the 'Captain' in the staff car. It appeared that on the spur of the moment she asked the Lieutenant to call her in sick and, out of misguided loyalty, apparently driven by a developing emotional connection, he complied with her request.

Both the Investigating and Base Commanding Officers accepted the assessment that Lieutenant O'Shaughnessy RNVR, was foolish in making the call, a fact he fully accepted. As a result, after discussion with senior officers, a pending possible commendation for his personal bravery connected with a recent rescue incident was discontinued and furthermore the Commanding Officer told him that he was relieved of command and was to be posted as a junior officer on a ship bound for the Far East. This action was taken because his telephone call would have been known about amongst 'Booth's' colleagues and the Commanding Officer felt that some punishment was required to be seen to have been awarded. Furthermore, in the seemingly most unlikely event that he was in some way connected to any German intelligence he would be of limited use to them in the Far East, where he is currently serving.

The Military Police in Inverness contacted this Section in London at 1220 on Sunday 12 July and the Duty Officer allocated the matter to me for investigation. After a discussion with the Inverness officers, I put together a team of our staff and civilian Police and we attended Sefton Lodge, East Molesey at 1750 the same day. We were required to force entry and found that there was nobody in the building. There were signs that there had been a hasty departure. Drawers open with some items still in there, as though some clothing had quickly been removed and the rest abandoned. The only filing cabinet was empty and in the garden was a forty-five gallon oil drum with one end cut off and it had been clearly used as an incinerator. Inside were charred remains of papers which had been burned. Neighbours later confirmed that a bonfire had been set the previous evening. From this I make the assumption that there was an arrangement for the 'Captain' or his assistant to notify Sefton Lodge of the success of the apparent operation to extract the Wren 'Booth' and either the man Jack or the assistant Ralph had reported problems. Alternatively, if no contact was made by a certain time the occupants were to assume the worst and follow a pre-arranged evacuation plan.

Over the following days I made enquiries with local residents which led to the following observations being ascertained. The principal occupants of the property seemed to be a man called Jack Smithson, a somewhat overlarge lady housekeeper named Gladys and the man Ralph Sheridan. They were very aloof with neighbours, and one told me, when he had asked directly, that Smithson stated that he ran several small businesses making clothing for the armed forces. He stated that he had several factories in the 'north' (unspecified) and he travelled there occasionally and also had representatives visit him. Upon enquiry all this proved unsubstantiated, but it would have provided good cover for him being absent from time to time and additionally for explaining a variety of visitors.

In short there was little by way of useful information from neighbours. Several items of partially burned material were found but nothing of significance except there was the charred edge of a British Passport and part of the first name was legible, it read "Stel……" which, I assume, might be the start of 'Stella'. Whether this relates to the person known as 'Sheila Booth' can only be pure conjecture.

Fingerprints were taken from the body of the deceased man, dressed as a Captain R.N. and these fingerprints matched one of several sets present at the Sefton Lodge house and the same prints were also found in the vehicle made to look like a military one and in which he had been found murdered. There was no match to these prints found to any on file. Interestingly, there were some other prints found at Sefton Lodge which also matched some found in the vehicle. This presumably is the missing man. Again, we have no records on file but they may be of use if this man comes to the notice of the police in the future.

My visits to Inverness, HMS Helicon and the York Police confirmed all the details provided by the respective officers involved, whose work I commend as being timely and thorough. In Inverness I additionally discovered that the Women's Royal Volunteer Service ladies remembered serving a Women's Royal Naval Service rating at the same time as a Women's Auxiliary Air Force corporal. They had little other by way of information beyond the fact that the WRNS rating was apparently starving hungry.

At HMS Helicon I interviewed some of the crew of the requisitioned tug 'Loyalty'. Despite being commanded by a young Sub Lieutenant RN, the main spokesperson was the Chief Engineer. I was left in no doubt that their former commander Lieutenant O'Shaughnessy RNVR, was a brave man and a much respected commander. The feeling was that he had been smitten by 'Booth' and just gone for a walk with her in the hope that a relationship might develop. They were categorical in refuting any suggestion that he was in any way involved with her previously, an opinion backed by the fact that he rarely went ashore except for appointments with the base Commanding Officer. Further, it was their view that he was not aware that she was seeking to avoid the authorities at the time he made the telephone call. Their view was what they described as him following a reasonable, if somewhat unusual, request from a girl in whom he was interested in getting to know better with a view to an ongoing relationship.

On my way north on Tuesday 14th July I stopped off at York Railway station where I made a number of enquiries with station staff, including porterage staff in the goods yards. The station sees a huge number of military personnel and even though WRNS personnel are much less in number they are not unknown and so there is no confirmed sighting of 'Booth'. I was able to inspect the items in the Navy issue kit bag believed to belong to this woman, but again there was nothing of significance.

Despite a watch being kept on Sefton Lodge for several days, there was no sighting of anyone seeking to enter which suggests to me that this was a highly organised spying cell with sophisticated arrangements for dispersal in the event of a breach of their security.

I reviewed the application 'Booth' had made to join the WRNS. Little there stood up to scrutiny in depth and about the only thing to be substantiated related to her employment immediately prior to being accepted into the Service. There was reference to an Uncle in the Royal Navy, by the name of Smythe, but contact with that deceased officer's sister revealed that he had no such niece. Two references were taken up in writing and had duly been responded to in writing and in glowing terms. The first was from her most recent employer which when checked was in order but the second, allegedly from a long-standing family friend and doctor was bogus as, upon visiting the address it turned out to be an empty apartment and there was no record of the named referee being a medical practitioner.

Whilst it seems clear that Ordinary WRNS Booth is not the real name of the woman who occupied that name and rank in the WRNS I did research the records held on her in that name. An identity had been created for her and a most professional one at that. Her passport, ration cards and other documents, which interestingly she left behind in her haste to join the 'Captain' on that day, were most exceptional forgeries. Her remuneration was paid directly to a bank account which had been set up during her time in the *bona fide* employment which immediately preceded her entry to the WRNS. The bank had sought and received apparently proper references, one from her then employer the other a note from a commercial landlord included in the rent book she produced. When she left the flat which she occupied during that employment she notified the bank of a new address and as proof produced a new rent book. In the event, and upon my investigation, this second address is an unfurnished and unoccupied flat in Hammersmith which I presume to be a dead letter drop used by the spy cell.

Finally, I checked her financial records. During her time at Cliff Hill House she regularly banked her pay cheques and withdrew very modest amounts. At HMS Helicon she was able to withdraw cash from her wages via the paymaster section and remitted the remaining amounts to her bank. To me it does seem that proportionately she was drawing out more during her time at HMS Helicon, where there were less opportunities to spend than at her previous posting where shops, cafés and opportunities for socialising were more accessible. Was she building a small nest egg? There is no recent activity on her bank account relating to withdrawals, payments or remittances. This means that apart from what 'petty cash' she drew from the paymasters in recent times she was not paying any other money out of her account. Her total accrued savings were £471-4s-7d. Despite having access to this significant sum (bear in in mind that the average wage over the past three years is assessed as a little over £6 per week and so under £320 per annum). She has not made one single withdrawal since she went AWOL. This suggests that she has gone to ground and is aware that to try to draw this money may reveal her whereabouts.

Assessment.

This appears to have been a high-risk operation, on behalf of a clandestine or subversive group, to go into a restricted area with significant chance of being detected. In fact the operation was successful in extracting a specific individual, clandestinely serving as a WRNS rating. What was the likely pressure driving the need to effect this risky extraction?

It is clear that the WRNS 'Booth' obtained her post by deceit. We may assume, therefore, that she was prepared to act as a spy or otherwise against the interest of our country. But neither of her two postings was at any significant level as to have access to information of great use to an enemy. The first was a lengthy deployment to a listening post at Cliff Hill House on the South Coast, at which she provided short term, time critical information to local commanders about contemporary enemy movements and communications; as such there was little that could be subsequently reported to the enemy that would be of assistance to them. Then the second, much shorter, posting involved her in day-to-day communication with vessels in the local sector, she would not have had access to the make-up, nature or timing of convoy departures. True she might have obtained general convoy details by deduction, but the evidence is that she rarely left the base any more than monthly. There was no evidence found of her having access to unauthorised radio communication facilities or apparatus.

Neither of her superiors at both of the postings held any suspicion of her whatsoever, beyond a general description of her being a shy and reserved person. So why might she ask to be extracted? If she did ask, why mount such a high-risk operation? She could simply have gone AWOL or contrived a reason to leave. Indeed, the evidence suggests that 'Booth' was surprised by the arrival of the 'Captain'. Furthermore, she used the reason of a sick parent to buy her ticket from Inverness, she could equally have used that same excuse to her base commander and then disappeared whilst on leave. Finally, and for me significantly, I believe that she asked Lieutenant O'Shaughnessy RNVR to make the telephone call to give her more time to escape, so that meant that she was not expecting the 'Captain' to arrive and may have had some reserve plan to evade him on the journey away from the base and which she needed time to effect. Overall my opinion is that it is unlikely that she sought extraction from this post.

Thus, in my considered opinion, the extraction was planned by the 'Captain' and, or, his organisation and it could have been driven by the fact that they had another role for her, but I discount this as by being AWOL she would have lost, what must have been, the hard won WRNS status. Much more likely, in my view, is the fact that he or his organisation were perhaps fearful that she was becoming disaffected and had therefore become a security risk and as such she needed removing.

So, having extracted an operative about whom he was suspicious, what then happened? In my view it is possible to surmise that she may have become aware that she was in trouble and either acting alone, or with the help of the man believed to be Ralph Sheridan, contrived to murder the 'Captain' and then the two of them could have made good their escape. As against that hypothesis there is no sighting of Ralph at Inverness Station at the relevant time. This is not conclusive since he could have remained in uniform and would easily have blended in with the many other male personnel. However, even that gives rise to the question as to why, in that case, did he leave his false navy papers on the front seat of the car and his more regular papers in the boot with his civilian clothing?

On balance therefore it would appear that 'Booth' somehow made good her escape alone. It would be remarkable if a single female taken by two men, apparently unwillingly and by surprise, was able to contrive to escape and kill at least one of the men. Unless she was either trained in single combat or had access to outside assistance.

Therefore, I have considered the possibility that she was assisted by others unknown and I also considered the possibility that 'Booth' was a double agent who had eliminated the apparent leader of a spy cell on behalf of ourselves and/or our allies. Contact with other departments of our own Intelligence Service has not resulted in their admission that this was one of their operatives. The American and Russian departments both deny their involvement and, even though one would expect that even if it was true, I can find nothing to support that being the case.

Nevertheless, the fact is that many months have passed and no evidence of 'Booth' has been found since she discarded her uniform in the York station goods yard. To me it is unlikely that she could have so completely disappeared from view without the assistance of some outside person or organisation to assist her resettlement. If she did, as on the face of things, somehow make good her escape alone, it would be truly remarkable.

Summary of Actions taken
It is now well over six months since this incident and all avenues have so far been explored to no avail. Unless and until 'Booth'

or 'Ralph' are identified the matter is unlikely to be progressed any further. In the light of this I have made the following arrangements.

Fingerprint evidence for Smithson and the man Sheridan have been added to national records together with a sample of those which, we have reason to believe, may belong to 'Booth'.

Police forces have been supplied with full particulars, as far as known, of both Booth and Sheridan and an added marker that, if identified, they are to be held for interview by this Department under suspicion of breaching the terms of the Official Secrets Act 1911 (as amended 1920 & 1939)

A memorandum has been sent to Armed Forces recruitment sections advising them to require their staff to take all possible steps to authenticate the existence and *bona fides* of referees to service applications. Where there is any doubt as to the status and whereabouts of a reference the application should be treated with caution.

Our Intelligence Central Index has been updated for any reference made to Sheila Booth, the two named individuals Smithson and Sheridan and to Sefton Lodge, East Molesey, with a marker that any such information is to be referred to this department.

Legal Section have been advised of the circumstances with a view to obtaining the title of Sefton Lodge for national benefit.

Maurice Smitherham
Senior Executive Officer 11 May 1943

Chapter 24

1995   Stella - Nova Scotia, Canada

Many people would probably support the view that life is precious. Yet human beings have, from time immemorial, engaged in shortening the lives of others. Why? In the years of the early humans I guess that we were just like animals, living lives truncated by the ravages caused by the absence of decent shelter, difficulty in finding enough food and coping with attacks by wild animals. Also, there would be attacks by other tribes seeking to gain any benefits of living that your tribe had managed to obtain. In effect those humans back then would be living like other top of the food chain wild animals of today such as wolves, lions, bears and the like. Over time, having moved beyond that fairly primitive state and learned to have decent shelter and regular food supply, we broadly learned to live reasonably together in an urban society. Yet this has most certainly not eradicated the fact that a large number of humans retain this this almost constant drive to be aggressive and to kill others of their species.

The world still has plenty of groups living without decent food and shelter, but in modern times many of the really destructive wars have been started by urban nations with generally acceptable, or even good, standards of living. So why do humans give up a good enough lifestyle to go to war? Tribalism, religion and the unchallenged power of megalomaniacs, and their cohorts of supporters, have a lot for which to answer. And where does that leave the ordinary citizen whose country's leaders invade another or who suffer attack from outside? Well, the ordinary person is challenged with choices that they did not personally seek or expect to have to face and which, in turn, interrupts their former life plans. Adapting to the changed circumstances creates both challenges and opportunities. Some have their future changed for them by the choice or conscription to join the fight. Others are bewildered and do not know what to do for the best, even if that means that their inaction will result in them becoming affected by the fighting anyway. Yet others see opportunities to advance themselves, like the wartime 'spivs' who had access to, and then sold on, black market goods in the Second World War.

For me that particular war which had initially entrapped me, eventually had, ironically, facilitated my escape, even though, in my case, it was 'out of the frying pan and into the fire'. From an oppressed position I became free of the constraints that had held me captive, but I rendered myself as a displaced person and had to live from hand to mouth, just like others in that position had to do. In that new state I lived in almost constant fear and I had felt forced to give up my child when she was born. All this then led to my mental collapse and, after I had got through the most florid aspects of my collapse, I had tried to contact somebody whom I thought would help me, but I was left adrift when no response was forthcoming. Life in High Royds Hospital went on with me spending a lot of time walking or sewing and from the latter I made a little bit of pin money.

Then in 1946 Pavel arrived at the Hospital. He had been in the First Polish Parachute Brigade, and trained at Ringway, Manchester and later in Scotland. He had been part of Operation Market Garden to secure the Rhine crossing near Arnhem. Some Polish troops had gone in by glider two days earlier, but he actually landed by parachute, near the town of Driel and many of his comrades were killed in the battle with the defending German forces. He fought there for four days before sustaining severe shrapnel injuries. It was several days before he could get proper medical attention. Although he recovered physically, he was mentally much more severely scarred and this ultimately led to his discharge from service. He wandered the country in a confused state and eventually, after some bizarre behaviour in Leeds, was committed to High Royds Hospital.

Like me he needed the freedom of the outside air and so we saw one another occasionally on walks in the grounds and eventually we got chatting whilst sitting on a bench. Pavel Jacek grew up on a farm near Krakow, he was four years my elder. We walked and met frequently and realised that we were two lost souls but, by some obscure mathematical equation, we found that in our case, two lost souls equalled one found soul; or almost. Together we talked and talked, each helping the other to improve our mental equilibrium. I sought and was granted a discharge from hospital in late 1946, having arranged to start work as a seamstress and I got a bedsit in Leeds. A few months later Pavel joined me, and he got building work, cash in hand. We saved as much as we could as both of us wanted to see if we could find a new life in a new country. We were married in Leeds Registry office and so Sarah Simpson became registered as Sarah Stella Pavel. A return to Doll's forgery friend, and a sizeable cash payment, got me a passport in the latter name and, in March 1948, with our accumulated money we purchased a pair of one way tickets from Liverpool to Halifax, Nova Scotia. Conflict on a broad scale engenders migration and it was the large-scale movement of people as a result of the conflict that had been the Second World War, which helped us get through the immigration hoops.

We travelled very light. My old knapsack contained all our clothes and valuables. On arrival Pavel got a large rucksack, as he called it, and in Halifax we bought a small tent and a primus stove. During that summer we camped and worked our way down the coast from Halifax to Saint Johns and then, upon hearing about a farming area northwest of Fredericton, we turned inland passing through that town and on into a very fertile valley. Here, with the help of a local village church, we found some temporary accommodation and the pastor found Pavel some work on a farm. Our one room apartment was fine, but I could not cope with being there all day, so I went to look for work. There was nothing formally available but after talking to various people the local hairdresser in the village was prepared to offer my seamstress skills for ten percent of whatever I earned.

Over the years Pavel and Stella, for I dropped the Sarah as soon as we got to Canada, established ourselves in a lovely little community. We both recognised each other's fragility and we made a decision to not have children. After thirty-seven years we have become rooted. We bought land and, after about seven years of saving, we built our small home. There are three acres of land where, when not working for local farmers, Pavel raises vegetables and sells any surplus. He was much more fragile than me and disliked social activities and, whilst I would have liked more, I guess I was glad not to be subject to too much intimate questioning about the past. Sometimes if your guard slips you can reveal little nuggets of information which allow people to make links to matters which you would rather avoid. So, we have led a fairly isolated life, but a happy one, in a latitude not far removed to that in which Pavel was used to farming in Poland, although the climate here, he says, is quite different to that of the central European conditions he experienced in his early years, and he says the winters here are harsher.

But now *anno domini* has caught up with us both and quite independently and coincidentally we have had our end of life sentences. For Pavel it is the heart failure which has led increasingly to his shortness of breath, swelling of his legs and feet and dreadful tiredness. His prognosis is up to three years, for me it's less. My speech started slurring about six months ago, people looked askance at me when I spoke, thinking I was under the influence of drink, but my diagnosis is one of Motor Neurone Disease and I have about half of Pavel's time, according to the medics. Not a problem as we are both *compos mentis* and have made some clear decisions whilst we are still able.

Paying off the loans for the land and the cost of building our house took a lot of our modest incomes but we treated ourselves to holidays in a small motorhome which we bought. We have both worked hard and built up some savings which will hopefully settle most of the medical bills for our care. The rest may have to come from taking out a loan on the house. But what is left will be bequeathed, when the second of us dies, to the local church, which was very helpful to us when we first arrived. We have stipulated that the church should use it to home a poor family and give them a start in life, like they did for us.

But there is one final thing I must do. When I walked away from that baby girl in Otley Hospital, I knew that the only way I could survive that experience emotionally was to mentally write her out of my life as completely as possible, and that, with all the other things that happened to me, I did manage to do. Pavel is the only person I have ever told of that event, the only person to know that I gave birth. I cannot now face letting slip that mindset, which I have worked so hard to maintain, by now acknowledging the child's existence, it might be too painful and all the 'what ifs' might cause me to breakdown again. So, I prefer to go to my grave without ever having sought to find that child. But Pavel said, whilst he understood that and supported me, there was somebody else who may wish to know who had brought her into this world.

After talking it through with him I was clear that I did not want that child to come looking for me and so I wanted to ensure that, so far as possible, our whereabouts could not easily be found. On the other hand, I accepted his suggestion that I should make some attempt to explain the circumstances of her birth to the child. At first I was unwilling, but in the end, even though after the passage of time it is unlikely that she will be found, I did conclude that I would make an attempt to send information which may get to her. At least it will assuage the guilt which, for reasons I do not understand, Pavel feels much more strongly than I do.

So, I have made some arrangements with a local man, who drives a big rig taking local produce over the United States border and down to Boston. He has gotten me some US Dollars and when I have finished my package he will take it down to Boston and post it there. That way it will look like we live in the United States and not Canada.

Whilst in due course I will have to write a covering letter to the solicitor and get out the other enclosure to go with it I will start my letter, which I will also enclose, in the hope that it may possibly find its way to my daughter.

To whom it may concern

My name is Stella Goldman born on Saturday 5 June 1920 in Woking, Surrey, England.

My parents were Jewish and father was an electronics engineer my mother a concert pianist and piano teacher; both were German Nationals but had lived and worked in England since, I think from about the year 1913. We lived in Woking until I was seven when we moved to Essen, Germany. Aged fifteen I was sent to finishing school in Switzerland. Although a bit rusty on some of them now I speak several languages English, German, French and I can get by in Italian and Polish.

Living in Switzerland for two years I did not experience the changes in attitudes and behaviour in Germany in relation to the Nazi approach towards Jewish people. When I was seventeen I went home on holiday from school to Essen, to see my parents. Whilst I was there I innocently enquired about travel to England, for a visit to our old home area in Woking. This foolish thoughtlessness of youth led to the travel agent informing the local Nazi's of my enquiry. Because my father was a very clever electronics engineer working in their programme of gearing up for war, I was taken as a hostage to my parents' good behaviour and more specifically father's electronic work. In Berlin, where I was taken, I was assessed as to how I would be employed and they identified my language skills and also, as a result of my childhood in England, my consequent excellent command of the English language. As a result of these factors I was selected for spy training. Whilst I was unhappy I nevertheless found it was interesting and I was well treated and I received genuinely contented sounding letters from my father, and so, at the beginning, my role as a hostage was not too bad.

My life changed when, over a year before the outbreak of war, I was allocated to a spy cell in south London. There I was raped and abused by the head man and he and his organisation went on to dominate me and scare me to death as well as giving me continuous warnings that any misbehaviour would lead to the death of my parents. Having felt they had me under their control they tried me out in an office job before the war and for a while I was happy there, but then they contrived to get me into the Women's Royal Naval Service.

I was only nineteen with little real-life experience and my parents lives, as I was frequently reminded, depended on my good behaviour and doing as my spymasters told me. But although I reported to my handler, I gave away no secrets which could really have helped the Germans. I was a low-level communications telephonist, I had two postings, neither of which allowed me to access the sort of information my bosses wanted. Then, in 1942 I realised that my father had sent me a letter which, by innuendo, tipped me off that things were not good for him and that, I assumed meant mother too. Indeed, I am sure that by the time I got the letter or shortly after they were dead. I felt released from my hostage status and so I planned to escape.

Over time I made preparations to escape and go to ground in England, but before I could put my plans into effect I was inadvertently involved in an amazing sea rescue, whilst on a programme of observation visits by fellow WRNS staff to a local tug boat to just observe their day to day work within the local harbour area. Perhaps overawed by the bravery of the crew, and especially with the Captain, I fixed a date with him, he was called Gareth O'Shaughnessy, and for the first time in years I felt a connection with another caring human being. We spent a summer afternoon together and my emotions were running high and I got a little carried away and he made me feel normal for the first time in years, and we made love. But that moment of bliss ended almost immediately when we came back to base to find my heinous spy master, Jack, and his henchman, were waiting for me disguised as members of the Royal Navy. Having realised that I was becoming disaffected, they had contrived to come for me with the purpose of eliminating me so that I could not betray their spy cell. I asked Gareth, as the tug captain was known to me, to report me sick so that my absence would not be noticed if I could contrive to escape.

In the event any idea of giving my captors the slip in some urban area at some later point, on what I assumed might be a journey to London, was dashed when the car was stopped, not long after my abduction. Jack made it clear that I was to die, but before this he sent the other man away so that he could rape me at gunpoint; which he did. However, when you know that you are under extreme threat you may be lucky like me and develop real strength to preserve your life at any cost. Whilst he was off guard after his exertions of abusing me I managed to strike him with the handle of a car crank which was to hand. He screamed and dropped his gun but not before a shot had been fired. His assistant came back at the sound of the shot and hearing his colleague crying for help he ran towards me. I picked up the gun and, in a struggle, I accidentally shot and mortally wounded him. Having suffered innumerable abuses by this Jack, and given that I had badly hurt him with the car crank and he was screaming for help, I shot him in the same way as I have subsequently seen

224

a wounded animal dispatched. I have never felt any remorse for this although I regret that the other man, who had never done me harm, had died at my hands.

When planning my escape I knew that the Military Police would look for me; having hurt this spy cell by killing their men they too would now be after me; and now, to add to all that, I was guilty of murder. So I ran, leaving clues that I was headed for Liverpool but I went, by circuitous routes to Leeds where a wonderful woman called Doll saved me. Then for reasons I will mention in a minute I became seriously mentally ill and was hospitalised. Whilst in hospital I met a wonderful Polish man whose ill health was due to his bravery and injuries sustained in the battle for Arnhem. In due course we married and in the confusion of the aftermath of war we manged to successfully travel together to North America. Over the years, like many other displaced European people, we have successfully integrated ourselves in this continent which is populated by so many people of different races and creeds.

We have had a simple, yet happy life together but we are now both suffering from ill health which is likely to be terminal within a relatively few years. I never wanted to write this. But my husband persuades me that, even though it may never reach its intended target, or is that victim I wonder, I nevertheless have a moral duty to at least try to explain things to a child which I abandoned. The details are as follows.

I was delivered of a baby girl in Otley Hospital on Saturday 3rd April 1943; she weighed 7lbs 1 oz. I did not name her and, whilst I gave her the colostrum that people now talk about, as I fed her for two days, I then abandoned her by design. If she ever reads this, I ask her forgiveness and I give below my explanation, or some might say rationalisation.

My parents loved me, but they were workaholics in their own ways. I effectively caused them to be put under house arrest in Germany before they had realised the way the wind was blowing for Jewish folk in that country at that time and managed to contrive an escape like their next door neighbour had planned. My guilt therefore is twofold; firstly that, albeit inadvertently, I caused the death of my parents, for I have no doubt that they were taken to their deaths; and secondly I abandoned virtually at birth

225

the only child I was destined to bring into this world. Believe me that is one heck of a lot of guilt which has, from time to time, weighed heavily upon me.

The guilt, together with the loss of my friend and saviour Doll, which in turn caused me to be homeless, led to my breakdown in mental health. Once recovered I tried to find the brave man, Gareth O'Shaughnessy, who had given me the first real human kindness in years, but he was either lost in the war or decided that the trouble I had probably caused him meant I was a bad bet, so I did not hear from him. But fortunately for me, my husband to be turned up as a patient in my hospital and we two wounded souls became lifelong mutual supports to one another. We moved to North America during the great migrations of the post war years and have made a happy life here in a rural area.

We have ourselves been members of a small church and they were here for us, in our early days and the congregation have always tried to help people who are struggling, one way or another. After our medical bills are settled there will not be a great deal left, apart from the house and land. I have decided that, as we have no children, to leave money in the vain hope that my natural daughter might get it, is too uncertain and so our wills have been written to ensure that the church gets our land and house, in the hope that some poor souls, like we were when we arrived, might be helped.

I have asked a solicitor in England to try to see if my daughter can be contacted, not for my sake as I will not be here, even if he succeeds. My dear husband says that this child, now woman, may be interested to know why she was abandoned. I assure her that my decisions were driven entirely by my need to survive. To escape the clutches of a nasty spy cell, to avoid being hanged for treason or murder or alternatively, spending many years in prison for being a spy, even though I did my best to ensure that I did not supply any information that would betray the land of my birth.

My fortune in being able to survive and ultimately to find happiness in life, came from being a free agent unencumbered by a child and I know that sounds harsh, but it is true. I did what I had to do and I have never had regrets. Once I settled here, even assuming I had wanted to find my natural daughter, which as I

226

have explained I did not, making enquiries about her could have potentially led to my identification and arrest and, apart for the consequences for me, I felt that I also needed to protect my husband.

And again, that is the reason why I do not include any means of identification in either my letter accompanying this or in this essay itself. I felt I might trust Mr Solly, the solicitor I saw in Leeds, to be honourable but a successor might not have felt the same and may have decided to open the envelope before January 2000 and then felt that immediate action should be taken to find this spy and murderess.

Dwelling on decisions made in times gone by is a waste of time. Nevertheless, I do sincerely hope that if this ever finds that daughter I bore that she will try to understand my reasons for abandoning her. That said I do sincerely also hope that she had a caring family to raise her and that she has had a happy life. You were after all a Saturday's child, one who, according to the rhyme, works hard for a living. That would be very apt, since I have had to do that too, so possibly it is something we may share.

Stella Goldman   22nd October 1995

Chapter 25

1997   Solly – Leeds

"Solly! Solly! It's the office on the 'phone."

"Gina, I am on the bloody toilet. Tell them to remember that I am now retired and that I will phone them later."

I could hear indistinct talking, interspersed with silences; then.

"Somebody has turned up with half an old one pound note and is asking for you."

More silence; this time it's me, as my mind races.

"Tell the office receptionist to make sure he does not leave, that I am coming to the office post haste. Tell her to ply him with coffee and biscuits and say I will be there as soon as possible and within the hour and order me a taxi for now or sooner. Oh. Tell her to be sure to locate the Horowitz file and have it ready for me when I arrive."

This is the day I dreamed may never come before it was too late for me personally to be the one to get to the bottom of this age-old wartime conundrum. I must hurry, I do not want to lose this person with the key to this ancient mystery and I want to be able to open the sealed papers over two years in advance of the deadline which has been imposed upon me. By the time I have finished what I had started in the bathroom, dressed myself, only glad that I had shaved first today, and got downstairs the taxi was just arriving in the driveway.

"Gina, you wonder woman you would have been an amazing asset on the reception desk at a busy solicitor's office in Leeds." I said with a smile.

"I was the most wonderful receptionist Hoffsteins ever had until some returning soldier swept me off my feet and filled my belly with the first of our two wonderful sons and then that awful man said; 'no wife of his was going to work when she could be at home caring for our offspring'. I suppose these barked orders and your uncustomary haste has to do with your interesting case of the torn pound notes?"

"Yes. Yes. Somebody is there with half a bank note so it must be the long-lost missing person. At least I very much hope so. Back when I land."

Who would have thought that the four or five miles to the centre of Leeds would take twenty minutes in the middle of the morning; but it did. Nevertheless, within a little over half an hour of the first call I was going up the familiar steps into the office; those very steps which I had, until recently, been used to regularly ascending every working day. The new receptionist, Jenny, informed me that the clients were in the best interview room.

"Clients? Plural?"

"Yes, Mr Solly. A middle aged lady called Mrs. Crowther and an elderly gentleman by the name of Mr. O'Shaughnessy. Oh. And here is the file you requested"

"Excellent, Jenny, most efficient and very helpful."

I went into the interview room to find the occupants had turned their chairs to the window and were watching the comings and goings of Park Square. They turned as I entered and despite clearly being much older than me the man rose fairly quickly to his feet. I went straight to him and with outstretched hand I introduced myself.

"Solly Hoffman. And you are?"

The returned handshake was firm enough.

"Gareth O'Shaughnessy and this is my friend Mrs. Rose Crowther." And the lady stood and returned my handshake.

"My receptionist tells me that you are the bearer of a torn wartime one pound note and I wonder if I might see it please."

The man handed me one half of the second of the missing notes, the serial numbers matched the other half of the remaining one in my possession which I had just extracted from the file. So now I had both of the two sets of torn notes complete again.

"Please tell me, Mr. O'Shaughnessy, how do you come to be in possession of this unusual part of a one pound note from the wartime years?"

"Well, it came to me in a letter from a woman who sent it to me in 1943 using my parent's address whilst I was away in the Navy out in the Far East. The letter was not forwarded to me at that time. When the war ended I got work out there as a ship's captain on small coastal ships working out of Singapore. My reason for staying was that I had married and the jobs over there were very well paid, so as a result my wife and I did not return to this country until 1949. Then, later that year, when clearing out my mother's home, I discovered the letter which enclosed this part of a bank note. It had been addressed to me at my parents' home and they had neither opened, nor forwarded, it to me."

"Well, well. So Sonia Horowitz had written to you but you did not receive it for six years and in that time the frequency of her contact with this firm rapidly diminished and then ended; until two years ago."

"Did you say the name was Sonia Horowitz? For the letter to which I refer came from a woman I knew as Sheila Booth."

We both fell silent and the woman spoke.

"Perhaps I can tell you Mr Hoffman, that all this is very confusing and is probably my fault because I should let you know that I only managed to track down Gareth a couple of months ago and…….. well…… I have been, very belatedly searching for my birth mother. You see I have known for some many years that I was adopted but had decided to not pursue trying to find out about her until a couple of years ago. It is, well it was, not a big issue for me, but the further I have gone on with the search I must confess the more interested I have become in getting to the truth. After a lot of enquiries and dead ends, I eventually traced Gareth to his home in South Wales, through the fact that some informal notes left with my birth papers suggested that my birth mother had some connection with a sea rescue involving a tug called the *Loyalty*. And Gareth, it transpired, was in command of the *Loyalty* at the time of the incident. He then dug out this letter and the enclosed half of a one pound note."

She handed me a copy of a letter, which I quickly read, noting that it was dated in 1943, addressed to 'Dear Gareth' and signed 'Sheila Booth' and was basically a request to contact her via our firm and it enclosed the half of the one pound note which they had brought to me today.

"So you believe that your mother is this Sheila Booth?"

"We do not know because the papers I have, which were left with me as a baby when I was apparently adopted, suggest that the woman who gave birth to me was called Sheila Johnson, or at least that is the name she gave, and she abandoned me two days after I was born."

"Most intriguing, as I knew it would be." I said. "Thank you for showing me this letter which you have explained that you actually first read in 1949 several years after it was posted. I begin to wonder if your Sheila Booth may actually be my Sonia Horowitz. Let me begin with the story from my end of the telescope, as it were.

When I was a very young man just beginning to work in this firm, which was started by my father and my uncle, I was given the task of dealing with a lady who came unannounced to the office one day. She told me she was Sonia Horowitz and she gave me a sealed letter and asked me to arrange for its storage until it was claimed by the bearer of one of two one pound notes which she had torn in half in my presence, handing one half of each note to me and retaining the other. It was most unusual, but she paid a generous fee for the service and so I created a letter, which she and I signed, and which was duly witnessed, confirming that our firm would hold the sealed package unopened and only release it to the bearer of either of the two torn one pound notes.

Within weeks I was in the Army and away for nearly three years and on return I enquired and was told that nobody had brought in either of the outstanding halves of the notes. Furthermore, I was told that there had been a period of regular telephone enquiries, by the woman we knew as Sonia Horowitz, apparently from call boxes. Her enquiry in each of these calls was to establish if there had been any contact made by a bearer of one of the notes. Gradually her contact declined and at some point, it ceased. From time to time in my career my mind has gone back to this most unusual event and the lack of contact, and indeed I have wrestled with the temptation to open the sealed envelope. In the event I am glad I did not, for out of the blue two years ago I received a letter signed by one Sonia Horowitz and postmarked Boston, Massachusetts.

As you have been kind enough to let me read your 1943 letter, enclosing the half of the one pound note, which you received in 1949, I am happy to read to you a letter from America, sent to me two years ago in 1995. As you will hear it has only added to the mystery of this most unusual of cases, so far as I am concerned.

'Rural North America

Dear Mr Solly (or successor, though hopefully not the latter)

I am most grateful to you for being so understanding when we met in 1943. You will be aware that I have not since been in touch with your office since probably about 1945 and so this letter will probably come as something of a surprise. However, you should find enclosed cash to the sum of one thousand United States dollars, in one hundred dollar bills, being an upfront fee for discharging the request I make below. Since I am not giving you my address for personal reasons, I am relying on the honesty I detected in you all those years ago, to discharge this request when the time comes.

Myself and my husband are both suffering from illnesses which may carry us off in the next year or so. My husband will have this package posted if I die first, which appears the most likely position. He is agreeable that you may commence to deal with my request as from January 2000, but not before, as he would prefer to not be around if you are successful in your endeavours on my behalf, even though I doubt you would be able to locate him. It is to that end that I am not advising you of our postal address or making any reference to my married name.

The enclosed fee is for you to arrange to make such enquiries as you can to trace a female child to whom I gave birth on 3rd April 1943 at Otley Hospital. I believe the hospital will have registered me as Sheila Johnson.

If you are able to trace that child then I ask that you provide her with the enclosed envelope, which is an explanation of my circumstances at the time. If after twelve months, and your best efforts to the value of the enclosed cash, you are unable to trace her, then you may do as you wish with all the papers you hold in my name as from New Year's day 2000.

Yours sincerely

Sonia Horowitz'

I can tell you that her *bone fide* was established as, in addition to the thousand dollars, which incidentally, accrued some six hundred and thirty one pounds and fifty two pence, when we exchanged it, and paid it into our client account, she also returned in her letter one of the halves of the set of two torn one pound notes. So, I can be quite sure that I was dealing with one and the same person whom I first saw in 1943 and, indeed, her signature was quite similar when you factor in the age of the lady at that time and her age now.

So already you may begin to see why I came rushing in here to meet you today. This conundrum has been an intriguing part of the whole of my working life and I was resigned to not being able to solve it for over another two or three years. Now your arrival brings me that chance and I am most grateful. Also, I noted from your reaction when I read out the birth date and location, Mrs. Crowther, that perhaps this was a significant date to you?"

"Yes Mr. Hoffman...... "

"Call me Solly, Please."

"Yes.....Solly, what you read out is both my date and place of birth. Sheila Johnson also the name that I was much later given as being the name my birth mother used when attending the hospital." She said looking at her companion, and he nodded and smiled at her and took her hand as tears began to form in her eyes and he spoke to encourage her.

"There Rose; your quest for your mother of birth appears that it may possibly have reached a conclusion. You have done so well, and I am so pleased that you have found this information. Equally it seems that, sadly, you will not be able to meet her, even in the event that you had decided that you wished to do so."

"Yes, that does appear to be the case; however there are the enclosed papers of course. They may reveal more of this story." I said. "Perhaps I should first open the letter she left with us in 1943?" And when they nodded agreement I cut through the heavily taped old foolscap envelope, expecting to find quite a bit of paperwork, there was in fact a small single slip only.

I read aloud "It simply says.

Dear Gareth,

If you are reading this I know that you must have received my letter and are willing, I hope, to give me the chance to give my explanation of events. You turned out to be a catalyst in changing my life and I have some hope that you may be able to advise me as to how to go forward from here.

Assuming that you are prepared to arrange to contact me then these are the options. You can write to me care of the Solicitors. I will be in regular telephone contact with them and can arrange to collect any post from them as they are unaware of my address. Alternatively, you could provide me with a telephone number and although I have no phone of my own I could arrange to ring you at a specified time from a telephone box. It would be lovely to hear your voice. Again, we could meet outside the solicitors office at a pre-arranged time, although I would prefer either of the first two options.

However, if your contact is as result of you deciding that you needed to alert the Police, or other authorities, and they have prevailed upon you to make this contact so that they can arrest me, then so be it. I know you are an honourable man, and therefore can fully understand that you may wish to do that, and I will completely accept your decision.

Do know that if the latter is the case, then I completely forgive you. But in that case I would still ask that you consider coming to see me in prison so that at the very least I may at least tell you my story."

Yours sincerely
Sheila Booth

Gareth shook his head and then said.

"So, as I feared when I read her letter addressed to me, via my parent's home in 1943 she was really reaching out to me as somebody she thought she could trust, and indeed someone, I assume, she believed might help her. That makes me feel awfully guilty, more, even, than I felt at the time, and I experienced the same feeling again when I re-read her 1943 letter just a few weeks ago after Rose had contacted me."

"Why was she reaching out to you in particular, do you think?" Rose asked him.

"Well, there is the mystery; it is not as though we knew one another for very long, indeed I only met her to speak to on two separate days. She was on the establishment of the local Wrens, and I first met her when she came to my ship, as part of a programme of allowing Wrens on the base to have a controlled experience of being on a ship in sheltered waters. The vessel was a requisitioned tug named the *Loyalty* and she was my first command. It was designed to be a day buzzing around in the safe waters of, Loch Ewe, a sea loch in northwest Scotland. She was to see what we did on what you might call our 'gofer' activities. Taking stores here, transporting seamen from ship to shore or vice versa and escorting ships to the bunker facilities were examples of our normal duties in those days. But then, quite unexpectedly we were called to an emergency to give assistance to an American ship drifting at sea having lost steerage and about to go aground in a gale and there was no time to land the Wren and so she was present at the rescue.

We left the relative safety of the loch and found the casualty and there it so happened that I took a big personal, and looking back now a pretty stupid, risk in entering the water to ensure that we got a line aboard the drifting vessel. This young woman saw that and I guess she would have been impressed and she subsequently invited me on what we must call a date. We spent one subsequent afternoon together and, whilst I did not fully understand all that she eventually was persuaded by me to say about herself, she made it plain that she was in an unhappy situation but had resolved to extricate herself from it in some unspecified way. She became very emotional and I comforted her. But then, as we walked back to her lodgings, we saw some people, one of whom she described as her former boss, and she said that she feared they had come to take her back to her former work and she was reluctant to go.

I must admit that I was very taken with her and, had she remained on the base, I am sure that I would have had high hopes of developing a relationship with her. You can tell I was very smitten given that I agreed to her emotional request to ring in the following day to say she was sick. This was, quite clearly to me in retrospect, out of order and my punishment was that I was relieved of my command and sent to the Far East. However, ironically it was there I met and married my late wife. Had I received the letter before I met my wife to be, then I would have responded and so I now feel guilty that I did not respond to her request for help."

"Well, be that as it may." I said. "We have already learned that she did in fact marry and moved to 'Rural North America'. So, she obviously survived and hopefully went on to a reasonably happy life, so that any guilt you may still have ought to be assuaged by that knowledge.

So far as I am now professionally concerned I am now keen to discharge my duties to my client, or almost certainly my late client. May I ask you, Rose, if you have any documentation relating to your date and place of birth?"

She pulled from her large bag a file of documents, representing the evidence of her searches to date, and we spent some time together and I was a satisfied that she was indeed born on the relevant date, in the relevant place. She explained the irregular birth certificate implying that she was the child of her adoptive mother when in fact she was not. I found the certificate and the circumstances surrounding its making, quite extraordinary, but clearly this was wartime and an elderly doctor, who may have used this ploy in the past, was unlikely to have felt he was doing anything other than being helpful, in both the long and short term. Then there were the notes supplied to her adoptive mother by the midwife, the very notes that had enabled her to generate her research. Having digested the information I summed up the situation as I saw it.

"Well, I am satisfied that I have discharged my duty to Sonia Horowitz and I have found her daughter as she requested; or perhaps I should say her daughter found me. In which case, I am delighted to be able to tell you that I feel able to hand to you the enclosure that accompanied her last letter to me of 1995. Do you wish to open it here?" I said this fervently hoping that she would agree as I was itching to know the whole story.

"Just wait a moment before you decide, Rose." The man interjected. "There is a distinct possibility that the note contained in the package potentially contains some very sensitive personal information, so, may I ask you, Solly, where you stand in relation to any confidential information which may be revealed? Because I half expect that we may come across information which might be better kept from the public domain."

236

Upright old gentleman he appeared, and there were clearly no flies on him.

"You have been involved with the Law?" I asked.

"I am a qualified master mariner and have been responsible for very many ocean going ships in my day. In that capacity one deals with legal issues involving employment, shipping management and the legal requirements relating to different cargoes and countries. Then, once retired I worked for a couple of years as a part time court usher and this brought me into contact with the day to day operation of the law and lawyers."

"Right, well then, to answer your question, I have a duty of confidentiality to my client, Sonia Horowitz. The duty of confidentiality applies to information about my client's affairs irrespective of the nature of the information. It continues despite the end of any retainer or the death of the client when the right to confidentiality passes to the client's personal representatives.

So in this case I have a duty of confidentiality to Sonia Horowitz and because I now must presume, from her most recent letter and the lapse of time, that she is deceased. In which case it would be reasonable for me to assume, in all the circumstances, that her daughter would be a 'personal representative', hence I can say, having perused all the documents here, that now my duty of confidentiality is now to Rose. Does that help?"

"Thank you, Solly. Sorry Rose, carry on with what you were going to say."

"I have no objection to you hearing what is in the enclosure, Solly."

I could barely conceal my delight at being allowed in on what I hoped would be the dénouement in this particular interesting, and long running, little story. I passed the thin package to Rose who opened it, extracted several handwritten pages and thoughtfully suggested that perhaps I could take her to get it copied so that we could all read it at the same time. And this we did, on return we passed a copy to Gareth and then all three of us began to read.

For about ten minutes we all read in complete silence as we devoured the clear handwriting covering, what turned out to be, some six closely written pages. Reading was a stock in trade part of my work until a short while ago, so I am a practiced and quick reader and I finished long before the other two. Looking at them both I could see that the unfolding story was having quite an impact on them both. I would have liked to say something, but I realised that this was nothing to do with me and additionally, I could imagine that there were some very impacting personal implications being generated from what each was reading. Therefore I stayed silent, wondering who would be first to say something. Perhaps unsurprisingly, since it was her story or rather the prequel to her story that we were all digesting, it was Rose who opened the batting.

"What does it mean when she says she lives in Rural North America?"

"I just think she does not want anyone to find out about her beyond what she tells us in this piece of writing." I told her. "Perhaps one could search on what we now know as her real name, or any of the alias names we know her to have used to see if there are records of entry into the United States or, I suppose, given the wording 'rural North America' it could even be Canada. However, maybe she had papers in another name, like the name of her husband which she interestingly does not give us. You could try, but, if I am brutally honest I think you are unlikely to find out more than we learn from this.

By the way, her recent confession makes reference to the fact that she killed two men and for my part and in relation to client confidence and, particularly given the facts of her enforced abduction and the way she was treated thereafter, not to mention that she is almost certainly deceased, I think we can keep that between us and leave that well alone. However, I have to confess the revelation, though serious and awful, nonetheless made me smile. You see, when I met her that one and only time I was trying to persuade her that there were other and cheaper ways of storing papers but she was adamant that they needed to be with a solicitor. So I asked what was so important in the papers and I said half-jokingly that I hoped that it was not a confession to a murder, which of course there was not in that particular envelope. I distinctly remember her in all seriousness looking at me and saying that she would swear on oath that she had 'not murdered one single person'. And of course that was the truth because she had killed two people.

238

I have to say that the story is fascinating and tragic all in one and I am so glad that she found some belated peace."

Rose nodded and then was silent for a while before she then said.

"In the past I have calculated forty weeks back from 3 April to the end of June or beginning July, of the previous year. So that would have been in the middle of 1942. When was the rescue that your tug *Loyalty* was involved in and which 'Sheila Booth', or more correctly Stella Goldman, observed?"

Rose paused after her question, and looked at Gareth. There was a pause. It could have been that he was trying to recall the date, but I rather assumed that he was buying time before answering. When he spoke it was to confirm that my latter assumption was the correct one.

"Rose, this comes as something of a shock to me, for it is the culmination of a line of thought which has exercised me ever since you told me when you were born, as well as revealing the details of your birth and the allusion made by your birth mother to her co-patient in Otley." He shuffled the photocopied pages of Stella's statement.

"Here on page two near the bottom, she refers to becoming 'carried away' after saying that her emotions were 'running high', well I can say that emotional state infected me as well and, to not beat about the bush, we made love and, if I can put this delicately, no precautions were taken."

There was another silence as they both began to join the dots. This could be the moment where a searcher for a long lost mother finds that she may be deceased but instead is able to throw her arms round an old man and cry 'Daddy'! However, in my line of work evidence is critical. So I said.

"You must both be beginning to consider the distinct possibility that you, Gareth, are the father of Rose, here. But may I just ask you to consider the wider evidence. It is possible that she engaged in other sexual contact just prior to her meeting with Gareth. But, in fairness given the way she writes about the importance of her meeting with Gareth, it is equally likely that she may not have engaged in other sexual activity immediately prior to this particular date. As against that she may have had other sexual contacts but the contact with Gareth may have taken on special importance because of what happened later that day. Then we know she was raped by the man she states that she killed and who had abused her in the past. Then she appears to then have gone on the run, and she mentions Leeds, so it is possible that she may have fairly quickly needed to turn to providing sexual favours in order to survive.

I do not mean to discount the point that Garth could be the father of you, Rose, it is just that it cannot be assumed on the evidence of one unprotected sexual encounter. On the other hand, whilst I have no particular knowledge in this area, having been a criminal lawyer, am sure that if you were so minded it would be possible to arrange for tests to determine to what extent, if any, the two of you were related. Be aware, however, that if you rule out that Gareth is related to you then you are probably going to find yourself in a position where you will never know about your paternity. You will both need to think about these issues.

If asked for an opinion, then I would say that the ultimate decision on how to proceed should lie with Rose."

Chapter 26

1997 Rose – Otley

That journey back home from Hoffsteins solicitors office in Park Square, Leeds, was quite ethereal. I do not think we said anything of any moment to one another. Of course we chatted about the visit and particularly the energetic and helpful Mr. Solly with his kindness and sensitivity. After his little reminder about the other possibilities in relation to my paternity, other than the possibility that Gareth could be my father he, quite sensitively, went off and left us to talk. But we did not seem to want to talk because we were, I guess, both trying to come to terms with all that had been revealed to us today. So, after a very few minutes, I suggested that we make our way home and Gareth, with obvious relief, agreed.

We went to the reception desk and asked the young woman to thank Mr. Solly for all his help, however, we told her that we had decided we were going to get off home after all. She told us she was under strict orders to not let us leave without Mr. Solly saying goodbye. So we waited a few minutes for him to re-join us and, after descending the stairs slowly, he was careful to usher us back into the conference room in which we had spent so much of the morning. We all remained standing as he gave us his views which he must have been considering in the short time he had been alone.

"It is clear to me that you have both discovered things that will have, to say the very least, surprised you this morning. Where you take that information you have gleaned from this statement of the woman we now know to be Stella Goldman is up to you. I do think it bears you spending a little time in coming to terms with it all before making any firm decisions. But may I offer some comment to Gareth in particular. You have expressed some understandable guilt about, in old fashioned parlance, having let this lady down. I do so hope that all such feelings may now be put to rest. She cried out to you for help when at a very low ebb in a life that had been very hard and you were one of very few, if any, to show her kindness after she was forced into her role as a low level spy. You should be proud that she held you in such esteem, but the fates decreed that the letter did not reach you. Yet you now know that she still survived, nay, even apparently prospered, at least in a relative sense, and lived to an age of, at the very least, the allotted three score years and ten. Even had you been so minded it is most unlikely that you would have found her in 1949, as by then she seems already to have managed to start her new life across the Atlantic Ocean.

Rose, my dear. Keep in the front of your mind that she did not abandon YOU, she abandoned a child which she could not cope with at that time. You have learned that your mother of birth was in an awful situation that was not of her making and her pregnancy was very much an unwanted extra burden at a very dark time. It must have been so hard for her to decide to abandon you, but she was in the most awful situation and felt that she had no choice. Actually, if you consider it, she showed extraordinary willpower to write out of her life, what turned out to be, her only offspring. She apparently either made a conscious decision not to have a child with her new found husband or she failed to conceive again and, either way, in a further display of singlemindedness she made the very brave decision to not try and find you. We will never know why but my guess is that there may have been various factors such as a horror of reopening some old mental wounds. The guilt about not gleaning better information for her spy masters which she might have felt led to her parents' demise. Concern that her actions in committing what she obviously saw as murder might lead her to have to face justice on that count. The re-opening of her emotional breakdown symptoms which led to her hospitalisation, and ironically that seems to have ended up being her salvation because she met her husband to be in the hospital. Then ask yourself whether, if she had re-surfaced many years ago, what that might have done to your relationship with your apparently legal birth, but actually adoptive, mother. Particularly if that had preceded your adoptive mother having told you about your adoption. If I may give advice for you to

242

consider it is this; your birth mother, Stella Goldman, asks your forgiveness and I advise that you afford that to her.

For me, this has been the most amazing enigmatic thread throughout my working life, and you both have been kind enough to let me share in your amazing discoveries today. May I confess that many times I was tempted to open the package which Rose, more properly, opened today? With a self-constraint, which has frankly amazed me, I decided that I would wait until the year 2000 as requested. But in parenthesis, as it were, I also resolved that should I become seriously ill, I would send for the papers because I could not go to my grave without finding out about it all.

There is little more that you will need a solicitor to do now and I assure you that the secrets revealed in these papers will stay between ourselves. Here is the full file on Sonia Horowitz, no other papers will remain in this office except for this receipt which I invite you, Rose, to sign, so that our records and accounts are kept in order."

I remembered mindlessly signing the small chitty which said that I, Rose Crowther accepted the cheque in sum of sum of six hundred and thirty one pounds and fifty two pence, being the return of the fee advanced by my mother Stella Goldman for the purpose of finding me. He said to me, that in all conscience, he could not take the fee, because we had saved him and his firm all the work and trouble of advertising to find me. He also pointed out that I had spent time and money in gleaning the information leading to our appearance at his office, so I had incurred expenses. He did mutter something about his Uncle Paul turning in his grave, but, when I queried what he meant, he just said it was of no consequence, just a little personal aside.

Our desultory conversation on the way home in the train and again in the car had masked our respective moods of contemplation, but after return, and the making of a pot of tea, I sensed that we both realised that it was time to address each other with our views on the discoveries of the day.

"So, you and your wife never had children, Gareth?"

"No. We did not. But that was not a conscious decision; at least not in the beginning. I suppose Dyllis and I were in some ways wedded to our respective professions and the nature of my work had a contraceptive effect upon our chances of children. I was often away for long periods and, whilst she saved her holidays for my leave periods, she could not effectively just disappear from her Ward Sister's role in the hospital, for the whole of my leave. We nevertheless both enjoyed being man and wife together whenever we had the chance and the probable consequence of conceiving a child was something we sort of expected to happen and were ready to accept, particularly in those early years. When nothing of the sort happened and we were getting into our forties we decided that we were not destined to be parents, and we did not wish to be the older parents of a child and so then we took a conscious decision to ensure that it did not happen.

We both worked well into our sixties and Dyllis had such a circle of friends that took up a lot of her time. Also, towards the end of her working life she transferred to a local hospice and even after she gave up paid work she still volunteered there. So we did not really miss having children."

"What do you think you would have done if you had discovered that Sheila, or Stella as we must now call her, had given birth to me and there was a possibility that you may have been my father and I was a baby in some care home or just fostered?"

"Well, I think you know me well enough to know that I would not have shirked my responsibility, and I am sure that Dyllis would have supported me. However, what I heard today raises so many questions. To start with I imagine that there are millions of men who have gone with a woman, and been the cause of a pregnancy, yet never get to know that this is the case. Many of them would be only too delighted to remain in this ignorance but some may be disappointed that they were never invited to be part of the life of the child they caused to be born."

"Which of those do you think applies to you?"

"Retrospective hypothesis seems to me to be dangerous ground especially in relation to this subject and with today's information fresh in our respective minds. Surely the issue is what is best for the child. You. From all you have told me, you experienced a happy childhood with devoted parents in a fairly idyllic environment. Had you been raised in poverty or by abusive, or uncaring, parents the story could have been different.

The motives and abilities of foster and adoptive parents must vary as much as in the general population who produce children within their own relationship, the only difference is that there is some vetting via a social worker for potential adoptees. But as I read the way things have gone in recent times there has been a push to close children's' homes in favour of recruiting foster carers more widely. I do note that some of those children's homes were not up to scratch, but equally I suspect that the bar for becoming a foster carer may have concomitantly been lowered as demand for such services have increased. I would suggest that a well-run, externally well supervised, children's home might provide a better experience for a child in care than a less than ideal singleton placement where the oversight is less and the child's unhappiness goes unnoticed.

So, back to what I think your question may have been driving at. If Dyllis and I had been faced with taking you out of an assumed care situation, then I know we would have done our duty. But the onus would have been on Dyllis to raise you as I was away so much of the time and would she have had, or developed, a resentment that could ultimately have soured your relationship?"

"Oh. Gareth. I do know that you would have done your duty and in many ways it was a silly question. I was very lucky to be taken on by Alice and Bill and to have had adoptive grandparents in Agnes and Ernest; also, as you say it was a wonderful place in which to be raised. But I am sure that you can see that today I seem to have both found and lost a birth mother whom I was trying to locate; and in the process it would appear that I have found the person who started me off, as it were. It is a lot for me to take in."

"Yes. It is a very great deal for me to take in too, but perhaps it is not necessarily such a big deal if we look at things more broadly. Sheila, sorry, Stella, was a victim of tyranny, by all accounts. She was personally abused yet felt she had to stand that abuse because her parents were hostage to her compliance. She had just been tipped off by her father that she need no longer be beholden to her abusive masters and then, still in in her

245

impressionable early twenties she had seen me take a reckless risk and succeed in a daring rescue. These things came together and when we met she experienced some emotional release and in that state you may well have been conceived. Had things been 'normal' we could, quite possibly, have made a life and a family life for you.

But things were far from normal and our respective lives took the course which they did. We all three of us in our different ways seem to have had happy lives. Stella is silent on her view of her life but reading between the lines she, and this man Pavel, seem to have been, if not happy, then at least content with their lives, their lot and one another.

The big thing now, as I see it, is that fifty five years have gone by since the events which appear to link us all three, you, Stella and me. Those lives have been led independently and apparently happily, or in Stella's case, more happily than might have been expected. What we have discovered today is that possibly, as Solly was keen to point out, I may have caused your conception. But that does not really join us in any significant way because of all that has happened in those fifty five intervening years. In particular I would be mortified if you were to now feel that, aside from my helping you in your quest to find your birth mother, you somehow needed to keep in touch with me because I may, I stress the 'may', be your natural father."

"You know there is a way to establish whether or not you are my father through testing. Is that something you would be prepared to do?"

Gareth was silent for a while. Then he said.

"I am not a great Church, or in my case I should say, Chapel, man. But I have, with passion, often sung that wonderful William Whiting hymn of the eighteen sixties, 'Eternal Father, strong to save'. Those chapel and church hymns of my youth come to me in times of trouble or concern. I call myself a Christian and the nearer I get to the end of my life then the more those elements of a religious upbringing come back to comfort me. Indeed, I worry about the youth of today who miss out on the comfort of a belief, however tenuous that may be. So, in short, I believe in belief.

There may or may not be a God, but I rather hope there is and I am happy to hold that belief without absolute proof. Therefore,

246

I think it is a question of what we each believe. A test may confirm what we think we know or it may not. In my case I would rather believe that it is highly likely that after all these years I have a daughter and both grand and great grandchildren. But you may feel different. You may need the certainty and I must leave that decision to you."

"Getting to know you Gareth has been an absolute pleasure. If there is to be a newly found 'natural' father in my life then I could do no better than you. Like you, I think that it might be less pleasant to find that a test showed that you were not the person who was loving and caring towards my mother at the time of my conception, for clearly on that day, and at that time she was as happy as she had been for years, and as she would be for several years to come. That feels like a very positive way to have been conceived. If a test showed that you were not my natural father then I would be left in limbo as to whom that might be and in what circumstances was I conceived. To say that you may be my natural father would mean a lot to me. To that end I would like to ask you to also assume that you may well be my natural father and support me in telling Sally, Michael and their children that this is the case. Would you be happy with that?"

He agreed; and we both embraced and then we set about making a meal.

Chapter 27

2000   Gareth – Otley

The sprightly, and apparently cheerful old man, joking affably with the physically disabled young woman, in a wheelchair, staffing the supermarket checkout, drawing a cheerful rejoinder from both her and the young man in the queue behind, and keen to be part of the repartee, is me.

What a huge distance I have travelled, both metaphorically and physically, since that other supermarket encounter of some three years ago with Mr. Tut and Mrs. Pie.

From my insular life in Lisvane, after the death of my dear Dyllis, via my bolt hole of an equally insular bungalow in Porthcawl, I am now leading a very happy family life in Otley. The change may never have happened had it not been for an episode which occurred the day after the meeting which Rose and I had held with Solly, in his office in Leeds. When I woke the following morning, I felt somewhat disorientated, but I put it down to all the excitement and revelations of the previous day. At home in Porthcawl I usually rose from my bed between six and half past and I noted on that morning in Otley that the time was approaching seven. So I swung my legs out of bed and sat, as usual, awaiting my brain's message of reveille to reach all my distant extremities. Possibly it never did, for the next thing I recall is that Rose was leaning over me as I lay on the floor, and I could just make out the distant sound of an approaching emergency vehicle.

Rose, and the ambulance crew together, 'got me stabilised' she would later tell me. Then after a blue light drive the hospital staff got me fully sorted out, so far as was within their wonderful powers at Leeds General Infirmary. Their diagnosis was a small stroke, leading to a brief loss of spatial awareness, which in turn led to a fall from the bed, on which I had been sitting. In turn this resulted in my becoming unconscious due to my head connecting with the adjacent wardrobe, and additionally my arm struck the bedside table. Quite a chapter of accidents, one might say from which the butcher's bill was lengthy. Sixteen sutures to the scalp, as they thought that the wound was too long and irregular to glue, a variety of technicolour bruises and a broken arm were the other obvious outcomes. All of these were relatively easily rectified over a number of weeks. Less obvious, and in many ways more significant, because not all of it was so simply rectified by a relatively short passage of time, was the damage caused by the stroke. But even there, in fairness, I still got away quite lightly; save in one particular, namely, I lost half the vision in each eye and that resulted in my being told I could no longer drive. The very down to earth ophthalmic surgeon asked me what my car was worth and, when I told him I thought it might fetch about three thousand pounds, he told me that was great, because I could sell it, put the money in an account and it would pay a heck of a lot of taxi trips.

As the effects of strokes go I was extremely lucky not to be more seriously impacted, but I must confess that I experienced the eyesight issue and resultant ban from driving, as a life limiting blow because I realised that it meant that my previous mobility, which, with my access to a car and ability to drive, I had taken for granted, would now be limited. No more trips to Aberavon Beach or the usual supermarket. My world would shrink to short walks to Porthcawl beach, and outings only to those places to which the local busses would take me. In the short term, plans were made for me to be released from hospital to stay with Rose and I was initially grateful, as clearly it would not have been easy to manage, especially with my broken arm, back home in Porthcawl.

As soon as I was out of hospital I realised that Rose had internalised, what she saw as, the fact that I was her biological father. Because of my illness on the day following the revelation in Solly's office, together with my few days in hospital, I was never part of any intra-family discussions, which must have occurred, about the possibility of my being Rose's biological father and the availability of paternity testing. I feel sure that in various telephone conversations with Sally and Michael down in

Bristol that, given their medical knowledge, they would have raised this issue with Rose. Clearly she had advanced the argument about belief and the others had accepted that was how she wished to proceed. So by the time I returned to Rose's house from hospital, I found that I had apparently become father, grandfather and great-grandfather so far, she told me, as the whole family were concerned. Suffice to say, for my part, coward that I am, I never thought to revisit any potential doubts about my status as the father of Stella's child. In my defence, albeit I had got off cheaply from the effects of the stroke and fall, I was still a bit disorientated and, to put it bluntly, I was very grateful for the care Rose was providing.

So I remained with Rose to convalesce and it was arranged that in a month or two Michael, Sally and the children would come up to Yorkshire for two principal reasons. One was to begin the planning for a return to the area, ready for Michael taking up his new appointment in the New Year. The other was for them, and particularly Sally to have the chance to meet me in what was obviously my new found status. And so it was that in that atmosphere of welcoming the long lost 'relative', that I had my first meeting with Sally.

And all became clear.

Prior to that meeting the impetus towards incorporating me into the family was apparently unstoppable. For my part, I felt unable to, as it were, rain on their parade and so accepted their insistence of being part of the family. And I admit that it seemed rather nice.

During my short term incapacity I had gratefully, and gracefully, accepted Rose's hospitality and care. But long before the plaster was to be removed from my arm I raised the issue of my return home to Porthcawl as soon as my arm was serviceable. This sparked a session of third degree in which she clearly adopted her usual professional role as a carer for the elderly. She quizzed me about how I intended to manage without access to my vehicle and I prevaricated. Asked what my ties were in the area, I admitted that they were not strong. The community ties around our married homes, because of the nature of my work and lengthy absences, had all been through Dyllis and they had mainly centred round her workmates and our neighbours in

Lisvane. When she had died her friends were supportive and kind for a while, but their lives moved on and, after all, they were not my friends, they had been Dyllis'. My retreat to Porthcawl had been to seek a quiet life in a bungalow, rather than continue to manage a large house, and with the bonus of a proximity to the sea rather than my remaining in a suburb of Cardiff. But I had no real contacts beyond the neighbours in Porthcawl, and even these were limited to pleasantries. So she had made a proposal to me.

She, Sally and Michael had been talking over the telephone and the bungalow that was let as a holiday home to paying guests could become my home, if I wanted, and they would offer me support, if I needed it. I was overwhelmed by this suggestion and after the dutiful initial 'I couldn't possibly impose on you all', I was delighted, when pressed, to agree. However, I was not out for charity and I still had my dignity and although they had talked about me paying a small rental and the household bills, I was having none of that. I insisted on a valuation and we negotiated that I should buy the bungalow at that independently set price just as soon as my Porthcawl property was sold. They were against my insistence but in the end the compromise was reached, whereby I would buy the property and the solicitors would insert a clause that in the event of my leaving, or my death, Rose, or failing her, Sally, had first refusal on its sale and could buy it back at the same price as I would pay. In fact, I have subsequently outsmarted them; because I have left the property to Rose in my Will, so she will get it back without having to pay.

There followed quite a difficult short period which I could not have faced without Rose and her help. She took time off work and drove us down to Porthcawl and took me to the estate agents and stayed with me for several days whilst we sorted the house. We only stayed for less than a week but in that time the house was put upon the market, with arrangements that the agents would supervise viewings. My car was sold to a local dealer and with her help I sorted my personal papers and other treasures and boxed them ready for transport north. Within a few months the house in Porthcawl was sold, together with a lot of my furniture which went to auction and local charities, as the cottage in Otley was let furnished and I only needed a few pieces of sentimental value to be transported up here.

So it was that in early 1998 I moved to Otley and I have experienced the most happy few years. I can potter about round the farm buildings, tidying up and keeping an eye out when all the family are at work, or school. My relationship with Ewan and Maggie has blossomed and indeed I occasionally find myself in charge of them for short periods, between school and the return of their parents from work. Also, on those days when Rose has collected them from school and then has to return to work herself. The children, like their parents, seemed to have accepted me for what Rose seems to want me to be; her biological father, a poor substitute, but substitute nevertheless, for the birth mother she had hoped to find.

My assumption is, and of course I never dared ask, that during my illness both Sally and Michael would have raised the issue of paternity testing with Rose. I suspect she represented my view, which she herself had accepted, about believing rather than proving. I suspect that the young couple would have warned Rose that by having me to live with them I could be inveigling my way into the family and perhaps my offer to buy the bungalow and give them the chance to recover it if I left or died, may have been sufficient to allow them to accept my *bona fide*. In any event they did accept me and I was very happy pottering about, caring for the two youngsters and going around with Rose; indeed it was she who took me for my weekly supermarket shop in town.

I do love them all, and after Rose's desire to have me and my need for support I have joined their family wholeheartedly. I am so sorry that I have not been able to reveal to them that I am indeed more than likely to be a cuckoo in their nest.

Rose had come to our first meeting in Porthcawl with Michael because Sally was required to work on what should have been her planned rest day, when she had initially arranged to bring her mother. When I arrived at their Otley home, Sally and Michael and the children were still away living in Bristol, even though they were planning to move back to Yorkshire for Michael to take up a post locally. She will have talked to her mother on the phone about all the information that had resulted from our visit to Solly. She will have learned of her mother's desire to see me incorporated into the family and no doubt she will have challenged that view and urged caution. But I had not met her before I was admitted to my short stay in hospital nor for some several weeks afterwards by which time Rose had obviously made up her mind that she wanted to accept me as her biological father.

And, to be fair, at that point I was quite willing to accept the real possibility that I was quite likely to be Rose's biological father. But then came the day, weeks after I came home from hospital that Sally, Michael and the children came north on their errand of house hunting and I got to meet Sally for, what was of course, the very first time. When the car arrived Rose helped me from the chair and we went together to the door and after hugging the children and her daughter she turned to introduce me to them.

"Folks this is Gareth. As you know from our 'phone calls I have adopted him as my Dad, as he most likely is. As we have discussed on the phone he is going to buy the cottage and come to live with us and I am sure that you will enjoy his company."

The children hung back a little, as they had only met me the once several weeks ago, but Michael stepped forward and shook my hand and offered what sounded like a sincere welcome and a 'lovely to see you again'.

Sally approached and gave me a hug and whispered.

"Welcome to the family. I know that finding you has made Mum very happy."

In this way I had my very first meeting with Sally, and her hug brought her face close to mine and straightway I realised.

Of course, my generation were brought up on homeopathic remedies for illness and learned about things from the so called 'old wives tales'. One of the latter is that some genetic factors can jump a generation.

This particular point must have undoubtedly come to my mind as I looked at this very attractive young woman who was introduced to me as Rose's only child. Rose believed I was her biological father, she had convinced her extended family on that point and up until that moment I was willing to be of similar belief. Therefore, on the basis of that assumption, Sally was my biological granddaughter.

But, just looking at her, I realised immediately that she was much more likely to be the child of somebody I had once met briefly in 1942.

A man, whom, I remembered, had worn the uniform of a Captain, Royal Navy, and beside whose left eye, was a bright red birth mark.

Just like the birth mark beside the left eye of the lovely Sally, as she stood before me on that, our very first meeting.

Epilogue

2001

The following entry appeared in the Death Notices columns of a number of newspapers and free press papers in South Wales in the summer of 2001.

"O'Shaughnessy, Gareth.

Friends are advised of the death, last January, of Gareth O'Shaughnessy, aged 88 years, husband of the late Dyllis, master of various merchant ships, a serving Lieutenant RNVR in World War II and unsung hero of the 'Loyalty' incident which took place off Loch Ewe in the summer of 1942.

Formerly of Penarth, Singapore, Lisvane and Porthcawl, he died peacefully in his sleep, after a short illness, at his family home in Otley, West Yorkshire.

He is mourned by his daughter Rose, granddaughter Sally, son in law Michael and great-grandchildren, Ewan and Maggie.

Friends who may wish to contact the family are requested to do so via Mr Solly Hoffman, c/o Hoffsteins, Solicitors, Park Square, Leeds. LS1 2NP"

Background Information

Loyalty's Legacy is a fiction in terms of characters and events, But I tried to set the story within geographical and historic realities. It is not meticulously researched, warranting footnotes and sourcing, but I have used real places and organisations that existed at the respective times. As well as personal knowledge I made a number of enquiries, I will not credit them with the term research, as they were not that thorough.

In many aspects of the story I drew on personal experience. I had a flavour of life in the Second World War as I was born in West London during it, and I have 1950s childhood memories of immediate post war life, together with the oral memories of my parents who lived through it. Like Stella, I used the Liverpool Street, Harwich-Hook of Holland Ferry, some twenty years after her, in 1960. Inverness station was first known to me in 1970, the same year as I first visited Loch Ewe and I have revisited that area over the years, most recently when writing the book. I used to walk through Park Square in Leeds on my way to Court and it does house several legal practices. The countryside between York, Harrogate and Otley is well known to me both by car and rail. Otley Chevin was a regular walking spot when I lived within four miles of Yeadon Airport (now officially Leeds Bradford Airport) between 1969 and 2022.

Save for Stella's first deployment to the South Coast listening post I have used and described only general geographic areas or specific places which I have personally visited. One exception is Abbots Hill House, that first posting for Stella. It was indeed a wartime listening post employing WREN officers and ratings. This I discovered when looking for a real posting where Stella was likely to get only time sensitive information which she would not be able to pass on quickly enough to be useful to the enemy.

During the Second World War there was indeed an HMS Helicon, a Royal Navy base at Aultbea on the northern side of Loch Ewe in the far northwest of Scotland. It was commissioned in June 1941, so not even a year before Gareth's arrival. The deep-water sea loch itself is extensive and permitted the

256

gathering of convoys bound across the Atlantic or, in Stella's time, to Murmansk in Russia; the notorious 'PQ' convoys. It was a refuelling base for naval and merchant ships so tankers, like my fictitious *Atlantic Catalyst* would have visited to deliver fuel oil. Incidentally I describe her as being of type 'T2' and indeed the Americans started producing such a class of tankers from 1940 onwards and quite a few were still sailing in the 1960s when I was at sea.

As described in the book there were several support vessels recorded as operating in Loch Ewe about that time and some of those I mention in the book. So far as I can find there was no tug there, although there may have been. A cursory search of Lloyds Register pre-1945 showed one small vessel called 'Loyalty' which sank in 1904. Loch Ewe was part of the Western Approaches Command, headquarters of which, as I mention, were in Liverpool and are celebrated today with a museum.

There was indeed a huge wartime Exclusion Zone around Loch Ewe and its perimeters were guarded as described and local residents were required to carry identity at all times. There are remains of wartime fortifications still evident and there is an 'Arctic Convoy' Museum in Aultbea. The book '*Loch Ewe during World War II*' (2014) by Steve Chadwick provided other helpful background.

The cover is a specially commissioned watercolour from my good friend and professional artist of many years standing, Rick Alred, who is best known for his Scottish landscapes. It captures an imagined view of a tug lying moored to a buoy less than a mile south of Aultbea. The view is looking west north west with Isle Ewe behind and a gathering convoy to the west. It is much as I imagined the tug's position when, at the start of Chapter six, Gareth is reflecting on the events at sea in the storm earlier in that day. In thanking Rick most sincerely for his work I am grateful for his attention to detail in seeking out, and representing, tug design of the era.

Today it is difficult today to appreciate the isolation of that part of the country, especially since a 2015 Tourist board promotion of the, now popular, North Coast 500 motor route, which passes through the area. Some understanding of how the area may have been in wartime have two personal sources. In

257

1967 I first visited my very good, and sadly late lamented, friend Ian Brown. He lived further north, above Lochinver (and setting for my first novel *Tragic Coincidence*) and even in those days many of the roads were single track. Ian also helped me understand the lifestyle of the isolated crofting families in the immediate post war years that he had experienced as a child.

There is a central issue, towards the end of the book, relating to establishing paternity. Today, where virtually every crime story uses DNA to pinpoint a person or offender, it is easy to forget that as recently as in the 1990s, when this issue becomes relevant in the book, DNA usage was only just developing. The big key to unlocking the absolute determinant of an individual's DNA seems to be, as I understand it, identifying the Polymerase Chain Reaction which was only established in the 1990s. Before that, and indeed from the 1920s, blood testing might have served to rule out a putative father as an actual father but could not necessarily prove paternity.

Then, finally, there is the issue of 'jumping genes' where a genetic abnormality allegedly skips a generation. I offer no conclusion to this unresolved debate other than point the reader to their own review of this contentious subject. Suffice to say that 'the old wives' tales' of my youth did hold that there was such a factor. All I can say in support of Gareth's conclusion, or belief, related to this issue, is this…...

…..my paternal grandfather had a decent head of hair in old age, my father was prematurely bald, I have a decent head of hair in my eighties, my son is prematurely bald.

Geoff Kenure 2024

www.ingramcontent.com/pod-product-compliance
Ingram Content Group UK Ltd.
Pitfield, Milton Keynes, MK11 3LW, UK
UKHW030113220225
455422UK00013B/111